TRAVELER'S REST

SUE CARTER STOUT

CrossBooks™
1663 Liberty Drive
Bloomington, IN 47403
www.crossbooks.com
Phone: 1-866-879-0502

First published by CrossBooks 04/06/10

ISBN: 978-1-6150-7048-0 (sc)
ISBN: 978-1-6150-7145-6 (hc)

Library of Congress Control Number: 2010920712

Printed in the United States of America
Bloomington, Indiana

This book is printed on acid-free paper.

CHAPTER

1

"No more, I quit. Y'all act like this is an occasion of some kind. It's no party, so let's not pretend it is. I guess we should have taken a picture of us in front of Dad's casket. The two pictures would go together, wouldn't they?" Shelby barked the words in rapid fire, moving closer to me as she spoke. "Mom, with pictures like this, I can make a scrapbook of my life going down the tubes."

"Please, Shelby, let me get a good snapshot of you and your brother in front of our home before we leave for South Carolina. That can't be too much to ask, can it?" I knew I was on thin ice but my daughter sulked back into position.

Through the lens of my camera, I saw my two children with tired smiles forced across their faces standing in front of the house. I couldn't blame them for looking so glum. A fly buzzed near my nose; I blew at it in retaliation. I shifted my weight to get a better balance and got ready to snap the shutter. As I did, Carter scratched his nose and Shelby fussed with her blouse. Her sandy hair curled around her face.

"Stop fidgeting," I called out. "On three, say cheese." A river of perspiration ran down my back.

"That better be a good shot, because I'm finished," Shelby mumbled.

"Okay. We're done. Let's relax." Claire ignored the latest outburst. "How about a Coke? There are bottles in the cooler." She motioned toward the steps.

"Sis, this isn't easy for any of us. We've just got to keep going." Carter wrapped his little sister in his arms.

Shelby pushed him away. "Easy for you to say—your life hasn't changed like mine. You get to stay here in Atlanta while I veg in the middle of nowhere—I won't know anybody or have anything to do in South Carolina. Try leaving your hometown the day after high school graduation. My dad wouldn't have let this happen." She folded her arms tightly across her chest and glared at me.

"Come on, Sis. Think about Mom, will ya? She's trying hard. This isn't her fault."

Shelby opened her mouth to fire back a retort as her uncle Pete rounded the corner of the house. "We're finished cleaning up inside. Isn't it time for the Realtor to do the final walk-through?" He hugged Claire.

"She flew through here in the middle of the morning, saying everything was fine," I responded. "The closing is at two." I glanced at my watch. "I need to head to the attorney's office pretty soon." I shrugged and held the camera up. "I'd hoped for some closure for us all. Shelby, forgive me. I just couldn't bear for our last memories here to be the slam of the doors on the moving truck or the echo of the empty rooms."

"I'm sorry, Mom. It just seems so unfair." She brushed a tear from her eye. "See you at Dinky's. I'll calm down on my long drive to nowhere."

"Group hug." Claire motioned and we all joined her. Shelby quickly disentangled her body from our arms and scampered to her car.

We waved as she plopped into her crammed vehicle and disappeared down the street. We stood there for a full minute after the old blue Toyota disappeared. With the emotional whirlwind in her car and headed to South Carolina, nothing seemed to fill the void. Words, which had seemed so plentiful this morning, now stuck in my throat.

Carter bent down, gave me a peck on the cheek, and told me he'd call tonight as he climbed into his car.

Pete enveloped me in a gentle embrace; I felt his shoulders shake as I heard a stifled sob. His familiar fragrance swirled around me. My brother-in-law released me and then put his hands firmly on my shoulders.

"You know, Sterling and I never dreamed this would happen when we borrowed the money for our company. We thought we had all the bases covered." He rubbed his forehead and continued, "This just shouldn't have happened." He lowered his shaky voice, and the pain in his eyes screamed out to me.

I summoned my strength. "Everything looked good. How could you have known this would happen? We both know that selling the house was the only possible plan with Sterling gone. It's not like you and Claire got out of this free and clear. You're both working hard. There's no good way out of this mess. On the bright side, your mother and I will love being neighbors." My calmness surprised me. "Thanks for letting Carter live at your house. It's easier for us all this way—he can keep working for you and going to Tech. Almost normal. If only it were that easy for Shelby."

Claire drew close. She took a deep breath. "She'll be in college soon and things will settle down. Remodeling Hollingsworth Hill and running the shop will keep you plenty busy. Hang in there and it'll be all right."

I swallowed hard and looked deeply into her green eyes, which these days were often filled with tears. We exchanged our pain in the glance.

"It still doesn't feel real," I whispered.

Claire squeezed my hand. "Almost a year now."

We pressed against each other as if standing there would keep the world from spinning. Our lives always so intertwined, now so unraveled. Claire grabbed the basket of goodies beside her and placed it in the front seat of my bulging car.

"It's a good thing Shelby has her own car," Claire said as she inventoried my packed vehicle. "There isn't an extra inch here."

I walked into the laundry room and gathered the remaining family member into my arms. Mercedes, my ancient black cat, let me know how much I'd inconvenienced her by leaving her in solitary confinement most of the day. She voiced her impatience even more as I placed the cat carrier in the back seat of the car.

"Shelby insisted she didn't have room for my baby to ride with her." I pointed to the groaning pet.

I waved a quick good-bye and slipped into the crowded vehicle. Driving away slowly, tears streamed down my face. There was some pleasure in feeling the moisture on my cheeks—a release, a cleansing. As I looked in the rearview mirror, my home appeared smaller and smaller. I had one more task to accomplish; I couldn't give in to the exhaustion I felt. I fought traffic, blasting the air conditioner until my face felt numb, and pulled in front of the lawyer's office with three minutes to spare.

I grabbed my briefcase and my cat, prying myself out of my sedan. Some business woman I was, lugging my feline to a closing. With the temperature expected to reach past ninety today, I had no alternative. I couldn't fight rush-hour traffic in Atlanta to retrace my steps to Claire's after the meeting to collect Mercedes. As I walked into the lobby with the hissing cat, I questioned my choice. When she puked in her carrier, I was positive it had been the wrong way to go. I ducked into the restroom, released Mercedes from her prison, and pulled fifteen paper towels out of the dispenser. I feverishly scrubbed the carrier clean, but nothing could eliminate my frustration or the nasty odor.

Convincing Mercedes to re-enter her cage was the hardest task of the day. With my head pounding and scratches all over my arms, I slipped into the office. The buyers glared at me, and their agent tapped his pen on the table. I heard my agent explaining his delay from the next room. I plastered yet another insincere smile on my face and fought to regain my composure. An hour later, I emerged with a check—a small amount for twenty-two years of life. *If only Sterling was here with me.* I dropped into the disheveled mess of a vehicle, apologizing to my cat for the long drive ahead. We shared dinner from a drive-thru, and I pointed my car north. As I crossed into South Carolina, with several miles left to go, I brooded over my decision to drive to Traveler's Rest this evening. I told myself it was necessary to be there early tomorrow to greet the moving van and supervise the unloading process. Practical but, oh, so difficult. *Come on, Abby, keep going through the motions. Good feelings surely will return. Numbness can't be a permanent state, can it? Wasn't I promised that goodness would follow me all the days of my life?*

Well, it must be following at quite a distance.

CHAPTER

2

I gazed beyond the porch screen to the tree-lined pond. The aroma of coffee brewing and bacon frying floated from the kitchen; my mouth watered. The sizzle of bacon had given way to the familiar ticking of the hall clock. Mercedes purred and rubbed against my leg. Familiar but now dramatically different. There was no Sterling. There was no home in Atlanta. That life was over. Hollingsworth Hill was the end of the road. What now?

People have suffered much worse than hiding in the arms of a loved one in times like this. Few race to their mother-in-law for comfort, I bet. I felt a smile flicker across my face.

Dinky emerged from the kitchen and placed a large tray of food on the porch table. "You looked rested." She smiled, pulling me into her tiny body for a long embrace.

She had the same wiry frame and no-nonsense hair as always, but recently she had stopped coloring her hair, exposing pure white strands. The lines on her face seemed to have deepened.

"I'm glad you're here, Abby."

Tears filled my eyes, startling me, as I relaxed in her arms. "Wow, I've really missed hugs." I wiped away a tear.

As if to announce her arrival, the branches of the live oak outside the porch moved as Shelby traipsed onto the porch. Her long curls fell on her shoulders and bounced with her movement. "My grandma fixes a great breakfast, huh, Mom?" She squeezed past me and placed the plates on the table.

"Pretty good for an old lady," Dinky said.

"You're not old. You're amazing," Shelby said with a chuckle.

"Sweetie, I'm so old I've started to brag about my age." She sighed.

"Dinky is amazing." I winked at Shelby. "She works circles around people half her age. You know we all do what she says and when she says to do it."

"Well, in that case, I'd appreciate it if you would snap to attention a little quicker, child." Dinky chuckled.

I took a deep breath and looked around as we sat down at the table. "I love this spot, Dinky."

The wide porch ran the length of the back of the home with comfortable furniture scattered all around. The daybed, with its big fluffy pillows, remained unchanged as it sat at the end of the porch—maybe a little faded, but still comfy. I touched the rugged wood of the table. *Our whole family gathered here for years, laughing and caring for one another.* I slid my hand down the surface. I flinched as the wood pricked my finger.

"So much the same," I whispered.

"So different," Shelby challenged as she passed the scrambled eggs. "I don't know anybody. It's going to be a long summer."

"Mmmm." I tried to sympathize with my daughter, but my eyes gravitated to the spectacular view of the lake. Beyond the water, I caught a glimpse of the mountains. The blue haze engulfed the distant view now, but the scene would change as the sun moved overhead. Those mountains reinforced that life marched forward—for Dinky and generations before her. People died and others kept going.

"Are you listening to me at all?" Shelby said.

"I'm sorry you feel it's going to be a long summer. My best memories from childhood were at this place. The summers flew by." *I doubt this summer will move quickly. I feel like life is being sucked out of me and it's sure to be a slow process.*

We finished our meal. I stood to pick up dishes. Dinky placed her arm around my waist and ushered me to the edge of the porch. We lingered there peering through the screens. I watched the sunlight dance on the water. The smell of fresh mulch around the nearby flowerbeds tickled my nose. I could have stayed in this place all day but Shelby grabbed the dishes and disappeared inside mumbling that we needed to get going.

"The old house looks far away," Dinky said. "Pretty site on Hollingsworth Hill, isn't it? I'm so glad Grandma Hollingsworth's home is being transformed. It's been sad watching it deteriorate."

I shrugged. "It'll be changed, all right. When Sterling and I bought the place from you, we thought it would be our retirement home. Now, the grand plan has diminished considerably."

"We both know you bought it to give me cash for opening the quilt shop. Well, really it was so you could keep an eye on me when I get decrepit. Elliot and I built our home on the property so we would be near when Grandmother Hollingsworth needed us. You're just moving here a few years before you planned. That's all."

"Oh, Dinky, I'm not capable. Sterling would have…."

"Nonsense, Abby." Dinky sniffed as she patted my hand.

I gazed down the worn path outside the porch. It sloped gently to the lake beyond. The scene had always invited me, almost lured me, to come and rest on the old dock. The path turned as it came close to the lake and continued to the old home place through the woods and then up the hill.

As I stared down the path, I heard Shelby say, "Well, Mom, are we ready for the day ahead of us? You seem far away."

"I was just thinking this path is my road less traveled."

"Sure, Mom. That tenth grade poetry stuck with you. Maybe it'll make the difference, right? Great." Shelby put her hands on her hips. "I assume you're traveling light on that road. I peeked at the new garage yesterday. It's not very big. Our home was gargantuan compared to this place. I doubt you've got room to store all the stuff." She threw her hands in the air.

"I sold the largest pieces. The garage should be big enough for the rest. At least until we finish the renovation of the old house. You're relieved you're staying with Dinky, huh?"

"Smart move, I think. And, speaking of moves, we'd better get going if we want to beat the moving van." Shelby pushed the screen door open and sprinted down the path.

"Abby, I'll join you later," Dinky said as she started inside. She turned and added, "We'll get through this day." Her eyes sparkled with a mixture of excitement and dread.

Shelby was now several feet down the path. Dinky watched her movement then she lowered her voice as she moved close to me. "I don't want to cause you deeper pain, child, but Rhonda Bell called again. Maybe it'd help you to talk to the woman. You know an accident took our Sterling." Her weathered face softened, and a gentle smile formed on her lips. "Why don't you talk to her soon?"

I crossed my arms and exhaled a sigh. Rhonda Bell's carelessness took Sterling. She said the glare of the early morning sun kept her from seeing Sterling. *I bet she was texting some stupid message. If so, her message got through, but my Sterling died. Maybe I'd deal with her tomorrow, maybe next week, and then again, maybe never.*

"I hesitated mentioning the call. The woman is on my mind all the time. I figure she invades your thoughts, too. Forgiveness frees both the forgiver and the forgiven, you know. Don't let this control you, Abby."

I trudged down the path. *Rhonda Bell—I can't deal with the move, the financial mess, my grief, let alone Rhonda Bell. I'm coping the best I can. Neither of us would be suffering now if only Rhonda had watched the road. Does she think I'll pat her on the back and assure her it was just an accident? Sure. I'm not about to let her off the hook that easy, even if the law did. Squirm, lady. That's all I have to say.*

I scurried to catch Shelby and forced a smile.

Shelby looked puzzled. "What's going on, Mom?"

The old place commanded my attention. It appeared older and more dilapidated than it had when I decided to sell my wonderful home. *What was I thinking?*

"Oh, it's been twenty years since the house was lived in. I don't know, maybe I plunged in over my head."

"Mom, don't tell me your doubts now. With my whole life a mess, I'm in no mood to hear your regrets," she said, her voice rising as she picked up speed.

I streaked ahead, overtaking my child. My face must have reflected my frustration—she looked startled as I flew past her and stopped in the middle of the path.

"Shelby, you know we could've lost our house after your dad died. When we started the business, we borrowed all we could on the house. I couldn't keep up with the debt and expenses of the large place by myself. I'm scared to death, but we've got to work together to get through this. You'll still attend the college you love. You just need to live off campus, that's all."

"That's all! You said I'd be moving into the apartment above the garage. I planned on it. Now that it's too late to do anything else, you tell me you can't afford to finish it. It'll have to wait till later. My dad wouldn't have done that. He kept his promises."

"Look, the sale of the house netted me less money than I thought it would. This place has already cost more than the contractor said it would. What do you want me to do? I could finish the apartment right now, but then both of us would have to live in it because I couldn't afford to finish the house. Would that satisfy you? I can't get a loan to do it all. No bank will give me one!" I shouted. "Shelby, I'm sorry. I just tried to do what was best for all of us, but I messed up big time."

Tears beaded up in her blue eyes. "Oh, Mom, I'm sorry, too. It isn't your fault." She threw her small frame into my arms. "I just miss Dad so much."

"Me too, sweetie." I stifled a sob that rose up from deep within me. I patted her on the back and turned. "I feel close to him here. You know, we met and fell in love in youth group. I remember...."

"That's all well and good for you, but what about me? What about the memories I'm leaving? What about the friends I won't see anymore?"

"Shelby, your friends in Atlanta are all scattering. College changes things for everyone. I lived in Atlanta and came here to college, you know. When I went back, few of my friends were still around. Time changes things."

"Yeah, I wanted to come here to school, not give up my life in Atlanta permanently."

"You're young. Your life is ahead of you."

"Sure, Mom. Hey, look, the moving van's here."

The bulky truck pulled into the field and backed into the driveway. The smell of exhaust and rubber greeted me as I opened the garage door. As the men unloaded furniture, Shelby yelled instructions. She ignored every attempt I made to communicate further with her. Each box was clearly marked "house" or "garage" but that didn't stop these men from parading each box before us for directions on placement. I scurried to keep ahead of them, attempting to organize as we worked. As the morning went on, the truck began to echo as the men retrieved objects. I sighed in relief as they placed the last pieces in the old house. One of the men shoved a clipboard and a pen at me and I pulled a check from my pocket. Shelby came out of the house and collapsed on the front steps.

"You did a great job of supervising those guys, Shelby. Thanks."

She giggled. "So, I like giving orders. I wonder where that comes from. Mom, I'm sorry I got ugly earlier. I feel so guilty dumping on you. The house will be great. This isn't a mistake."

"We're in a crunch now, but as soon as the house is remodeled, we'll finish the apartment. It'll be a great place for you, you'll see."

"Good, because I'm not leaving home for good till I'm thirty."

"You say that now." I snickered as Dinky's car pulled up.

"Come with us to see my lovely accommodations," I said. The three of us trudged into the home place. Looking around the living room, we began to laugh.

"Boy, at Dinky's I don't have any closet space, but you just don't have anything in this place, period." Shelby shrugged.

"At least the new roof won't leak." Dinky put her arms around each of us.

The first glimpse of trouble had come when a hard storm brought streams of water into the old place. The contractor had said the old roof would do for a while. He was wrong. Next, I replaced broken windows caused by dead tree limbs and paid for the trees to be trimmed—expenditures the contractor hadn't anticipated. Then, when the existing well wouldn't pass inspection, my initial plan went down the hole along with more money. So, another change was required. Instead of finishing the garage apartment and living there comfortably while the renovations were made to the small home, I was moving into the living room. I would live in the middle of the remodeling. *Oh, well, it'll all work out, somehow.*

I gazed at my bed, nightstand, desk, and computer. They silently testified to my poor planning and lack of money. We pushed boxes to the side to create a walkway into the tiny bathroom across the hall.

"It was just so difficult deciding what could stand the extreme temperatures in the garage. Storage companies wanted a fortune for climate-controlled space." I lamented. "I have the window air unit in here until the central system is completed. The choice to bring all these boxes inside might destroy the little sanity I still have. *I ran out of room in the garage just as Shelby thought I would.* I'll have to move everything again when the floors are being refinished."

"Let's face it, Mom, things are a gigantic burden that take our time and limit our vision," Shelby stated grandly.

"My, what an impressive statement. Where were you all those years when I was collecting these lovely possessions?"

"Oh, I was probably teething on the stuff as you collected it." Shelby shrugged as she put her arm around me and we made our way to the door. "It is definitely time to celebrate with a pizza. Things are looking up, Mom." She glanced at the containers. "The boxes nearly reach to the stars."

Easy for you to say. I used to look up and see the stars. Now I feel like every move puts me deeper in a hole.

"So, when are you coming to work? You sure can't spend all your time in this place." Dinky held out both arms, taking in the desolate space I now called home. "Wanda is so relieved you're taking her place as my partner. She can't handle the stress with her heart. I don't mean that there is lots of stress, mind you. She's just getting older." Dinky grinned.

"What a history you two have shared—all the years working together. Lots of people have learned to quilt at the shop, haven't they?"

"Yes. I hated to see her retire, but I'm so glad you're joining me at the Quilter's Circle. You know I'm too old to do this alone."

I patted Dinky on the arm. "I think you have more energy than anybody I know. The shop was a good decision all those years ago, wasn't it?

"It was. It's a good decision for you, too. God has plans for you. You just can't see Him at work right now, with all the sorrow. Grief just makes us more dependent on Him. Dig deep, Abby. Youth is so refreshing."

"You must be thinking of the kids, then, because I am no spring chicken."

"It just depends on your perspective. To me, you are a perfect age, with your whole life yet to be lived. In fact, you are just now coming into your own, maturing and yet young enough to be full of energy. What a combination! Remember, I wasn't much older than you are now when we started the shop. Think of all the lives that have been touched through that seemingly insignificant choice. And now we'll start a new business venture. As Shelby says, who would have thought?"

Insignificant choice? This isn't my choice. No one asked me if I minded having my world turned upside down. The things I have given up, not only my wonderful husband, but my home, my job at the college, and my friends—it's been forced on me, not a matter of choice.

CHAPTER

3

After pizza, I plodded back home. Mercedes meowed her displeasure as I opened the door. The feline had tolerated being alone all day. As I surveyed my vast domain, I suppressed the urge to join her lament. *No, I'm not a helpless victim. I just need to take charge.* I delved into the boxes, elated at finding a pen and paper. My mind raced as I forced myself to write out the dreaded to-do list. *I can do this. It's not that big a deal.* I flopped onto the unmade bed and began writing. I fell asleep with my list in my hand.

The next day, my enthusiasm diminished as I surveyed the scribbled tasks to be accomplished. I visited Dinky's bank and opened accounts. Everyone seemed to know Dinky and welcomed me to the community.

The rest of the world knows our Dinky as Jane Ann. Her three brothers tagged her "Dinky" when she was four or five and smaller than most. It stuck over the years. Actually, I can't imagine a more endearing term for the small woman. In fact, my children were shocked the first time they heard someone call her Jane Ann. She's just Dinky to her family. There was no need for the great Grandma, Nanna, Meemaw debate when grandkids came along. She is Dinky to all of us.

I braced myself as I entered the license branch; I was sure this would devour the morning. Again, my expectation of impending disaster proved wrong. Another short line, another cheerful face, another job completed. I released the built-up tension. This was no Atlanta.

Gloom challenged my perky thoughts as I pulled up at the post office. *This is the United States Post Office—it presents a problem, no matter what town's name is written across the top of the building.* I reluctantly grabbed my stack of papers: a manila envelope with a house key on its way to my Atlanta agent, twenty new address cards, and change of address information. I bounded toward the building. As I pulled the door open and stepped inside, I felt something bump against me. Thanks to the bright light outside and the extra dark sunglasses nestled on my nose; the interior seemed a dark pit. I struggled to recover my footing as my documents slipped to the ground. I grappled to catch them as a gust of wind propelled some further from my reach. A snort of laughter alerted me that I was not alone. I whirled around stomping on one piece of mail while picking up two others. Another chuckle. I straightened up in time to bump into a man on his way down to retrieve the fluttering objects. Our eyes met somewhere in the skirmish. In a split second, we exchanged glances. I labored to regain any remaining dignity. There it was again—laughter. It put me in my place. The sound took me back to the grade-school playground. I was sure the beautiful, blonde Cindy Tucker was standing over me chuckling as I lay sprawled on the hot pavement. Looking more closely, I realized the person in front of me was a brunette, though she was hauntingly similar to my nemesis, Cindy. I guess she saw my icy glare in spite of the dark sunglasses perched on my nose. Alerted to impending danger, she hustled to her red BMW with amazing speed. Mr. Smile handed me the tossed documents, grinning as he did. He introduced himself as he attempted to shake my hand. I shifted the material in my arms but missed his outstretched hand. I didn't catch the name. He welcomed me to the community as he handed me more cards. Before I could respond, he sauntered to his truck. I feebly yelled my thanks and turned around, holding tight to my things as I reentered the building. The line gave me time to fuss at myself. *Great, now there's someone in this community who knows I'm certifiable. Thank goodness, it's not like I'll ever see him again. It can't be that small a town.*

As I approached Hollingsworth Hill, I relished the breeze that stirred the gigantic limbs of the oaks near the house as it floated into my open car window. *It won't be long before I am settled. Hmmm, great roof. I like my choice of shingles. It was a quick decision, but it looks terrific. This place will be finished soon, and I can start enjoying life. Sterling would be proud.*

As I retrieved the bags from the trunk, I heard Dinky's voice.

"Hi. I was on the path and saw you drive in. It is so nice to have a neighbor, I thought I'd come for a visit. I've been meaning to tell you, I haven't noticed any activity on the old place for a while. Not since the men finished the roof. Maybe they've been here and I just haven't seen them. Want to look around?"

As Dinky stepped onto the porch, I hurried to unlock the door.

"I love this place." Dinky whispered.

"Good memories," I said softly as we entered the large main hall that ran from front to back. Perspiration puddled on my lip. "I've been too busy moving in to notice what's been accomplished. This entrance always looked like a stately mansion. I love the high ceilings and wide hall. Grandmother Hollingsworth always put the Christmas tree right here." I pointed to the spot. "I did notice they put the French doors in the dining room. They really open things up. That was probably a splurge I should have passed on."

"Oh, it'll be so lovely to have a patio out here." Dinky pointed beyond the doors. "I'm so thrilled we relocated your plants from home before you listed your house. They look like they've always been here. You'll have memories of Atlanta as you enjoy them."

"My dining table will be great here. You know, I sold my beautiful formal table and china cabinet, but the harvest table will give a more casual look. Actually, all this room needs is paint and a new light fixture. The wallpaper in the rest of the house might slow me down some, but surely, painting can't be too time-consuming. Maybe this isn't the gargantuan task I pictured," I declared enthusiastically.

"Of course, the floors need refinishing and the ceilings repaired all over the house," Dinky added. "Ya know, stripping wallpaper isn't easy.

Abby, it's stuffy in here. We haven't experienced any real heat yet. Your window unit can't cool the whole house. I thought they were going to install your central system before you moved into the house."

"I did, too. I should've been on top of this before now. I've been on overload too long."

We walked into the hall again. "I guess I've made some decisions that will put a strain on my budget, but it'll look great in the end."

"You've always been clever. Your home in Atlanta was lovely but comfortable at the same time. It was a nice home with flair. Sterling always loved what you did. Your 'magic touch', he called it."

"His billfold and my magic—an unbeatable combination. I wish we were doing this together. Nothing is the same," I said as we walked.

The original house was a box with the living room, dining room, and kitchen on one side of the wide hall. A tiny sitting room, two small bedrooms, and a gathering room were on the other side. My plan for a small master bedroom, which would fit between the existing house and the new garage, had been scratched from the blueprints long ago when the roof began leaking. "I guess I'm lucky I got a new roof."

"Why don't you call Mr. Johnson? You know, his wife is a friend of mine, and I've tried to reach her, but there was no answer. They don't seem to have an answering machine," Dinky stated.

"I guess I can't ignore it any longer," I agreed. "I procrastinate a lot these days, Dinky. I just don't seem to be myself."

I dug into my pocket for the phone, made the call, and luckily got an answer. "Hi, Mrs. Johnson." Dinky frowned as she heard me saying, "Oh, no. Hmm. Oh, no."

"Not good." Dinky sighed.

I looked at Dinky. "He's been in the hospital, but he's back home now. He's doing rehab, and, of course, he can't work. Junior was supposed to continue the job. She thought he'd been working here for days. She doesn't want to stress her husband, but she'll try to find out what happened. Mrs. Johnson reminded me that I knew that her husband wasn't in good health—he just took the job as a family friend."

"Junior Johnson is going to do the job? That'll be the day. I thought Ted Johnson had other men to do the work. The ones who built the garage, where are they?"

"I don't know, but Junior must be bad news, huh?"

"That's putting it mildly. Let's hope that it's all a misunderstanding and when the Johnsons contact Junior, he'll bring that nice crew back and let them work."

I drove Dinky home and found Shelby stretched out in front of the television. Her work schedule was a huge problem, some days she went in early, some days she worked until closing. No facet of the job appealed to her, the work was boring, the staff difficult to get along with, and the manager demanding. I listened carefully, trying to find some way to encourage her. Nothing seemed to help. I heard a vehicle go by the house and headed for my car. I saw a junky pickup truck sitting in front of the garage, and I breathed a sigh of relief. *It was just a misunderstanding. I can't wait to finish and move in. Then things will smooth out.*

I raced to the house. Country music blasted from somewhere; I heard it before I stepped into the house. I followed the sound from the main hall into my bathroom. There stood two rather interesting looking characters, who obviously didn't see me.

"I told ya, I didn't pay ya to think. Just do what I tell ya," said an overweight man. He was middle-aged with a wild, thick head of hair and long sideburns. I could see a faint resemblance to Mr. Johnson. He wore a tool belt around his middle, which disappeared under a very large belly. He smelled as if the plaid shirt he wore bore several days of accumulated sweat. I hesitated to go closer.

"I tell ya, I don't think they want this bathroom gutted. Why don't we ask first, just ta see?" said the thin, balding man who stood with his foot on the toilet lid.

"Hi there, gentlemen, I'm Mrs. Hollingsworth. I don't think we have met." I extended my hand.

They looked at my hand and frowned.

"Can we turn off the music and discuss what needs to be done here?" I asked.

Still no comment. I walked over to the radio and turned it off. *Now we'll all be able to hear.* I said, "I'm sorry to hear Mr. Johnson won't be able to continue. Which one of you is Junior?" *As if I didn't know.*

A toothless grin spread across the heavyset man's face. "I'm Junior. Don't I look like my old man to you, lady?"

"Where are you planning to get started today?"

"Today? Today? Why, we ain't gonna be here long today, got too much goin' on. My mom called and said you were busting a gut over this job, so we came to tear out this mess so we'd know where we're going," Junior said, pointing to the bathroom.

"Maybe we could drive over and talk to your dad. Could we just go with his plan? Where are the men on his crew?" I uttered without daring to breathe in.

"Ah, those guys, they must carry their feelin's on their sleeves like babies. They got mad and won't work with me. I don't care either. We kin do it ourselves." Junior nudged the other man, who grinned. "Now, what was it we're goin' to rip out of here?"

"Nothing, nothing," I said, my voice going up an octave or two. "Let's wait until we discuss this with your dad. Maybe he could supervise the operation from home and tell you what he wants done."

"Hey, lady, are ya saying ya don't think we can do this? 'Cause we got better things to do than jaw with some fancy pants fresh from Atlanta," Junior said indignantly.

"No, no. I just want to talk to your father—besides, he has the blueprints for the remodel." I tried to sound reassuring.

Junior mumbled for me to follow their truck if I wanted.

"What's the big deal, lady?" he yelled as they picked up their things to go. As I started for my car, I saw Shelby leaving Dinky's house. I waved for her to come to the house.

"Do you have time to take a ride with your mom, Shelby? It would really help me," I asked.

She agreed begrudgingly. I felt better knowing that I'd have company for the short trip. I saw the strange look on Shelby's face as she moved closer. First it was a look of surprise, then disgust. I followed my daughter's gaze to see Junior Johnson standing at the edge of the woods. He was relieving himself in front of anyone who would care to see. I screamed at him to get off my property that minute—I'd find someone else to finish my home. Junior turned around, shrugged, and the two men got in the truck.

"We won't come runnin' when ya call and beg, lady, just remember that," Junior yelled. "I wouldn't sleep with that window unit plugged inta that ancient electrical if I was you." He laughed as he gunned his truck and flew down the lane.

Shelby and I burst out laughing.

"What a hoot!" Shelby laughed.

"What a hoot, indeed," I said.

CHAPTER

4

We scrambled to report to Dinky. One minute, we all laughed, the next we were nearly in tears. Shelby departed for work, leaving Dinky and me on the back porch sipping sweet tea.

The old wicker rocker creaked as Dinky tapped her foot on the floor methodically. "Laughter is medicine for the soul." Dinky sighed.

"Oh, Dinky, I'm so vulnerable."

"God will provide."

"I hope He provides new electric service to my home before it burns," I said, informing her of Junior's last comment. She jumped up and called Mrs. Johnson, casually asking the name of the nice young man who wired the garage. She came back with a name and number. He answered on the second ring; he'd be out tomorrow.

"Say, did you decide where you were going to church this Sunday?" Dinky said.

I groaned. "That is one thing I can control. I'm not getting up until noon. I'll make a decision about church next week. I'm exhausted."

"I know you're tired, but why not just join me this Sunday for church? You can visit other congregations later if you want, but everyone's been praying for us these last several months. They would love to see you."

When Dinky brought up the subject some time ago, I stalled. Now, I agreed to go. I was too tired to argue. After Sterling died, I'd become sporadic in attending our church. I justified my truancy by telling others of urgent matters that needed attention. I dreaded going in the doors of a new church even more than my church. The whole process was unsettling, but attending as a single and a stranger was more than I wanted to tackle. Especially in the Hollingsworths' home church, people would inevitably dwell on the subject that I desperately avoided. I was weary of people's pity. It was a mini-death every time I went over the requested details of Sterling's tragic end. Shelby must have felt threatened as well. When I mentioned going to church, her only response was a scowl. If my children were with me, maybe I wouldn't feel so single. The term "widow" had been safer. It covered me in its shelter for the first six months, now single followed me everywhere. At the bank, at the hair salon—anywhere I introduced myself; the issue was front and center. Oh, will Mr. Hollingsworth need a signature card? Will there be someone joining you for lunch? The car is titled in just your name? Every utility company, every charge card, everything was just Mrs. Abigail Hollingsworth. It didn't feel right.

The thought did occur to me that, as a single, maybe I needed to be around other singles. Surely, I wouldn't stick out like a sore thumb in that kind of a group. I wasn't sure that Dinky's church would have a group of not-so-swinging adults, but I decided it was probably a harmless place to start. Besides, this way I wouldn't say no to my adorable mother-in-law. Maybe next week I would try another church.

On Sunday morning, I drove Dinky to the front entrance to the church. As she shut the car door, I realized that dropping her off was a dumb move. I would have to walk into the church by myself. I might as well have put a sign around my neck saying, "Hey, I am single." I fussed at myself as I ambled through the main door. Several people greeted me. Dinky was on the far side of the entrance, so they seemed to be welcoming me, not Dinky's daughter-in-law, and not that poor widow. No one seemed shocked that I was alone. I was the one with the problem, and I needed to work past all that. Several people invited me to their Sunday school class. The most interesting detail was that they were all sizes, shapes, ages, and colors. It felt good, as if they were welcoming me to my new home. *I've blown something else out of proportion. I've got to get a grip.*

I chose a class and took a seat. With young and old, mostly women and a few couples, the room seemed to explode with excitement. After the class, I was optimistic as I found my way to the sanctuary. Tension melted as the music penetrated my ears and then my heart. The service moved quickly to the sermon. The preacher, Pastor Roy, was a heavy-set, middle-aged man with a booming voice and a mass of red hair. I'm not sure what I expected, but his message soothed me one moment and challenged me the next. I worshiped in a way that I hadn't in a long time. It wasn't Abby, the widow (that poor, pitiful girl). It was Abby, the individual, coming before a Holy God and seeking fresh insight from His Word. It was okay that I was there without Sterling and my kids. It was even okay that I was more aware of my need than I'd ever been. My tears formed freely. It was nice that Dinky was sitting next to me, but her presence was not a necessity to my worship experience. It was just God and me. It felt good.

I'm sorry I've moved away from You, Father.

As we strolled to the car, Rhonda Bell crept into my mind, but there would be no unpleasant thoughts today. My son was coming to visit. When Carter called Thursday, Dinky and I were ecstatic. We'd all be together. What once occurred often, almost without thought or planning, was now a rare experience, a treat for all.

I forced Dinky to relinquish the cooking chores; I had invaded her kitchen with gusto, sticking everything in the oven before church. Now the aroma penetrated the small kitchen. I heard his car. I yelled for Dinky, and we ran out to greet our young man. I shouted to Shelby. As his vehicle came to a standstill, I noticed the broad smile on his face. Something else caught my attention. What was that black thing sharing the front seat with him?

"Oh, my, it's a pup, Dinky," I whispered.

Carter struggled to gain control as he corralled the moving ball of fur. He grabbed the end of the leash and helped the squirming baby to the ground.

"The neighbors send you their love. Their Lab produced a great litter, and she's the best. They said she has a good disposition. Here's their note."

I perused the card. They appreciated Sterling and me. We softened their rough times. They hoped I'd think of them occasionally as I enjoyed the puppy. They were praying for me.

"What a generous gift. Come here, Lexus. Mercedes won't appreciate you, but I do." I leaned down just in time to receive a slobbery kiss.

"Oh, brother, I hope the dog impressed with the name. Mom, your clever names were always embarrassing. Let's see. Tootsie, Snickers, Skittles—did I name them all, Shelby?" Carter said.

"Yeah, and Toffee and Taffy were on the short list. Great choice, huh? At least Lexus is luxury, not calories." Shelby hugged the puppy.

"I always felt sorry for the poor animals." Carter chuckled. "I've matured since then, though, and I realize how close I came to the cutesy factor. Having three last names is no picnic."

"You are a pup." I cocked my head and looked my son in the eye. "Sterling Carter Hollingsworth is a fine southern name. Your father's first name and my maiden name—who wouldn't be proud?" *I insisted on Carter as his middle name, because I hoped it would please my father to give my boy, his only grandson, his family name. I should've known better—having all girls was a curse he wore proudly.*

My sister, Betsy, stopped for lunch on her way from visiting grandchildren in Columbia. We chattered as we consumed pot roast, potatoes, carrots, and my blueberry salad. I fussed at myself, realizing I hadn't prepared a real meal for the group since Sterling's death. I meant to, I even planned to, but something always interfered. Now, I studied my family as they devoured their dinner. Carter's face seemed so mature. Had it been a gradual change that I'd just missed? He looked like his dad—the strong jaw, the broad shoulders, the same mannerisms. That complete package had won me at fifteen. Now, those characteristics haunted me as I looked at my son. My attention shifted to Shelby— frail, fearful, and anxious. I faced the inevitable fact. My frustration was escalating because she was so much like me. The men were faithful, stable during every wind of trouble. She and I were emotional, and easily convinced that a tornado was on the horizon. When Sterling died, I prayed for her continually, now, I stumbled over rote prayers, which seemed to bounce off the ceiling and come reeling back to me.

Shelby unloaded her woes onto her brother's wide shoulders. "There isn't a decent-looking male for miles. You know, you've entered a female compound here. I won't have a date till I'm twenty-five at this rate."

"Or till you start college in a few weeks," Carter retorted.

Betsy looked at me. "Well, sis, just in case there is a date in your future, I have something we need to discuss."

"Oh, no, not in front of the children—or me, for that matter." Dinky laughed.

Betsy proceeded with a sigh. "I know how difficult it is to enter the dating scene, so let me instruct you. Unfortunately, I have experience in this realm. I've been alone for several years, you know."

"Oh, this ought to be good." I put my hands on my temples.

"Listen, before you accept an invitation, I'm going to give you three documents that need to be completed by your prospective date. One form is for a physical, the second a psychological, the third is a financial."

"Heavy on the psychological, girls!" Dinky shrieked.

"Oh, and who will be reviewing these papers?"

"I think Claire, Dinky, and I can handle the assignment. These documents must be submitted even when you're asked to go for a Coke, okay? You know how things can escalate. We wouldn't want you to fall prey to some smooth talker."

"So, what you are telling me is there is no way I'll ever being going out, huh?"

"Sounds like it to me." Dinky chuckled.

"Wait a minute. What about Carter and me? We want to review that stuff too. What about it?"

"Bribes will be discussed later, my dear," Betsy said. "Well, look at it this way, sis, at least you won't be hurt if you never get out there. You just don't know the kind of men who are lurking around every corner. Ugh. A girl can't be too careful."

"I'm not interested in the whole process. I've already asked God to send me someone in a miraculous way, or I will stay single. But, if I did risk dating and got hurt, I guess it would at least prove I'm alive. Pain is a part of life, you know." I had hit my stride by the time I finished. *So there, Miss Betsy.*

Betsy reached over and pinched me. I jumped. "Yep, you're alive. Lighten up, sis. I don't have those documents drawn up yet. So, we both have time to let God work. Fair?" my sister mocked.

"Fair."

"Girls, girls. What am I going to do with you?" Dinky sputtered.

My Sterling was so like his mother—gentle, caring, full of faith. What if I possessed no faith of my own? Perhaps I had just coasted on Sterling and Dinky's faith. I quickly slammed the door on such thinking. Something from the dark crevices of my mind shouted that I was a phony. They were the real people of faith. Could I be a faith groupie? Digestion was impossible.

Betsy picked up the dishes and took them to the kitchen. She needed to get on the road; she was exhausted. I suggested a trip to the pet store. The kids were eager. I knew Lexus wouldn't survive a night in my small place without a kennel. More to the point, my belongings were in imminent danger. Finding a spot for the cage would pose a problem, but I'd deal with that later.

As adorable as Lexus was, she was unruly. Carter and Shelby commanded, then cajoled her, while she pranced and plunged through the store. My job was to pay for all the adorable items. I charged the enormous amount of supplies while I chided myself for my weak resolve. I didn't have the money to spend on frivolous things. A pet was definitely unnecessary. I wondered what Sterling would do. I knew it was too late to think about it now. I should've sent the dog packing. When the amount appeared on the register, I scrutinized the items carefully. The cashier looked annoyed as I retrieved several toys to delete from my bill. The completed transaction would still have an economic impact, but it'd been softened some.

When Carter left, Lexus and I headed for the house. She struggled to climb the front steps, slipping as she pulled at the leash. I finally carried my new baby to my sparse quarters. Carter had placed the large kennel near the hall. I encouraged Lexus to explore her new surroundings before I confined her for the night. Mercedes wasn't impressed. She greeted this interloper with an extended hiss. She arched her back as she uttered some of the strangest sounds ever to come from my beloved old feline. Clearly, she didn't appreciate the intruder. I advised her to embrace change and climbed into bed. I wish I could say Mercedes took my advice but instead she paced, hissed, and swatted at the kennel until I gave up and put her in the bathroom, shutting the door to any objections. Maybe she'd think about her bad behavior and things would be better tomorrow. Maybe.

The dog cried. I wanted to join her. The afternoon's spending spree tormented me. I'd long ago eliminated pedicures, movies, and new clothes. A meal in a restaurant was a luxury. I wasn't planning a six-month check-up with the dentist or an annual trip to the doctor. I hoped I had enough money to make my house livable and send my children to college—that was all. Fear grabbed my attention and my pocketbook.

I rolled over for the fifth time and fluffed the pillow. New fears surfaced with every movement. My friend Ken came to mind. After Sterling's death, he had volunteered to help me with taxes. Taxes had been Sterling's thing, certainly not mine. As we gathered my documents together, I explained to Ken my struggles since my economic downturn.

Ken listened intently. He seemed to be processing the information—the analytical type. He flinched at my creative bookkeeping methods.

"Ken, do you think Sterling is watching from heaven?"

Instead of thinking the question over, he immediately responded, "No."

"How can you be so sure?" I shot back.

"Abby, if he saw all your financial struggles, he wouldn't be in heaven. I'm sure he's been spared all the grueling details of this life."

Hmmm. Tonight I found comfort knowing Sterling escaped my turmoil. I gave up trying to sleep and stumbled to my computer. I recorded the dog expenses and winced as the new total popped up. The puppy howled. Sleep didn't come gently, but I convinced myself things would improve tomorrow. I could see bushy-haired Annie humming "Tomorrow, Tomorrow" as I finally gave up the fight.

The electrician came promptly that morning and gave me an estimate for rewiring the entire house. I fidgeted as I looked at the amount. It was less than Mr. Johnson estimated, but I was dealing with an unknown person. Would Sterling fork over that amount of money to this unknown man?

"Ma'am, let me give you a list of my clients. I wouldn't want you to jump into this much work without knowing something about me."

I called one of the reference numbers while he waited, got an answer, and heard from a satisfied client. I asked him when he could start the work. He could get to it later in the month.

"I'm afraid I'll burn the house down before then with the window unit."

He scratched his head. "Ma'am, I'll put you next on the list. That'll be next week. My commercial client will just have to wait." He hesitated. "Unplug the air conditioner until then, will you? You have great electrical in the garage, but you're courting disaster, plugging that thing in here."

I rushed to the home improvement store as soon as he left and bought a heavy-duty extension cord for outdoor use. I stretched it from the garage to the front window and pulled it into the room. I wouldn't fry now. I swatted a fly and shoved the window down as far as it would go.

Saturday morning, Dinky called. She had heard of a woman who worked at the local home improvement store and had built her own home.

"I know the chances are slim that anything will come of it, but maybe she can point you to a contractor. It's worth the try," Dinky said.

I called the number and Kelly Jo said she'd love to see my project. Forty-five minutes later, she scurried into my house. As we walked through the den, she paused and looked at the back yard. "What a view—the lake from the side, now the mountains and the valley from here. Oh, Abby, this is neat. No wonder you're doing this."

There was a bounce in my step as we finished our inspection.

"Well, I kin see now why you'd move to this old place, but next to your mother-in-law? How's that working for you so far?" Kelly Jo asked as nonchalantly as if she'd asked what the temperature was.

I bristled a little. "It's working great, thanks. Actually, after Sterling died, my house in Atlanta was a luxury I couldn't afford. I already owned this, so here I am. Dinky is my rock and my business partner," I finished with flair.

"Well, I never heard o' such a thing! Nothing like doing business with your in-laws ta keep ya awake at night. Ex-in-laws, to boot!" Kelly Jo's voice echoed through the house. "I've got to teach ya some independence. I never count on nobody for nothing."

That bounce in my step ended in a thud. Trying to change the subject, I asked about her family.

"I've got two girls—one on her own, the other a senior in high school. I've got a man around. Nothing much. He's sort of a barnyard dog, ya know. He keeps others away, so I'm not bothered, if you get my gist," Kelly Jo said, smiling.

Now, there was something new. Talk about getting out of my comfort zone. I was baffled. What could she mean, she "kept him around?" Was he caged somewhere? How was he like a barnyard dog? I was thinking of getting out of my comfort zone, not into another universe entirely.

"Say, how bout comin' ta my house? It's nothin' as grand as this, but I'm proud of it. I have a home and I'm debt-free. Let's grab a bite on the way. I don't live far from here," Kelly Jo declared.

The love she felt for her home reflected in her voice. *Why not?* I called Dinky and encouraged her to join us. She passed on the invitation; she'd had a busy day. Shelby was working, per usual, so nothing was keeping me. I put Lexus in her cage, much to her objection, and climbed into Kelly Jo's truck.

She pulled into a gas station. Her truck jerked and rattled, then stopped. She filled her tank and went inside to pay. It was growing dark outside, but not as dark as my thoughts. I tried to pray. Sterling and I had prayed for our day, for friends and relatives, for our children. As I sat in this unfamiliar vehicle, waiting for the stranger to come back, I realized I used to pray from a position of comfort and ease. No more. Had the decisions I made been stupid? What if Pete couldn't pay me for my part of the business? What if Dinky and I couldn't work together? What if I just couldn't make it alone? The door slammed as Kelly Jo climbed into the truck. What was I doing in this stranger's vehicle going who-knows-where? What if I never returned?

CHAPTER

5

Kelly Jo started the engine, swiveled in her seat, and stared at me. "I guess I was a little rough on ya back at your house. Sometimes I get carried away. I forget there are other ways of livin'. I need to learn...."

"Did I have a deer-in-the-headlights look when you got in? I must admit, I've never had the privilege of getting to know a self-made woman—not up close and personal. I've got a lot to learn. Maybe we can learn from each other."

"Just maybe," she replied.

The vehicle wound through scrub trees as I felt the pull on the engine. I couldn't see it, but I knew we were climbing. We approached a clearing and I saw a tiny log house. I slide out my side of the truck as she opened the door. Inside, Kelly Jo flipped on some lights, but it was still difficult to see. A counter separated the small living room and the tiny kitchen. Dark wood covered the walls and the floors. There were no rugs on the floors, no paint on the walls. Kelly Jo pointed beyond the kitchen to a bedroom. There was a loft overhead, with winding stairs to her daughters' area.

"My family helped me put the logs in place—I cut all the trees myself. My dad helped with the plumbing, and an electrician wired the place. I wish they could help you, but they're both up in years. I did everything else with the help of a strong neighbor kid. I heat my home with wood." She pointed to the wood stove in the center of the living space. "I have my own vegetable gardens and preserve most everything I need. I figure I don't really need anybody."

"Ah, what a contrast, huh? You and me, I mean."

"Well, I figure I kin show you what I know about stripping wallpaper, patching plaster and painting if ya want. I'll be on the look-out for a good contractor, too. I've got a lot I kin learn from you. I kin feel it."

I was still reeling from the day as I took baby Lexus outside for a walk. There was a slight breeze as I picked my puppy up and stepped onto the porch. As I climbed into bed, Mercedes purred and joined me.

My dream visited me that night. It was always the same. I stood with an umbrella for shelter as raindrops fell from large tree limbs above me. A fine mist covered me as the wind drove moisture wherever it wanted. A sea of faces passed by. "He is better off where he is. Isn't it comforting that he didn't have to suffer? We will all join him in heaven someday." The voices echoed into the vast distance. I stood alone. Raindrops penetrated my thin-soled shoes. The dampness seemed to have moved into my bones, my heart, and my soul. The mist disguised the tears running down my cheeks. The charms on my bracelet pinched my arm in the dampness. They felt as if they were digging into my heart.

I woke from the all-too-familiar dream with my heart pounding in my chest and my fingers digging into my palms. *Calm down, Abby.* I breathed deep and hard. I rubbed my clammy hands on my pajama pants. *The same dream, always the same end.* I rolled out of bed; my feet hit the floor hard. Mercedes meowed and jumped down in disgust. Lexus howled. So much for a good night's sleep. I opened the cage door, and Lexus raced out. I dropped into my chair and turned on the computer. The hours dragged by as I patted Lexus with one hand and played a game of bridge with the other. As the light shone through my makeshift curtains, I began praying, but God seemed as illusive as sleep. Nothing seemed to satisfy my broken heart. A wave of bitterness, anger, and resentment assaulted me. I couldn't take it—life wasn't supposed to be this way. Why didn't God prepare me before all this happened? I could've gotten a better education. Sterling and I shouldn't have gotten a second mortgage. One minute I was doing all right and the next I exploded into a torrent of uncontrollable tears. Where was God in all my pain? I'd attended Bible studies for years; I knew God allowed things to come into our lives for our good, for our growth. It all sounded too simple now. My life was spinning out of control. *I should be coping with this, in fact, I should be seeing the light at the end of the tunnel by now.* What was wrong with me? Had I been too quick to sell my home, leave the familiar? Why had I left my safety net of friends and church family? I'd prayed; it seemed to be the right thing to do. My stomach churned as I thought about working at the shop. I wasn't just going to start work there. I was now an owner with more responsibility, more pressure, more brain fog. I had a hard enough time just paying my bills or making the slightest decisions.

The sound of the phone pierced the stillness.

"Hey, Abby, I see your lights are on. I wondered if you'd join me in my morning walk. The days are warmer now, so I walk early." Was the woman always cheery? It grated on my nerves.

I slipped on shorts and a top and stumbled out the door. The path ran through the woods and beside the lake and connected the two houses. I'd heard stories all my married life of Sterling and Pete's grand adventures when they were young. The grandkids had taken their turn playing cowboy and Indians as well. Later, Elliot and Dinky kept the path clear by walking daily to keep him active. Now it was our turn. We talked of simple things, the weather and our plans for the day.

Dinky stopped at the bend in the path. "I know you didn't know Elliot when he was a young man who came courting, the new father proud as punch, or the hard-working businessman. When his business ventures went sour, he changed. Those last years, you know, he'd go out, sit on the dock, and look out over the lake for hours. When I'd ask him what he was thinking about, he'd say 'the if-onlys, I reckon.' He lived in the past more and more. I should've made him go to the doctor. I should've done more." Dinky's voice softened. She cleared her throat. "Well, I got really mad at God when Elliot died. I spent a lot of time sorting it out before I came to the obvious conclusion. My life is a blessing. The good and the bad go together in the end. I just can't see it all the time. Well, I started praising and thanking Him for who He is, and I got closer to Him again."

"I'm glad you find comfort in God."

"It isn't something you settle once and for all, sweetie. I thought the struggle was behind me till Sterling was taken so young. I started into the if-onlys myself. If only he had not gone jogging, if only that woman had paid more attention, if only he'd survived. It wasn't until I started praising God and thanking Him for the good coming out of the situation that I began to heal. You know he didn't suffer. Remember, the doctor said that." She looked into my eyes. "He said how much the challenges in the new business had made him lean on God for strength—more than ever before. He had a wonderful wife and two great children, so he left his mark on the world. He was in the middle of church activities and never lost sight of helping others, so what more could I have wanted for my child? When you think of all the wasted lives today, I'm so fortunate I had him in my life, even if the time was short."

I felt the tears well up in my eyes as we walked. Finally I said, "I'm not there yet, Dinky. I don't know if I ever will be there. I'm not the spiritual giant you are. I have overwhelming hatred toward that woman. I just can't seem to get past it. You knew what I've been feeling, didn't you? The if-onlys were sure knocking at my door." I stopped and looked at Dinky, then hugged her. "Thanks for loving me," I said. We walked on, the crunch of our shoes against the dirt made a booming sound in my ears. "I guess I lost sight of the things I'm thankful for. You are truly a gift, Dinky." I wiped away the tears.

"You'll get it all worked out."

The day was warming as we finished walking and Dinky started home. In the last hours, I'd experienced every feeling possible. It was time to get off this roller coaster. My Sterling loved this place. *I could sink my feet on the solid ground here.*

As I stepped into the house after my walk, I heard the sound of the phone. Two calls this early seemed strange, but I recognized Claire's voice as she began leaving a message. I'd avoided her calls.

"I thought I needed to call early to catch you!" Claire commented as I answered the phone.

"Well, how are you?" I said with a sigh.

"I need to know how you are. Sorry to call so early."

"I just finished walking with Dinky. It's great to hear your voice."

Claire chatted about job and family. "Well, you know I love you," she said.

"Yes, I do."

"When I got your last email, I knew I had to call. Because I love you, I have to say this to you." There was an awkward pause, as Claire seemed to summon the courage to continue. "Is God in charge, or is what happened a big mistake? Which do you believe it is, Abby?"

Tears bubbled up instantly. "Whew! You aren't mincing any words, are you?"

"Well, which is it? I haven't experienced what you have, it's true. Maybe I don't have the right to ask you, but which is it—God in charge or a cosmic blunder?"

CHAPTER

6

Claire was right. I'd behaved as if all the events of the last year were some uncontrollable error, as if God was off the throne and the world was spinning wildly. I was acting this way because that was exactly how I felt. First Dinky and now Claire. *Why couldn't they just leave me alone?*

Somewhere deep inside I knew I was to live by faith, not feelings; I just vacillated in the application of the fact. I'd told others these truths—even lived them from time to time—but more often than not, I responded to feelings and nothing else.

"After Sterling died, I questioned God. I couldn't believe He would take such a wonderful man in his prime. It seemed to be a tragic mistake. God reminded me He knew the number of a person's days from the moment He created each of us. Okay, it couldn't be a mistake," Claire said. "I continued to wrestle with the situation. I felt impressed that because God knew Sterling's days would be short, He gave you to him so his days would be good. I saw the way you loved each other."

I sobbed. I thanked her and said I needed to get off the phone. I promised to call soon. My body froze in place as the tears poured down my cheeks.

Lord, all this is too much to bear.

I listened closely, hoping I'd hear a resounding, *All right, my child, I'll take it all away,* coming down from heaven. Instead, I heard the purring of the cat at my feet and the whining of a pup who wanted to play.

It was obvious that I needed to trust. Trusting was easy—in theory. Trusting seemed hard, if not impossible, when applied to everyday life. It had been easier when Sterling shouldered the load. I wasn't sure what trust should look like in this situation, but I was open to finding out.

After the Johnson fiasco, the unfinished house screamed of my incompetence. I couldn't handle this alone. Now, I stood motionless in the middle of my chaotic house, giving the situation over to God.

I paced through my vast domain for what seemed a long time. The phone rang. Kelly Jo screamed, "I found him!"

"Hi, Kelly Jo. Who did you find?" My immediate thought was that she'd found her barnyard dog. He must not have been lost, because she continued screaming into the phone.

"There's a man who finished a house like yours. A guy at work told me bout him. Maybe he can help." She gave me the number.

I called, left a message for Nathan Christopher, and prayed some more.

I couldn't waste another minute. I was opening the shop. I met the challenge kicking and screaming—only on the inside, but kicking and screaming nonetheless. I had fussed and fumed so long that I now had a tremendous headache and an upset stomach. I took aspirin and washed down some Pepto-Bismol with my orange juice. *I'm not going behind enemy lines. Get a grip, get a life.* Gasping, I exploded in laughter. Had it come down to this? Was this the bottom of my pit? Had I wallowed long enough that even I was sick of it? The only way was up from down there.

I danced around the bare space then dropped into my chair. There were many things to be thankful for. Sterling and I loved each other until the day he died, and I adored my wonderful children. I chuckled as I thought about my awesome mother-in-law and what a blessing she was. *Oh, God please forgive me. It has taken me so long.* Gratitude poured out where the anger, pity, and hatred had been. I'd never experienced a more moving encounter with the Lord. I lived Christ's amazing gift of grace right there in the cluttered, jumbled mess of my very chaotic life.

I picked up the phone and called Rhonda Bell before I could change my mind. After much sobbing, we agreed to meet the next Saturday. In spite of my objections, she insisted on coming to my home. Things were right between God and me. They'd soon be right between two fragile human beings trying to make it through this journey called life.

After all that had occurred this morning, I still arrived to the shop early. Dinky was at the dentist's office and assured me she'd be at the shop before the doors opened. I'd dreaded working at the store ever since I moved to town, but now I felt exhilarated being there. The aroma in the room was a curious, yet familiar, mixture of old floors and new fabric. The sunlight coming through the windows exposed tiny dust particles dancing in the air, but when I looked around, the room appeared spotless. The ticking of the large wall clock and the hum of the automatic coffee pot penetrated the space. I glanced up at the old tin ceiling and the high windows along the long narrow room. It had originally been the local drug store. The soda fountain and stools remained. For some time, Dinky had dreamed of creating a café in the quilt store. The way I felt that morning, it was more than a possibility. I swiveled to face the front window. It held books and sample pieces mingled with antique sewing objects, all put together artfully by Dinky. The back corner was home to a large bookshelf and a couple of old wicker chairs with a lamp squarely between them. The cutting table, which occupied a prominent spot in the middle of the shop, was one of the old drug store counters. Cutting mats, baskets of scissors, and rotary cutters were ready for use on the top of the antique surface.

I turned on the sound system near the cash register. Immediately, instrumental music filled the air. At the rear of the store, I peered in the darkened classroom, which was next to the office. I turned on the lights and went into the office. I jumped when Dinky touched my shoulder.

"I guess I should purchase a louder buzzer for the door. Then you'll know when someone comes in," she mumbled.

Dinky had a stiff upper lip—literally. Even though she'd insisted on going shotless, the dentist persisted. Her swollen jaw testified to the outcome. I guess the dentist was not aware of the Hollingsworth code—pain is okay, as long as we're able to talk when we get out of the chair. She'd be miserable for a while, by the looks of it.

We had no more than exchanged greetings when my little Dinky mumbled through the stiffness, "What's going on?"

"Oh, you mean I don't look puffy and the dark circles aren't so bad this morning? Well, maybe, just maybe, I got sick enough of moping around that I actually applied some of the wisdom I've been getting. I called Ms. Bell. We are meeting next Saturday." I beamed.

Dinky took my hands and yelped "thank you Jesus" between swollen lips.

The day raced by as friends, new customers, and delivery people came into the shop. Mr. Perkins, the locksmith from next door, startled me as he stomped into the shop through the back door. He shouted his frustration at the misuse of his private parking spaces. When he had rented the space years ago, there had been an agreement, he said. Now women got out of their cars, walked past his store, and came into our shop. Dinky smiled sweetly and told him she'd continue to remind customers to park elsewhere. He pounded his fist on the counter, turned, and mumbled as he exited. *Note to self—keep the back door locked.*

As Mr. Perkins left, I heard the pleasant jingle of the front bell and turned to see L.J. Adams, a friend of Sterling's from high school days. We'd run into him and his wife occasionally when we came to South Carolina for visits. L.J. received a promotion with his company, and they moved to Charlotte. Over the years, we heard rumors of his success, and eventually we read in the local newspaper that he was the majority stockholder in his corporation. It seemed he was quite influential.

"Good to see you, L.J. What brings you here?"

"Looking at you brightens my day."

We hadn't heard from L.J. for years. That is, until Sterling died. I had been amazed to receive a sympathy card from him, telling me of his wife's premature death six months earlier. Later, a second card—thinking of you—had arrived saying that he had retired from his firm in Charlotte and was moving back upstate to start a consulting business. He hoped he'd see me there. He dropped by Dinky's to visit shortly after I moved to town, and we'd caught up on each other's lives. It was strange, however, for L.J. to come to the shop. Not many men ventured beyond the doors of a place with nothing but fabric and women.

This man seemed particularly out of place. Most men in the store were over seventy, and they strolled through the store with a curious mix of boredom and fear—fear of a wife with the credit card in a fabric store.

"You must be having a bad day to risk coming into a store full of women to brighten your day," I said.

L.J. must have been around fifty, with naturally blond hair sprinkled with distinguishing gray streaks. In fact, as the sun streamed in the window, I admired the highlights. *I'd have similar highlights—when I could afford it.* He had few wrinkles, and his muscles stood out in the knit shirt he was wearing. I hadn't remembered the confidence he displayed. Maybe success had given him that air; it bordered on cockiness. Maybe I was just jealous of such self-assuredness.

"I made a business call a couple of blocks away and remembered how close the store was. I just took a chance we'd get to talk."

I looked around the busy shop. "I don't think I'm getting much chatting done here today."

"In that case, how about dinner?"

"I'm sorry. I'm really busy."

"What about tomorrow evening then, or next week?"

Dinky called from across the store. "Abby, would you tell this customer about your class on antique reproduction quilts?"

I hurried to the woman's side, telling L.J. how nice it was to see him again. Maybe we'd get together sometime for lunch. He talked to Dinky for a moment and left.

My favorite visitors that day were the "P" sisters. They lived down the side street within a stone's throw of the shop. Years ago, their family had owned a large farm, which encompassed most of what had become the downtown area. As each sister had married, the parents had given her a plot of land and everyone helped build the home. The youngest sister had inherited the old home place, which stood regally down a long lane near the other houses.

"The 'P' sisters are Polly, Patsy, Penny, and Pansy, Abby," Dinky said as two sisters came in the door. "There are plenty of rumors—gossip really, about this lively family. Each daughter was a beauty. Each married well and lived lavishly. In fact, they were the cultural figures of this area for decades."

"What rumors?" I asked.

"They concerned the demise of their husbands. I'm sure it was a coincidence that each husband met his end in February. I don't mean the same February. As they aged, every couple of years, one would go. A couple of the sisters even remarried and, of course, the new men died in February, too. That gave this lovely group of siblings the nickname 'the crazies'."

"I'm sure I'll like them. They seem sweet. Classy, actually." I chuckled.

"I'm hope you like them, dear. They come in every day. Not all at once, mind you. Each sister makes a grand entrance, dressed beautifully in the latest fashion, but always wearing her wide-brimmed hat."

Pansy strolled into the store wearing her hat. She adjusted it with flair and told me every well-bred Southern woman knew sun was her enemy. It was to be avoided at any cost. I felt like grabbing my sunbonnet.

Anyone who visited the shop was welcome to stitch on the donation quilt, which occupied the space close to the classroom in the back. Before Pansy left, she reminded me of the reason for working on the charity quilt. "As concerned citizens, we donate our time and talents. Poppa said to."

The sisters' concern included being watchdogs of the quilts. Each one walked around the quilt, humming as she inspected the piece. When a sister noticed big stitches, obviously quilted by someone of little skill, she attacked. She ripped out the offending work and proceeded to replace it with perfect quilting. Each bragged she was a better quilter than her sisters were—Mama said so.

Penny and Pansy must have been the older sisters. They were petite but wiry, looking rather severe as they went about their patrol of the quilt. Polly and Patsy were round and energetic. They displayed several rings on their fingers, which they pulled off with great gusto before quilting. They tossed the large stones into a pouch and then put the pouch in the oversized purse. These lovely women certainly added to my day. Each one brought me some special treat from her kitchen to welcome me to the store. Polly was the last one to visit. "I've quilted longer than I should. We're having dinner at Penny's house this evening, so I must go. You know, Patsy and I have to look after our older sisters. No telling what they would do without us."

"You all seem pretty lively to me. Didn't you all walk to the shop?"

"Most certainly. Penny is nearly twenty years older than me, of course, but she walks every day and insists on serving dinner for us all when it's her turn. I try to arrive early to help. This evening is special. We're viewing our gardens for the flowers we'll be taking to the Garden Club Show. So good to see you, my dear."

As she left the store, I admired the marmalade she'd given me and began twisting the cap. I was ready to sample the lovely gift when another customer came from across the room.

"Don't eat that," she whispered, looking around to see if anyone was listening. "The ladies are all cat people. Some say there are half a dozen or more in each house. They don't clean much these days, so I wouldn't try the great-looking wares. I don't believe the rest of what people say about the sisters, but sanitation is important, after all."

"What do people say?" I asked.

"Well, the sisters are proud of their beautiful oleander shrubs. Their properties all display lovely specimens. Even though oleanders don't thrive here, they still have beauties."

"What do the oleanders have to with their food?" I chuckled.

"Probably nothing, but remember in your southern history, the stories of the grand ladies of Charleston who apparently mixed the deadly plant into their good cooking and served it to British troops encamped around the city? There were deaths you know." She tilted her head and raised one brow. "Well, people speculate oleander might have something to do with the tidy deaths of eight husbands in all."

"Why, I can't believe it," I said softly as I dropped the tantalizing marmalade into the wastebasket. *I guess I'm just not daring enough to want to be part of the whole oleander mystery.*

On Friday evening, I reflected on the first week of work as I drove home. The fog in my thinking was lifting. I was capable. I had enjoyed the week. As I drove by a little church, the board outside caught my eye. I couldn't believe the words written there. That day of all days, there it was; "Have you trusted God with something impossible lately?" I hadn't noticed it that morning. You see, I had spent most of the day thinking I really didn't need to see Rhonda Bell face to face. Why should I subject myself to such emotional turmoil? *After all, you've forgiven her, isn't that enough? Just call her this evening and tell her everything is all right between you two.* Now this sign—God certainly had a sense of humor. *Wow, Lord, I get it. I'll trust You for strength for tomorrow.*

CHAPTER

7

Saturday morning, I grabbed the leash and headed outside with Lexus. We didn't work as a team yet, but there was a glimmer of hope. I told myself she soon would understand and cooperate with the whole leash thing. In the meantime, her enthusiastic tug ensured a vigorous walk. Mercedes, on the other hand, spent much of her time perched atop the many boxes I was storing in the space. The huge cat wound her way through them, hissing and growling at the animated little pup. I hadn't heard Mercedes growl before Lexus came along, but she often demonstrated that talent now. Of course, the cat was just the fun Lexus had been looking for. She leaped into the maze of boxes, wagging her tail. She always looked confident she'd found a playmate, only to return with a beaten look, her tail tucked between her legs. I couldn't imagine what occurred in the blackness of the maze of boxes. The amazing thing was this happened repeatedly, with the same results. *The little gal is hopeful—the eternal optimist.*

This morning, the squabble between Mercedes and Lexus was a desirable diversion. Actually, a firing squad at dawn was beginning to appeal to me. I wasn't sure which one of us would be facing the gun—Rhonda or me. Either way, the issue would be settled. I told myself again that I wasn't the one with the problem. I functioned quite nicely without seeing the woman who so carelessly took away the most terrific man I ever knew. What good could come of meeting each other, anyway? What was Dinky thinking by encouraging this?

As I heard a car approach, I opened the door. A yellow car stopped some distance from the house, behind a clump of trees. Why so far away? Was she planning a quick escape or something? I planted a wobbly smile on my face. I shivered. How would I get through these next few moments?

Rhonda appeared frail, fragile. At the cemetery, Sterling's cousin, sitting behind me, leaned over and whispered something about that woman having a lot of nerve, coming to the funeral of the man she just killed. Anyway, I hadn't ask Sterling's cousin how she knew Rhonda. I hadn't really cared. She was there, big as you please, standing in the rain across from the family. She had stared at me all the while.

Trust, lean. I motioned for Rhonda to sit down on the rocker on the porch, but instead she collapsed on the swing. *Great.*

"This seems welcoming." Rhonda smiled. "We can be closer here."

I explained that the house wasn't ready for company. Since I couldn't picture the two of us on the swing together, I sat in the rocker. Rhonda pulled a tissue from her purse, which she twisted in her hands as she glanced down.

"I came to beg your forgiveness. I can't live with myself. I see the whole thing in slow motion over and over. I'm having a hard time sleeping." She looked away. "I think I'll probably lose my job, if not my mind. I don't know what to say to you, but I'm so sorry. I know I can't expect you to forgive me." The swing creaked as it moved back and forth.

This was the moment I'd been waiting for. I started to speak when my vocal cords tightened and I gasped for air. I became lightheaded as I struggled to respond. *God, I don't want to forgive her. It's too easy for her. Shouldn't she have to suffer more? I'll never have an end to my suffering.* Saying I forgave her would be so final. It would mean an end to thinking and praying about forgiving Rhonda. I suddenly realized that it had actually become a comfortable place to be—angry, nearing rage at times, justifying my feelings before God. Now, I'd truly have to release the whole thing.

I managed to open my mouth. "There is nothing else I can do but forgive you."

Rhonda sobbed, her whole body moving up and down in spasms, her head bowed as she tapped her feet on the floor, pushing the swing back and forth.

I felt nothing. I wished desperately for any emotion. We just sat reliving our personal losses.

"I really didn't want to have this conversation," I stated as she sniffed into her Kleenex. "It was the right thing to do."

"What I don't understand is how you could ever forgive me. I can't forgive myself," Rhonda muttered as she looked into her tissue. "I came here hoping someday you'd forgive me, but I didn't think it was really possible."

"I tell you what, let's walk to my mother-in-law's house. Dinky would love to speak with you." What a strange situation this was—two broken women bobbing up and down on the sea of life and giving each other a lifeline. God is amazing.

Dinky greeted us with a warm smile. "I've been praying for you ever since Sterling died," she said, extending her arms to the burdened woman. Rhonda responded by crumpling into Dinky's chest and sobbing. They talked, then Dinky suggested we pray together.

There, in the wonder of that moment, a new child of God was born. After Dinky prayed, Rhonda poured her heart out to God, shaking as tears flowed in repentance. The release of all her torment was evident as she finished her prayer. We walked toward Rhonda's vehicle; I heard the sound of the trees blowing in the breeze and the crunch of our feet against the gravel. Mentally, I checked "dealing with Rhonda" off my list as I pictured my life becoming normal again. As we turned the curve in the lane, I saw a sporty convertible by the Crepe Myrtles. Rhonda seemed to pick up her pace, she quickly strode to the car and opened the door. I started to speak, when I glanced at the front of the yellow vehicle. There in the bumper was a huge V-shaped dent. My stomach sunk. My hand touched the surface, then ran the length of the indention. I lingered, speechless, as I pictured my Sterling's body violently thrust there. I looked at the hood. There were dents there, too. My knees buckled.

"I haven't taken it to the body shop yet," Rhonda said. "At first, I couldn't bring myself to fix it. Now I can't because the insurance money is gone."

I turned and threw myself into Dinky's arms. My sobbing echoed in the trees that surrounded us. Dinky swiveled me around and marched me up the steps. I heard her muffled voice say good-bye to Rhonda. As she slammed the door behind us, I heard Rhonda shout something garbled from the other side of the door. I threw myself on my bed and curled up in the fetal position. I pulled the covers over me, surrounding myself with darkness. I heard Dinky pacing. When the pacing ceased, I opened my eyes and pulled the covers down. She stood with her arms lifted up and her mouth moving. The soft words of prayer were hardly audible. Knowing my warrior Dinky was there for me, I rolled over and fell asleep.

I gritted my teeth and rolled over. How long had I slept? Light forced its way into the room at the edge of my makeshift curtain. I stumbled into the bathroom and found a note taped to the mirror. Had I really slept through the night? Dinky was picking me up for church. Church? Ugh, Sunday morning. I knew I couldn't escape Dinky even if I crawled back in bed. I was ready to leave in fifteen minutes.

Every word the pastor said penetrated my soul. I was a beloved child of the King, just as the Bible said. I couldn't give into the self-pity that knocked at the entrance to my mind. I wrestled with the scenes from the day before. I tried to make sense of what I'd experienced. No clarity came. When people began rustling around and chatting, I realized that the service was finished. I longed to sit there alone, but Dinky's pat on the back urged me to move. We ate lunch with the group from church. I listened to the conversation and smiled a forced smile. Dinky tried to comfort me as we drove home. I trudged into the house to take a nap. I needed one in spite of sleeping through most of Saturday. The familiar beeping sound greeted me—five calls. I pushed the button. Rhonda Bell. She couldn't forgive herself for her insensitivity. Could I please forgive her? The second call, Rhonda asked if I could call her. The next call was from L.J., asking to have dinner together. I'd deal with that later, maybe much later. The next call—Rhonda. The thought of forgiving the woman was much easier than the act. Maybe I would call her sometime. I was about to erase the last call without listening to it when I heard an unfamiliar voice.

"Hi, Mrs. Hollingsworth, this is Nathan Christopher. I got your message, and I'd love to see your project. I don't have much time to give to your remodel, but my dad might. He taught me all I know. He'll come with me. Give me a call on my cell if we could come around three."

CHAPTER

8

What...Mr. Christopher...today! I quickly dialed his number, changing clothes as we spoke. I phoned Dinky to join us. The roaring sound of a big engine alerted me to the Christophers' arrival. With long legs, quick smiles, and gray hair, both men were handsome. The older of the two was closest to me and extended a large hand my direction. After we exchanged greetings, I swiveled to acknowledge Nathan Christopher. My arm was still in midair when I looked directly at him. My smile turned to astonishment, my arm frozen in place.

A faint "hi" tumbled from my lips as I struggled to regain my composure. The eyes—the wrinkles when he smiled—it was the man from the post office fiasco. *Drat it—small towns. He's seen me at my clumsiest.* I shook his hand and turned quickly toward the front door.

"Haven't we met before?" The young Mr. Christopher moved closer and inquired. "I've been trying to place you since you came out the door."

"Well...." I began.

"Wait...you were at the post office the other day, when that rude young woman ran you down."

"Oh, were you the gentleman who helped me?" I responded awkwardly.

"So, you two have met. Nathan didn't tell me," the father interjected.

"I guess it wasn't as memorable a moment for you as for me, huh?" Nathan grinned.

"It was a memory I'd rather forget." The edginess in my voice was evident.

Dinky arrived with precision timing. Buck, Mr. Christopher Sr., assisted her up the steps, introducing himself as they went. There was nothing to do but follow them.

Great start, Clumsy.

I shook off the rocky start as we ushered the men through the house. The younger Mr. Christopher rubbed his hand on the partially stripped walls in several rooms.

"Wallpaper causing you problems?"

"You can tell the history of the house by the layers that I've stripped off. I didn't realize how hard that job would be. That's why you'll see some painting going on at the same time. I switch jobs when I can't stand steam and sticky paper anymore. Painting doesn't seem so bad in comparison."

He smiled and nodded his head. "I had the same problem working on my house. It gets to be a grind after a while."

The men admired the workmanship on the garage and the hall that connected the garage and the house, which would be home to my laundry room. Buck crawled under the house. He climbed into the attic, examining the wiring and heat ducts. They both squeezed into the unfinished apartment bulging with belongings and measured the space.

Nathan studied the trim work needed throughout the house. He measured and wrote down his calculations. He said his old home presented similar problems, but he was happy with the finished results. This would be time-consuming but possible.

The inspection complete, we sat down on the front steps. With the quality work accomplished so far, Buck was confident he could proceed without surprises. "My men and I can do most of the work.

I'll need Nathan to work on the finished carpentry when he has time. None of my men can match his work."

"I got through college and seminary working with my dad. His company was responsible for building apartment buildings and condominiums all along the east coast. Now, working with my hands is great therapy."

"Son, don't say that too loud. I intend to charge her for your therapy. All kidding aside, I sold my business and tried to retire, but I just couldn't sit and do nothing. I have two men working for me now," Buck said.

"I couldn't let him retire," Nathan said with a smile. "I sold my home and moved into the parsonage before Dad came to live with me, so he was driving me crazy. There certainly isn't anything for him to remodel there. We both tend to throw ourselves into our work. Dad is back working, and we are both happy."

We discussed the cost. Buck was relieved he wouldn't have to strip wallpaper. I told him Kelly Jo had shown me how to repair plaster, so I would be responsible for completing the paint and wallpaper work. That would help me stay within my budget.

He calmly explained, "I can finish your home for the amount you have to spend, but we'll have to stick to the existing home. Unless you have more money somewhere, the apartment will have to wait. I think we could improve the house tremendously with just a small amount of money. You don't need the little sitting room up here, do you?"

"It depends. What do you have in mind?"

"What if we combine the two tiny bedrooms, the sitting room, and the bath areas? Son, let's measure and see if that wouldn't produce two good-size bedrooms and a bath you can move around in."

After measuring, they gave me the cost.

"That sounds good. The money from the sale of my home in Atlanta was all I had. I guess I knew all the unexpected expenses had robbed me of my choices. I just hoped I could get the apartment ready for my daughter."

"Remember how much you loved the old place when Grandmother Hollingsworth lived here? You'll still get a laundry room and new kitchen. The bedroom idea sounds fine, doesn't it? You'll give it your own touch, and it'll be great," Dinky said. "Shelby can live at my house or in one of your new bedrooms."

"Okay, I'm ready. I guess I knew I couldn't have everything I wanted. At least I won't be consumed by bills when this is all over." I felt almost giddy at the thought of release from financial doom.

"Good girl. I like your grit." Buck chuckled and slapped me on the shoulder. "I wish more people thought like you."

"It's out of necessity, I assure you."

"I'll put the costs down on paper so you can be comfortable with the whole process. Hey, kiddo, don't look so glum. You'll be enjoying your wonderful home before you know it." Mr. Christopher's booming voice calmed my fears as we shook hands.

"Looks like the Hollingsworth family and Christophers will be seeing a lot of each other," Nathan said as they walked to the truck.

I smiled, but as the dust from the vehicle settled, the enormity of the situation settled in. I knew the master bedroom was beyond my reach, but there would be no apartment for Shelby.

"Sweetheart, I'm excited for you." Dinky's normal enthusiasm seemed somehow canned at the moment.

"Well, I guess I don't really need all that space. But Dinky, I have to consider Shelby. I promised her a space of her own."

"She'll just have to understand. After all, she has a perfectly good room at my house," Dinky said.

"I can't pay for her schooling if I'm paying for a larger house. I don't know if she'll understand or not," I said. "I've noticed that she hasn't unpacked much at your house. Seems temporary, to say the least. Dinky, what if we paint the room? Shelby can get new bedspreads, maybe even drapes. That won't break my bank, and she might feel more at home. What do you think?"

"I think we should get Pete to move some of my stuff to the attic. The room could use some freshening up."

All those plans sounded exhilarating until I put them on my list of things to do. I'd have to take the time to make Shelby feel at home, even though other things screamed for attention. We set a date with Pete and Claire—the Hollingsworth clan would come to the rescue and paint the room. In the meantime, I threw myself into the day-to-day work at the house.

I was more aware all the time that puppies needed lots of attention. My big plan hadn't included a dog, especially not a puppy. Motivated by guilt more than desire, I began walking Lexus as much as possible. I rationalized that huffing and puffing on the family trail would be good for both of us. Well, I huffed and puffed as I pulled the reluctant dog away from every tree, big and small. How she could manage to entangle herself in every tree was beyond me. When I couldn't take the time to walk, I played ball with her. She raced after the ball happily for a while, then I raced after the ball while she watched.

"Put the dog in the crate, and do what you have to do," Betsy said one day as I recounted my plight on the phone.

Betsy had never been an animal lover, but I'd try her advice. It seemed very effective for a couple of nights. Then, one night, as I went into the bathroom, Lexus became anxious. Her anticipation turned to disappointment as I turned to leave. I heard her cry turn to a howl. Leaving her in the living area in her kennel wasn't the answer.

"Abby, the unfinished part of the house is large enough to let her roam. What can she hurt?" Claire suggested after I whined to her.

I had new resolve—I'd let her explore. She found her favorite tennis ball and carried it around the space. Then, she amused herself by dropping her ball and retrieving it. Why not?

With the pocket doors closed between the dining room and my living quarters, the rest of the house was empty. I needed to finish painting the dining room woodwork that evening, so I opened the gallon can. When I turned to retrieve the paintbrush, I heard a plopping sound. Lexus was in the paint. Well, actually, her ball was in the paint. With all the space in this home, she'd chosen to drop the ball in the bucket of paint. She stood looking at me, her tail wagging, her head cocked expectantly, whining. She'd already taken a dip into the paint in hopes of retrieving her beloved sphere, but with no luck. Now, her adorable face was covered with paint. Of course, she began to prance around in the colorful substance enlarging the affected area. I grabbed at the ball. She thought we were playing. She wrestled with me until we were both a mess—and totally exhausted. The plastic on the floor saved us both.

At the end of my patience, I pulled a sheet of plywood, which had found semi-permanent residence in the kitchen, to the door and blocked her way into the rest of the house. I let Lexus roam the house for a few minutes, then slid the wood back and put her into the kitchen.

"Now, you can stay there, hear me, and you won't get into anything. The kitchen will be the last room I tackle," I said sternly.

Dinky was fixing dinner, so I threw myself into my work. I was becoming nimble on the tall ladder, and the crown molding was no longer daunting. I was seeing progress. Tonight, I'd finish the dining room completely. I loved the light bluish-green on the walls. After watching HGTV once too often, I had applied a light gold to the ceiling. The woodwork and mantle were all creamy white and beautiful. *Sterling would have loved this room.* Confidence was building with every brushstroke and every strip of wallpaper off the wall, but negative thoughts were always there to squelch my enthusiasm. Those thoughts were familiar, comfortable at times. If I got past losing Sterling, other losses invaded my thinking—loss of home, loss of income, loss of friends, loss of family as well. Next, I thought about the remodeling job. What did I really know about the Christophers? It didn't seem reasonable that Mr. Christopher had been so successful and, now in his golden years, he chose to work rather than hitting a golf ball or traveling. It even sounded as if he might be living with his son. Why? Hmmm. I'd better look into that whole thing. *What would Sterling do?* My stomach churned.

Kelly Jo was coming to help me patch the ceilings. I needed to be focused, that's all. I needed to ask Kelly Jo to go to church. I would look for an opportunity.

"Wow, it looks good!" Kelly Jo yelled as she came into the room.

I jumped. "I try to tune out the sounds around this old house. It has sounds of its own, you know. Even the trees close to the house scrape against the windows. I could get carried away listening to it all." I turned off the music.

"Later this week, my barnyard dog is cuttin' some of the wood you said we could have. If ya want, he kin trim around your house. I kin use all the firewood you'll let me have in exchange for the little work I'm doing with you."

"That would be great." I put my hands on my hips. "So, why is it that you call him a barnyard dog, anyway? Doesn't he have a name?"

"Sure—Buddy." She laughed. "I call him barnyard dog because of my past. I've jumped into relationships with bums. My girls have different daddies. Neither stayed around long enough to make them legal. That's probably the luckiest thing ever, since both the guys were losers. Anyway, Buddy is lots older than me. He drinks some, but he works every day and helps pay the bills. He don't cuss a whole bunch, drink too much, or hit anybody. Most of all, he stays away from my girls. You know what I mean? I figure with him around in my barnyard, I won't go makin' no big mistakes again, and maybe my girls won't either.

"I got it," I said, though I wasn't sure I really did.

CHAPTER

9

We worked until Dinky called us to dinner. When Kelly Jo and I entered Dinky's living room, colorful quilt squares lay on the floor. Dinky hugged me. "Look at the progress. The blocks are arriving every day. We received Betsy's today. Since Shelby won't be here tonight, I thought we'd admire them."

"Everybody at the shop encouraged me to make a memory quilt for Shelby," I told Kelly Jo. "We're keeping it a secret from her. We chose these fabrics and sent pieces to each family member." I pointed to the multicolored floral and the mottled green cloth. "They added other fabrics as they constructed their blocks."

"We've received blocks from all the Hollingsworth women and most of Abby's family. The P sisters heard about it and insisted on contributing squares as well, so it's growing larger than we planned," Dinky said as she ran her hand over a block.

"Wow, look at the fabrics and the fancy patterns. I love it," Kelly Jo said. "Can I make a square? It's like the quilts on my mother's frame when I was a girl."

"Do you quilt?" Dinky asked.

"I grew up in the mountains—everybody quilted. We needed the blankets. I can make a pretty fine quilt."

"We have a couple of women my age who work part-time at the shop, but we sure could use a young woman at the shop some, especially at night, when one of us teaches a class. The other women don't like to be out at night. Would you be interested?" Dinky said.

"My hours at the home improvement store used to be the same each week, but lately I've gotten fewer hours—just an hour here and an hour there shaved off. Everybody has. I'd really like some extra money coming in. I'm a hard worker. When can I start?

"Give me your schedule and I'll give you some hours," I said as I reached for a pad of paper.

"The memory quilt is a great idea." Kelly Jo picked up some blocks and admired them.

"It's hard to believe my baby is going to college. Maybe this'll help both of us make the transition."

"Kids grow up so fast, don't they?" Kelly Jo mused.

"I made this star block because Shelby and I looked at the stars a lot when she was small," Dinky remarked. "We shared wonderful memories on the dock, swinging our feet and enjoying the night sky."

"The stars always looked so much clearer out here than in town. It was a good time in our lives, wasn't it?" I sighed.

"Yes," Dinky said. "Shelby showed some interest when I constructed a prayer quilt for church. That was when she first came here to live. That gave me the idea of creating a quilt for her. We'll do the construction at the shop." Dinky picked up pieces.

"It's really coming together, isn't it?" I said as I moved close to look at one the blocks.

"Having Shelby's quilt up at the shop for friends to work on will be like the old days—quilting bee style. There'll be plenty of prayers said over it, that's for sure," Dinky said. "I hope Shelby feels love every time she puts the quilt around her."

I tried to sound casual as I handed her the last of the blocks. "It's a struggle getting through to her. It's like we left all rules when we left our Atlanta home. She doesn't act like I'm her mom anymore," I confided softly. "I don't know what to do, do you?"

"She does act like she can do whatever she wants. I've tried to pull the grandmother card and tell her she had to come home before I went to bed because I worried so much I couldn't sleep till I knew she was home. It didn't work. She's been staying out later and later. She reminded me that if things had been different, she'd be living in a dorm by now and she'd be doing what she wanted to do."

"She's been dealt lots of disappointments in the last year or so. I just hoped she'd be coping with things by now, but I still have to take one day at a time," I said as I stacked the blocks by the table.

Kelly Jo gave me a hug, and we cleared the dishes. "Once they think they're too big for our nests, they try flying on their own, whether they're ready or not. I guess it's always been that way. One of my girls threatened to find her father and go live with him when she got real ornery." Her voice softened. "She found the bum all right. It broke my heart when he totally rejected her. Sometimes I guess they jist have to learn on their own."

"We've just got to make the nest more appealing," Dinky said with resolve. "I'm glad Claire and Pete are coming next weekend. We'll move things around and paint. Getting her settled ought to help, don't you think?"

Dinky insisted on cleaning up and urged us to get back to our task. We said little as we worked that night. By the end of the evening, we had finished plastering most of the ceilings.

Kelly Jo giggled. "You're doing a good job with painting and stripping the paper off the walls." She stretched her arms out to encompass the room.

"A fresh coat of paint changes a room enormously. A new life is surfacing for me too." We cheered. "I just hope Shelby can get settled."

"It's hard at that age. She'll be fine."

As we cleaned up, Kelly Jo suggested I rent a wallpaper steamer. Spraying and scraping the paper was tedious and produced poor results. Surely, a steamer would help. As Kelly Jo went to her truck, I dragged myself into my room. Dinky had confirmed my fears. Shelby was avoiding her, too.

I'd tried numerous times to pin Shelby down to a shopping date, with no response. Now, I resolved to try harder. After several more calls, my persistence brought results. She informed me Thursday afternoon was the only time available. When Thursday morning finally arrived, she mysteriously had things that had to be done that afternoon. I dug my heels in, insisting on dinner. Reluctantly, she slid into the seat beside me, and we headed off.

I glanced at Shelby as I drove. A scowl covered her face. I had begun the summer hoping it'd be one of bonding for the two of us, but that hadn't happened. I'd sheltered Shelby after her dad's death. I didn't want my daughter to grow up as quickly I had when Mom died. I deliberately gave her room to be a kid again. Instead of blooming in her new freedom, Shelby had distanced herself more and more. We had to connect somehow.

Dinky often told me that the first job of love is to listen. I would make every effort to keep that in mind.

Father, help me to listen even if I don't like what I hear.

Shelby made few responses to my small talk.

We ordered. I took a deep breath. "Sweetie, I know it hasn't been easy for you this summer. Please, talk to me. I miss you."

"Oh, Mom, I'm just trying to get through the summer. I don't have anybody to hang out with. I'm bored to death."

"It's been rough. I pray for you often."

Shelby glared at me. She lowered her voice and leaned across the table getting in my face. "Mama," she hadn't called me that for years, "I don't find comfort in your prayers. God isn't a part of my life anymore. I really don't want to talk about it." As she finished speaking, tears formed in her eyes. She glanced away, finished her meal, and fussed with her napkin.

I put my hand on top of her arm. "Honey, it doesn't seem fair that you're experiencing all this. I lost my mother, so I know some of what you are going through. It gives me great peace to lift you to God daily."

"I don't feel the peace." Shelby whispered. Her eyes narrowed as she leaned in close to me. "How can you talk about peace and God? I heard you screaming at Dad the night before he died. Didn't have any peace then, did you?"

"What are you talking about?" I gasped.

"I was walking past your bedroom and I heard you say Dad lied to you. You don't deny it, do you? My dad went to his death with those words in his mind. Does that give you peace?"

"You don't know what you are talking about, Shelby. Married people have arguments. We talked through the situation and made up."

"Yeah, well, you two talked through a lot of things in high pitched voices those last few months. My dad would still be alive if you hadn't yelled at him all the time."

"Shelby, you don't know what you're talking about."

"Well, fill me in, Mom. Let's hear you justify what I heard."

My tongue stuck to the roof of my mouth. My hand shook as I reached for my glass of water. I tipped the goblet over sending water everywhere.

"Great, Mom. Just stop the religious jabber and take me home. When you're ready to be real, let me know." Shelby jumped up and walked out of the restaurant.

I paid and we drove home. I stopped at Dinky's long enough for Shelby to slide out and slam the door. She headed in without a backward glance. I parked in front of my house and sat with my hands firmly gripping the steering wheel. My head fell onto my arms.

The scene in our bathroom the night before Sterling's death danced before me like a scene from a movie. First, in slow motion; then faster and faster. How could I tell my daughter about the argument? I thought she was in bed asleep before I started talking with Sterling. I hoped she would never know the betrayal I'd felt that night. I'd stuffed the scene in the recesses of my mind.

The picture began again, this time with clarity. I'd run into the grocery on my way home from work. When I tried to check out, my credit card was rejected. The clerk had smiled and suggested I try another card, something must be wrong with that one. We tried all three of my credit cards—I wrote a check assuring her my husband would clear up the problem.

"Mine closed the credit card accounts and took all but fifty bucks from our checking account when he left with another woman. I hope you have your own money tucked away somewhere. I'll never trust a man again, I tell you." The clerk smirked and handed me the receipt.

As we prepared for bed, I told Sterling what happened. He mumbled something about hoping he could work it out before I found out.

"Work what out?" I chuckled nervously. "Did you cancel the credit cards and forget to tell me?"

"Now, Abby, it's only temporary. The cards are maxed out. I'll take care of it."

"What do you mean, maxed out? Why didn't you tell me? That's not something you just forget to mention? In all the years we've been married, we've always paid our card each month."

"You know that job Pete and I thought we landed a couple of months ago? It fell through and the little things we've been doing have hardly paid the business expenses, let alone our living expenses."

"So why didn't you just get that line of credit you talked about when you first started the new business?"

"We did, long ago. Abby, there isn't anywhere else to get money. We've got a good contract starting in two weeks. We've just got to coast till then. You'll see, it'll work out. I've always provided for my family and I will now."

"I could've gotten another job when this first started. I told you I should. How could you do all this without telling me, Sterling? You lied to me."

"Oh, Sweetie. I thought I was sparing you the worry. Heaven knows I've worried enough for both of us." Sterling held his arms out and we sobbed as we clung to each other. When I started to let go, he wiped his eyes and told me not to worry. We comforted each other in the privacy of our bed as only two frightened lovers can. The next morning he left me a note on the bathroom counter telling me how sorry he was—things were going to get better. I read the note minutes before I received the call that he was dead.

I asked Dinky to pay for her son's funeral. It was one of the hardest things I've ever done. Betsy helped with my bills until I received the money from a small insurance policy. Pete and Claire popped in almost nightly with dinner and often filled the pantry until we moved. Claire taught Spanish at the local high school—she had for year. Now she taught at night at the local resource center, as well. The business had affected all our lives.

That had been months ago and the shame came back fresh and new. I couldn't dismiss Shelby's ramblings, garbled and twisted as they were. She was in pain. I looked in the rearview mirror at her betrayer.

As I opened my front door, the answering machine beckoned me. Lexus bellowed from her kennel. It was probably another call from Rhonda. I'd deal with the message later. I felt like a whipped puppy as I took Lexus for a long walk and poured my heart out to her. She listened sympathetically—I felt the love. It'd be days before I quit pulling the conversation with Shelby out and rehashing it in my mind. How could we get past all the hurt?

Upon my return from the walk, I punched the dreaded button. Instead of Rhonda, L.J.'s voice reverberated in my small space. He was hoping we could go to a movie tomorrow evening. I dialed the number on the phone, and he answered on the first ring.

"I was hoping you'd get back to me this evening. How about dinner in downtown Greenville, then a movie closer to home?"

"I'm tied up tomorrow evening, but thanks for asking me."

"Then lunch."

"I'm working from eleven until closing. Maybe some other time."

"Well, the pancake place isn't far from your shop. If we can meet at 9:00, you'll be at the store in plenty of time. Deal?"

Why not be in the company of someone who could take my mind off my troubles. Besides, at this point, it looked like a good deal. "Okay, 9:30 and it's a deal."

I stumbled over Mercedes as I headed for bed and muttered, "Good grief, old girl, you're a black cat in a dark room, run for cover."

Good grief—what an odd statement. I'd used that term for years. Was there really such a thing—good grief? Why couldn't I just grieve the loss of my wonderful husband? Why did money and family have to muddy the whole thing up. I loved an incredible man—not superhuman—but incredible, none the less. We'd had our disagreements but even that last huge argument had ended in an embrace. What I wouldn't give for that now. I felt Mercedes settle in at the end of the bed as I drifted off to sleep.

CHAPTER

10

Buck Christopher and his small crew arrived by 7:30 in the morning. Dinky was pacing in front of the house when I opened the door at 7:25. Until now, she'd shown no interest in the actual process of remodeling so I wondered what inspired the new enthusiasm. As Buck came into the room, Dinky beamed.

"It was great talking with you the other day." He smiled.

She looked down ever so shyly. "Yes, for me, too."

Dinky looked at me. I looked at Buck. He looked at Dinky. Suddenly I knew the source of Dinky's enthusiasm.

"Oh, yes, Abby. Buck and I went for a cup of coffee after we all picked out the cabinets the other day. You were on the way to the shop before we made the plans. You were opening that morning. Remember?"

"Ahhhh," I mused. Dinky's face spoke volumes.

I struggled to get back on the subject. "Buck, I'm so thrilled that we're getting started. By the way, the plunger and I are becoming friends. I hope my plumbing is high on your list."

"Your electrician is almost done, and the plumber starts tomorrow. Maybe you won't need the plunger much longer. Plan to be in your new home by Christmas," Buck stated.

"That is wonderful, isn't it, Abby?" Dinky said. "I'm planning on staying here this morning. You know, in case there are any questions. I got one of the girls to work with you this morning."

Oh, boy. I doubted that Buck would have many questions about the job, but I had a million questions for Dinky. Those questions would wait. I was going to be late for breakfast with L.J. if I didn't leave right away. I kicked myself as I drove to the restaurant. I had a class to teach, and I needed to prepare for it. Why had I let L.J. talk me into eating breakfast with him? I was still on the run as I reached the restaurant. Eager to slide into the booth, I smiled at L.J. and headed for the seat. Instead, he rose and hugged me, a little too long for my comfort.

"There's a festival in the mountains this weekend. I thought it'd be great to grab lunch and walk around for a while. What do you think?"

"I can't Saturday. I work all day. Really, I can't do much right now. I've got more than I can handle with remodeling and working at the shop."

"I've been on this journey through mourning longer than you, Abby. I remember fearing commitment. I think that's what you're going through." His tone was condescending, to say the least.

"I'm committed to several things. That's the problem. I'm committed to my family, my work, and my house. That's really all I can manage right now."

"I'm not asking for much—two friends spending time together once in a while. Don't you get sick of eating alone and watching television?"

"Actually, that would be a step up from my existence. I don't eat out much, and I'd like the luxury of an hour of television. But, I guess there's no harm in friends grabbing a bite to eat once in a while."

"How about Sunday evening?"

We were nearly finished eating when I checked my watch. I waved at the server, who produced a bill.

"I'm paying, Abby. I asked you out."

"I'm sorry, but if we're going to go places together, it has to be with the understanding that we pay our own way or I can't go."

"Control issues, huh?" He grinned.

During the mad dash to work, I fumed at the things slung at me with my eggs and sausage. First, commitment—I'd been married for over twenty years. What was that, if not commitment? Second, control—I didn't think I was the one dealing with those issues. Actually, I felt out of control. L.J. seemed to win every time. Being an assertive male could be attractive, but this bordered on being aggressive.

My phone rang as I pulled into the parking lot. I glanced at the incoming number.

"Hi, Dinky. What's up?"

"Abby, the electrician just fell through the ceiling. He was running the electrical in the den and missed his step."

"Is he all right?"

"I'm so glad Buck was here. He called 911 and they came quickly. He was dazed at first and in pain. They thought he might have broken bones. He'll call us as soon as he knows anything. Abby, there is more."

"More. What more?"

"He crashed down close to us. It was frightening. Abby, the ceiling thundered to the floor right along with him. That old plaster flew everywhere."

"Oh, no. Are you okay?"

"Buck and his men are working to clean it up. He'll let you know what it will mean."

I hung up and buried my head in my hands. I had just finished touching up the plaster in that room. A gasp escaped from my mouth. I had a class to teach; I couldn't bail out of it. Six girls were learning to sew. This would be the third class, and it was going well. I'd taught them the fundamentals and the girls were now making pillows. I wanted to rush to the house and see the damage for myself but the clock was ticking and I had things to do. I finished duplicating information about today's lesson just as the girls hustled into the shop. They giggled as they set their machines up. They were attentive as I reviewed and demonstrated what they were to do today. They began sewing the pieces they had cut last week.

I kept waiting for Dinky to make an appearance, but the cleanup must have been extensive. As I forced myself to think about the electrician and his health, all I saw were dollar bills flying past me into a deep pit. I foolishly told our sales clerk I could handle things until Dinky got there, so I was operating the shop as well as teaching the class. Pansy finished quilting. She was making her way to the door when she stopped and turned to me.

"Abby, I have got to say this quickly—Penny may be coming soon. We sisters have found quilt supplies around her house. When we asked her about them, she had no memory of buying anything. She's been getting more absent-minded lately, but nothing like this. I just don't understand how this could happen to our family."

"What kind of things, Pansy?"

"Well, new scissors, thread in interesting colors we would never use, and thimbles, two of them still in the package. Penny seems confused about them. When we looked in the quilting bag she always brings in here, there was more. We are so sorry, but we sisters will pay for everything. Here are the things still in the packages, and we have a list of other supplies. Here, you look it over and give us a bill." Pansy's face reflected deep pain as she handed me the supplies and list. "This is so unlike Penny. You know that her husband was the mayor for many years. No scandals there, I tell you. He ran a tight ship in our little town. Well, this is so unlike our family. Mama and Poppa would be mortified."

"I'm sure Penny didn't mean any harm. I'll look over your list. We'll keep this just between you sisters and me."

"But the bag she carries—we don't want this to continue being a problem. We can't tell her not to come."

"I'll keep her bag behind the counter. It will be for her safety. I'll tell her I wouldn't want anyone walking off with her things by mistake. That ought to solve the problem, don't you think?"

"It really would be for her safety, wouldn't it? Oh, thank you, Abby. That will relieve us tremendously. In fact, we will all put our bags behind the counter so she won't be suspicious. I'll tell the sisters, and we will start keeping a better watch at home, too. It is just our little secret, right?" I shook my head in agreement, and she literally skipped out of the shop. *What precious women. Mama and Poppa did a good job.*

I kept expecting Penny to arrive. When I heard the buzzer, I assumed it was her. Instead, someone from my past fluttered through the door.

"Melissa Ann Grimes, is it really you?" I would recognize her anywhere. She was the same as ever—perfect hair, perfect figure, perfect clothes, well, just perfect.

"I can't believe you moved here. After Atlanta, this must seem like a quiet little burg," Melissa Ann gushed, elongating her syllables in a soft southern drawl.

"Quite the contrary, I love it. How are you, anyway?"

After telling me glowing reports of her flawless life, she put on her sad face. "Arthur and I just found out about Sterling last week while we were at the country club gala, and I set out to hunt you down. We just happen to be having friends over Saturday night, and you simply have to join us. Some of our mutual friends from the old days will be there. They are begging for you to come. I just won't take no for an answer."

"Well, then I will save my breath and simply say yes," I said, and we both laughed.

She gave me directions and told me the proper dress for the evening—not too casual, but certainly not fussy. She flew out of the shop, having accomplished the niceties that she aimed for, leaving me to wonder what I'd been thinking. I could picture her crossing "Saturday night—Abby" off her list as she moved on to the next social obligation for the day.

Oh, great. You could've told her you'd get back to her after you checked your day timer. Penny rushed into the store, soaking wet. "It was just gentle rain until I reached the door, and now look. It's a downpour."

"Oh, Penny. I'm so sorry," I said. "Wait just a minute." I turned to the young girls. "You're all doing a great job. Let's look at your work, then we'll discuss putting the pillow together. Next week, you can take home the finished project."

I directed Penny to the bathroom, gave her hand towels to absorb the moisture, then went back to the class. After we talked about each girl's project, they gathered their things. I answered questions and said good-bye to them. I watched them scurry to their awaiting cars. Penny had been quilting, but now she followed me to the office. I noticed her bag was wet, so I wiped it off with a towel. I casually asked if she'd like me to start keeping her belongings under the counter while she quilted so nothing would happen to them. She seemed genuinely pleased with the attention. She was filling me in on the latest squabble between Pansy and the mailman when Dinky called.

She wouldn't be in; things had come up. *Yeah, things like Buck. Hmmm.* I did some paperwork and then sent an email message to Betsy. The holidays were coming up and I had devised a plan—it was simply brilliant. I'd go to our sister Eleanor's for the family Thanksgiving dinner if she would. She usually celebrated Thanksgiving with her children and Christmas day with our family. Maybe I'd be lucky and she'd say she couldn't go. At least then, I wouldn't be the only one letting Daddy down. He'd still disapprove, but I wouldn't be the only one under fire.

Penny retrieved her bag and started for the door. I yelled for her to wait a second. I'd take her home. I turned off the lights and trudged to the car as thunder boomed in the distance.

On the drive home, the whole Melissa Ann Grimes thing began to bug me. It festered during my struggle with wallpaper and erupted after dinner at Dinky's house. I actually stooped to asking Dinky to call Saturday and tell Melissa Ann that I was ill and couldn't come to dinner. I was embarrassed to ask her, but desperate times called for desperate measures. In a way, I was sick. It had come to me as I drove home that evening that I actually had never cared for Melissa Ann.

CHAPTER

11

Seeing Melissa Ann Grimes put another kink in my already twisted ties to the past. The threads of rejection were intricately woven into the fiber of my being from a very tender age. Memories of Traveler's Rest started with Grandmother Carter. I seldom saw her until I was five. I guess Daddy had his fill of caretaking by then, because he sent me to Grandmother's for that summer and every summer after that. My older sisters stayed at home while I felt the sting of Grandmother's tongue for three months every year.

The most consistent comment to other people was, "if they'd known when to stop having children, I wouldn't be forced into this role. My precious boy endures so much with an invalid wife that it's the least I can do to take the child off his hands for the summer." There would be a deep sigh followed by a pat, a hug, or a smile from the listener. I seldom received the same.

That was, until I met Dinky. Grandmother dropped me off at vacation Bible school like a person drops off discarded items at Goodwill. After that, Dinky began taking me to church and home for dinner afterwards. Later, I stayed all day on Sundays. As I got older, I spent more and more time with the Hollingsworth family. I lived for the gatherings, a youth group junky.

Melissa Ann was a member of the youth group. She was the popular girl. While everyone else struggled with zits, her skin radiated health. She developed a body before I even thought about that kind of thing. She glided gracefully across a room, while I stumbled into the corner, watching and wishing I could be like her. The boys followed her around like little puppies. She made it known that she was number one in the pecking order; I guess we all agreed.

When I turned fifteen, things changed. After all, I was the new girl every summer. During the school year, Melissa Ann had successfully landed Arthur—the big catch. He was the large fish in our little pond. He was handsome, bright, and, more importantly, his family was wealthy. She had one problem. That summer, Arthur and Sterling both noticed me, I guess for the first time.

Considering me a threat, she singled me out. "It is such a shame you are so pale, Abby. Maybe with the help of the tanning booth, you wouldn't look so sickly." On another occasion, "I'll give you the number of the orthodontist here in town. My teeth are naturally straight, but I hear he does wonders with teeth like yours."

These remarks elicited nervous smiles from the other girls—better me than them—and mystified looks from the guys.

I was vulnerable. We all knew it. All the buzzard had to do was swoop down for the kill. That day came when she flitted into Dinky's house with two garbage bags brimming with clothes. In front of the others, she dropped the burden on the floor and said, "Mom cleaned out my closet and told me to get rid of last year's things. So here, Abby, I hope you can use these."

She delivered the remark with the skill of a heavyweight champ, with regular one-two punches that hit the mark. I was down for the count. Her only error was in timing. I stooped to pick up the bags as Dinky flew into the ring, swooped them up, and said, "I'll be glad to take the contributions to the church myself. No need for sweet Abby to do it." I'd never heard that tone of her voice before, or for that matter, since.

Actually, Melissa Ann's blatant rudeness had been a turning point of sorts in my life. Dinky became my protector, my mentor, my defender. She squelched Melissa Ann at every turn. The girl had missed the obvious fact. I was interested in Sterling. I hardly knew Arthur existed.

Sterling later said I loved Dinky so much I figured I'd better fall in love with him too—the two-for-one special. We often laughed about it, but that was when I was the loved, secure wife of a wonderful husband. So, here I was. I couldn't live in the past. I couldn't cling to Sterling. I couldn't ignore the fact I was the new girl in town again. This time, I was going to the ball without my prince. Why did my first real adventure as a single woman going to a social gathering involve Melissa Ann Grimes? As I thought the whole thing over, the solution became clear to me. The only way around pain and self-deprecation was to avoid the situation altogether. Unfortunately, Dinky didn't come to the same conclusion. She refused to help. She smiled sweetly as if I were joking. Where was my defender when I needed her? She casually mentioned she was going to a movie with Buck. I told her I'd be glad to give up my evening and be her chaperone. No amount of whining changed her mind.

Arthur and Melissa Ann lived in Greenville, only fifteen minutes away. I gave myself a little pep talk on the way. I wasn't the poor little stepchild. I was handling life. I could mix and mingle. How hard could it be? I pulled my shoulders back, adjusted my purse strap, and walked up the lovely brick sidewalk. I took a deep breath and rang the doorbell. Looking around as I waited, I noticed several cars on the street. As the door opened, I heard a blast of voices coming from inside. I stepped into a buzz of conversation. There were certainly more people than I planned on seeing. *Oh, well, I'm ready. Bring it on.*

Arthur greeted me, took my hostess gift, and yelled to Melissa Ann. I walked into the living room, and a dozen people turned to stare. Dread gripped me as I realized the obvious—couples. Oh, great. I saw friends from the past, and I smiled and relaxed. After all, it'd be fun to catch up with their lives.

From the kitchen, Melissa Ann emerged with hors d'oeuvres, which she placed on the coffee table. Following close behind her was a distinguished gentleman, twenty years older than her, who shot across the room to greet me.

I assumed we would shake hands, but instead he hugged me. "My dear, I'm Winston Carrington. I've heard so much about you. What a delight to share the evening with you." He kept his arm tightly around me.

"Hi," I said as I felt my face begin to burn. Was it hot in here, or was it just my temperature rising? I concentrated on being poised. I don't think it worked, because Melissa Ann quickly escorted me into the kitchen.

She spouted Winston's pedigree—influential family, banker, and wonderful dancer. *Hmmm.* He and his wife divorced years ago. Some young thing took her place. It sounded like there had been a succession of young things.

"Winston was with us at the country club gala when I heard about your poor Sterling. He voiced interest in meeting you. I really thought it rather strange, since his money seems to attract sweet young women from all over. Well, anyway, I thought this would be a great thing for you. I mean, Winston can really treat you right. You should see some of the gifts he gives his friends. He thought it'd be nice for us all to share dinner together. If you play your cards right, it might lead to something more."

I smiled and returned to the group. My mind whirled with new names, new faces, and a new pain in my stomach. I kept my distance from Melissa Ann, but it was impossible to shake Winston. After a long dinner, I excused myself, saying I wasn't feeling well. Winston hugged me and handed me his business card. He assured me that he would be calling. *Great. I am certainly no sweet young thing, Mr. Carrington. What came over Melissa Ann and Arthur?* I dropped into the seat of my car. *Next time, I'll ask more questions.* I looked into the rearview mirror as my wrinkles jeered at me. *Sweet young thing, huh? Well, let him pine away for this one, I'm out of here.* Winston and his cheerleaders faded from view.

Driving home, I rethought seeking Winston's favor. Why, I could be a trophy wife—no more worries about finances. I could get used to lavish gifts. I quickly mumbled, "Not interested, Lord, just thinking. Please, protect me from any other Winstons who might be looming out there? I'm waiting on You."

Apparently, I arrived home from the Grimes' house long before I was expected. There was a party going on at my house. All the lights were on, and as I peered past the boxes into the den, I saw two figures gliding across the floor. There was a beautiful waltz floating through the air, and Dinky and Buck moved smoothly to the beat. *What do I do now? Awkward moment.* I decided against barging in. I'd give them time by taking my pup for a walk. They'd probably leave soon. The song ended, and I heard laughter. I slipped into the garage as quietly as possible, giggling as I tiptoed through my chaos.

When the daily temperature had become livable, I had decided to move Lexus's cage to the garage. The close proximity of the kennel to my bed had bothered me on several levels. My toe caught the wire cage on more than one occasion, but I could have lived with that. The problem was Lexus snored. Now, my heart pounded as I foraged my way across the storage area. Lexus began barking, anxious to get out of her crate. I plunged across the space and let her out. She came bounding to me, barking with glee—Mom was home. Her wagging tail told me that her business outside couldn't be stalled. I crept toward the exit, begging her to be quiet as Dinky and Buck came through the door.

"Oh, Abby, I hope we didn't startle you. We heard barking and came to check on this little gal," Dinky said as she patted Lexus on the head.

"Hey, Abby, we were just trying out those beautiful wood floors to see if they were smooth enough to be finished," Buck said uneasily. "Won't be long before we have to move your stuff out totally and do the floors."

"Buck, she caught us." Dinky blushed. "I bet you've already guessed that it wasn't just the house I've been interested in lately. We've talked about dancing for a while, and thought we'd better practice here rather than on a ballroom floor at the senior citizen's center with everyone watching."

With that, Buck took her hand, which he patted as he looked at the floor. I might not have had eye contact, but I certainly saw that grin. They looked like a couple of teenagers, a little embarrassed by the situation, yet captivated by each other.

"Abby, we've planned to invite you to dinner for some time now. I guess I feel the need to tell you my intentions toward this beautiful woman. I know we've only been seeing each other for a short time, but …." Buck started strong but stopped with a whisper.

"Abby, darling, I was the one who delayed saying anything to you. I know you've had a lot of adjustments in the last year. I don't want to complicate things. I mean, I'm still here for you."

"Dinky, stop right there. I'm thrilled to know that you two are enjoying each other's company. You have a right to a life." As Dinky and I hugged, I felt Buck gently place his hand on my shoulder.

We were all entangled in the leash, so we twisted until we were free. I followed my pooch outside. The cool night air hit my face. I'd never thought about Dinky being in love again. I wrestled with the concept. I was shocked that self-pity oozed hot and ugly as I trudged in the darkness.

In the morning, I wrestled with a strange feeling in the pit of my stomach as I drank my second cup of tea. Just as I was getting settled in a new comfort zone, change was coming again. If Dinky's life didn't end after Elliot, then maybe there was a future waiting for me. I wasn't sure I was up to having a future.

The next Friday evening, everyone gathered to disassemble furniture and prepare to paint Shelby's room. Carter had promised to help this weekend but, at the last minute, he was too busy to come.

"We seldom see him. His head is usually stuck in a book when he is around. He has dinner with us once in a while, but with his night class and his new study partner, Alex, he's gone most of the time."

"I haven't heard him mention Alex, but he seldom mentions the guys at school. But, I haven't heard a girl mentioned either. We haven't talked much since his dad died. My relationship with my children seems to be a casualty of Sterling's death." Claire hugged me extra hard that evening.

Saturday, Claire and I painted the walls. I felt like a pro after all the painting I'd been doing. Shelby and Pete moved furniture into the room after hanging blinds. I actually heard Shelby giggle as they wrestled the mattress up the stairs.

Dinky winked at me. "This might just be the medicine needed for our girl."

"I hope so." We placed the bedspread on the bed.

"Thanks," Shelby said as she looked around the room. "This looks great."

I anticipated a quiet family evening together, but Shelby disappeared after putting her clothes away. Dinky and I took Claire and Pete to my home and showed them the progress. Dinky marveled at the workmanship and gushed at the ease of the building process. Claire gave me a look. I raised one eyebrow. She could fill in the details for herself. Dinky suggested playing Scrabble. The game was slow, but the subtle interrogation Claire gave Dinky was hilarious. I'm sure Buck's ears were burning by the end of the evening. It's a shame he missed it. He would have caved quickly under Claire's questioning.

Monday morning, I listened to three messages from Winston before erasing them. I was heading to the shop when the cell rang. "Abby, how about dinner at Capri's tonight? Buck just called and suggested it. I'm hoping this will be the first of many evenings together." Dinky sounded like she was bouncing off the ceiling. "Nathan has some time to work at the house. Since the cabinets are going to be here soon, we thought it'd be a great time to get together and coordinate it all."

"Sounds wonderful. You know, the wallpaper stripping isn't going well. I'm really sweating—literally—to get the wallpaper off so Nathan can complete his trim work."

Dinky chuckled.

"Are you coming in this morning?" I said.

"I'll be there. I love you." Silence. No details for me, I'd have to wait.

Kelly Jo came by before heading off to work at the home improvement store. As she left, three other customers came in. I was cutting fabric when Dinky arrived and waved as she went into the office. I tried to get away from the customers to speak with her. Instead, she popped out of the office and through the back door.

Pooh, I wanted the scoop on what is going on. She yelled something about beating the storm as she ran to the parking lot. *I guess my questions would have to wait.*

It had spit a fine mist all day, but the rain that once was a distant rumbling was now a booming presence. It was a deluge. I hurried to the door, thinking Dinky might come back inside, but she disappeared into the fog. We closed at five on Fridays. With the temperature dropping and rain pelting, there were no late shoppers. I flipped the sign on the door to "closed," locked up and slipped into the office to catch up on paperwork.

I called Shelby and asked her to coax Lexus outside before she left for the evening. We both knew the job might require venturing out in the elements with the puppy. Shelby mumbled, but finally said she'd take care of my baby. I'd head straight to the restaurant when I finished paying the bills.

The electrician called to say how sorry he was for the long delay. He'd be back on the job next week. He asked about the damaged ceiling, and I assured him that Buck and his men finished the new ceiling. We agreed to discuss the cost when he finished the electrical work. Thirty minutes later, my stack of papers was dwindling when the phone rang. I didn't recognize the number, so I decided not to answer. *Probably a customer wanting me to open the store for a spool of thread. The machine will get it.*

As the answering machine told the caller to leave a message, I heard Shelby's voice. She screamed something about my not answering my cell phone, and I could hear other people in the background. What was going on?

I grabbed the phone. "I'm sorry, Shelby, I didn't hear my cell ring. Is something wrong with Lexus?"

"Mom, get to the emergency room right now. It's Dinky. The police called the house as I was leaving. Mom, get here, we need you." She sobbed.

"Okay, which hospital, what happened?" My heart pounded wildly.

A woman came on the line, gave me directions, and assured me that everything possible was being done. "What do you mean, everything is being done?" There was silence.

CHAPTER

12

"What would we do without her?" Shelby sobbed.

"God knows how precious she is to us all," I said.

"Oh, yeah, like He knew how important Dad was to me—He took him anyway. Don't talk to me about God."

Tears streamed down her face. She stood in the waiting room, her frail body shaking. As our eyes met, she sobbed and clenched her fists. I reached out to embrace her. She pushed my waiting arms away and rushed from the room.

Buck sat there, his head buried in his hands. I collapsed in the chair next to him, my knees shaking.

"Abby, Dinky loves you both so much. She talks about you both all the time." He raised his head. His voice faltered. "She lights up when she talks about her Shelby. Abby, Dinky's going to be all right... yes, she's going to be just fine."

I wept and Buck paced. My watch told me thirty minutes had passed since Shelby stormed out. My body told me that was a lie. It felt like it had been days since this whole thing started. As I bent over and burrowed in my purse for a tissue, I heard footsteps and saw Nathan in the doorway.

"I just spoke to Dr. Cline." He looked at Buck.

"What did he say?"

"Jane Ann is in surgery, and they'll know the extent of her injuries soon. Dr. Cline's shift is over in half an hour, but he promised to check in with us before leaving."

"Thanks," I said.

Buck told Nathan the little we knew. Jane Ann had been driving in the downpour; a man failed to stop at the traffic light and smashed into her car. She was unconscious when she arrived at the emergency room.

"There is nothing to do but wait," Buck finished with a sigh.

Nathan started to put his arm around my shoulder, then seemed to change his mind. "We can pray," he said and took my hand.

The three of us huddled together in the sterile room and placed Dinky gently into His hands, praying for her physical healing and emotional strength for us all.

"Father, please protect Shelby. Show her that You are in charge, even in the most difficult circumstances. We give it all to You," Buck prayed.

We remained huddled together, then realized Dr. Cline was waiting. He reported there was internal hemorrhaging and a broken hip, but he was confident the surgeon had successfully repaired everything. The bottom line was everything looked good, considering.

He left as quickly as he came in. "Everything looks good, considering? What does that mean?" Buck mumbled.

"Dad, he is just being conservative in his assessment. We'll hear more from the surgeon in a while. Well, this certainly isn't the Friday night we planned, is it?" Nathan smiled as he turned to me.

"No," I said. *Oh, Lord, I need my Sterling right now. I would give anything to be nestled in his arms.*

Two hours later, Pete, Claire, and Carter arrived. Shelby stomped in behind them. She'd been sitting alone in the front entry. There was a trip to the cafeteria, a blur of Cokes and coffee as the night wore on.

Around midnight, the surgeon appeared, apologizing for the lengthy wait. He'd been busy with two surgeries after Jane Ann.

"She is stable, and her good general health points to a good outcome. I don't foresee any complications. She is in the critical care unit so the staff can supervise her for the night, but I don't expect any surprises. You can see her tomorrow."

We moved to yet another waiting room. Carter suggested taking Shelby home. *We need Sterling.* Nathan accompanied them to the car, saying he'd return tomorrow. Buck, however, remained. He'd remain for many days.

CHAPTER

13

I felt my phone vibrate in my pocket. Startled, I jumped, nearly knocking over the tray perched on the edge of Dinky's hospital table.

Kelly Jo screamed into the phone, "Mr. Perkins disappeared! Abby, do you hear me? Mr. Perkins is gone."

"Do you mean he was kidnapped? Did he wander off?"

"No, no. When I came by his shop this morning, I saw his store windows were empty. Abby, there's nothing there. I raced in to call you, and there's a message on the machine. His children moved his things out. They had ta do it in the middle of the night. I don't know. I closed last night, but didn't see anything going on then."

"Kelly Jo, what did the message say?"

"His son said with the economy the way it is, the family decided Mr. Perkins should work from his garage at home. He said if they owed any money to contact him."

"Good timing, Mr. Perkins. That's all I can say." I thanked her and said I'd talk to her later.

I should've prepared for this. The man had rented space in our building for over twenty years—long before Dinky bought the place. It seemed the economy had taken its toll on our aging antagonist. We should've known the ever-growing list of complaints was leading to this. In the last couple of months, he'd made a point to tell us about his leaky sink, the funny sound in the air conditioner, the flickering lights. Of course, the parking problem had seemed to escalate as well.

I slipped the phone into my pocket, adjusted the sheets around my sleeping mother-in-law, and tiptoed out of the room. It was nearly ten in the morning, and I needed my first cafeteria run of the day. When the hospital stay was over, I had to diet. Right now, my Coke and pretzel break was an essential midmorning activity. As I rode the elevator to the main floor, I fumed. Mr. Perkins—the turkey—had deliberately moved out in the dark of night instead of waiting for a more appropriate time. If he needed to leave, why not the end of the month, the end of Dinky's hospital stay, or at least during the day? Coward.

As I plopped into my favorite booth, I dug in my purse for a pen and paper. I found an empty envelope. It would do the job. I scribbled my concerns on the back. Our newly vacated storefront now became concern number one. Number two on my list was the money we were paying in wages while Dinky remained hospitalized. The part-time help rescued me in so many ways, but it still cost money to staff the shop. I sighed as I placed my home remodel in lowly third place. *What would Sterling do in this situation?*

"You look deep in thought." Nathan's voice was recognizable without looking up.

"Hi." I forced a smile. *Why was this man always around when I was at my worst? He must have pastoral radar to seek out and comfort grumpy little widows.*

"I was on my way up to see Dinky when I noticed you here. Apparently, I picked a bad time." He started to leave.

"I'm not the best company right now."

"As a professional, let me give you some advice." He smiled and waited for me to respond.

I motioned for him to sit down. "Well, let me have it. I wish someone could advise me. Our profit at the shop has dwindled, my daughter confuses me, and my dad drives me crazy. Last, but certainly not least, my tiny living space is now in shambles."

"Dad said they tore the walls down between your rooms in the front of the house last week. Do you have a working bathroom yet?"

"Sort of. It's really a good time for the bedroom demolition since I've spent nights here anyway. It all adds to the drama of my life."

"Well, my professional advice is to give yourself room, and I don't mean physical space. Then…."

"What do you mean, give myself room?" I scoffed.

"Don't be so hard on yourself right now. Your life's complicated. Give your struggles to God."

"Easy for you to say."

"Sure, and I do it all so well. The man of the cloth hears directly from God—is that what you think?" He laughed.

"Something like that." I chuckled. "Now that you say it, it sounds sort of silly."

"I haven't eaten. Can I join you?" I nodded, and he went to the counter. He slid into the booth across from me. We talked about lots of things—my past, my responsibilities, my hopes. I tried to turn the conversation to his interests, but he skillfully diverted my efforts.

"Thanks for your help. I'm not used to handling life on my own. It's nice to have someone to listen to my craziness." I put my lips together tightly, wishing I could retract the statement.

"Everybody needs a friend. I'm one, and you know Dad is a safe person to ask about those business questions."

"Thanks." My phone rang. Nathan got up to refill his drink. I moaned. "Oh, hello, Dad."

"You still at the hospital, I suppose. I hear you aren't coming to Thanksgiving dinner with us. Is that right?"

"Yes, I'm still at the hospital. Dinky is improving, but I need to be here. The accident has slowed the remodel, too. On top of that, I have a business to run. I'm having the traditional fabric sale the day after Thanksgiving. Really, Dad, I don't know if I am coming or going."

"All I hear you saying is that Jane Ann is more important than spending a few hours with your real family," he said emphatically.

"I'm sorry if that is what you hear. I can't do anything about it. I emailed my regrets to Eleanor. By the way, I haven't heard from her any more than I have from you. I leave voice messages, but neither of you return my calls. Let's see, it was July or August when you last answered my call, right?"

"I'm calling now, aren't I? Don't get that tone with me, little girl. I'm still your daddy."

"Daddy, you of all people know what it is like to lose a mate. Surely you can smooth things over with Eleanor and be a little more thoughtful to your baby girl, right?"

"I should've known I couldn't talk sense into you. Good-bye."

"Good-bye, then, and give my best to Katherine." I flipped my phone shut.

"You're fortunate to have so many loving friends and family members, Abby," Nathan said.

"Hmm, sure. It's grand." The words left a fowl taste in my mouth.

He tilted his head slightly. "Sounds like there are unresolved issues there."

Oh great. Just what I need, a caring professional.

"Oh, we just have a complicated history. That's all."

"Sounds like the present, not the past. It's harder to carry that stuff around than to let it go. Dad and you not close, huh?"

"We aren't buddies, if that is what you mean. Never have been."

"People can change, you know."

"Haven't seen much of that." I shrugged. "With Dad and Rhonda Bell both bothering me all the time, I'd love to see changes."

"I've seen many people carry a burden for a long time when they could forgive and move on with their lives."

"What do you mean? You don't think I've done enough? I forgave Rhonda, and then I saw her car—she's still driving around with the dents in her car from Sterling's death, like a trophy of her kill or something. As for my dad, what do I forgive, who he is?"

"All I'm saying is you don't have control of them, but you do over your thoughts."

"I've done all I can to forgive Rhonda, I guess I just don't want to be around either of them."

"Love them from a distance, huh? Do you think they haven't suffered enough? Seems like you're inflicting pain on both of them until they've paid for what they did. Will it ever be enough?"

"Well, that's up to God, isn't it? I used to pray about Daddy. I still pray occasionally for Rhonda. The rest is up to God."

"I wouldn't have said anything, but they just seem to have a hold on you. I've seen how you react to their calls. Just think it through."

"Dad doesn't need anything from me. In his mind, he's the father of the year. I guess you're right about Rhonda, though. I don't think she deserves forgiveness."

"You and I didn't either, but God extended it to us at a great price."

"Yeah. I get it straight in my head. Then I hear their voices or know they've called, and the emotions of the past come out."

"Rhonda may never deserve your forgiveness. Your father either for that matter. It really isn't about that, is it?"

"I've done everything I can."

I hoped Nathan would get the hint and leave me alone. He sat across from me staring at me. I shifted in my seat; it became as hard as a rock. *I forgave Rhonda Bell. Isn't that enough? Didn't work with Rhonda, won't work with Daddy.*

Nathan put his hand on mine. "Just tell me to mind my own business. It's all right." He smiled. "I need to see Dad and Dinky. Will you be all right?"

"Yeah, peachy keen." I forced a smile.

I shifted my glance to my feet. Tears flowed as Nathan disappeared.

The cafeteria was preparing for the lunch rush. I bought a chicken salad sandwich, then slid back into the booth. *Lord, I almost lost my second mom. Can't you give me a break? Do I have to deal with family, too?* I picked up my pen and began writing. My list of three major things became a page of problems.

Buck called, asking me to come to the room; Dinky was stirring. He hoped she was waking up. She'd remained motionless since the surgery. As I walked in, she moved and moaned. Buck leaned closer.

She whispered, "What about the other driver?"

She looked around the room, smiling, then she whispered Shelby's name softly. Nathan smiled at me. I frowned back. He told Buck to call if he needed anything, and he turned and left the room. Dinky said nothing more. Buck said he was spending the night, so I left to do laundry at Dinky's house and pay bills. On the drive home, I doubted I'd do any of it. I called Shelby as I drove past Dinky's house and saw no lights. She was out with friends from work, she said. I traipsed into the house and collapsed, fully clothed, into my comfortable bed in the middle of my messy living room.

When I pulled into the back parking lot of the store the next morning, Kelly Jo, Polly, and Patsy were waiting in their cars. I shut off my engine and moved toward the back door. I waved them in and began turning on lights as we walked into the office.

"We have a plan for you," Kelly Jo said. She hesitated, then took a deep breath. "We'd like to start that sandwich shop that Jane Ann is always talking about. What do ya think?"

"It isn't a priority right now. There are state regulations which can become a huge thing." I hoped I'd squelched that line of discussion.

Kelly Jo forged ahead. "My friend works with the state and told us what was required. We're not talking about anything fancy, just fresh muffins and cakes, like that real popular place in downtown Greenville. We'd be in charge of it. Maybe we could have two or three lunch specials once we got started."

Polly jumped in, her hands waving and bejeweled fingers fluttering. "We've been driving around Traveler's Rest, and there just isn't a good lunch place anywhere near the old part of town. Sure, people frequent the newer area with Wal-Mart and all. The fast food places are there, but there's a need for something different. We even thought about putting a couple of tables outside next spring. What do you think?"

"I can't take on anything else right now, I'm sorry."

"We'll be in charge of running it. We want to help bring in a little more revenue. We know it hasn't been easy with Jane Ann's accident and all. Maybe this would pay the extra salaries. We sisters have been so burdened for you. We've been coming in more and staying longer just to help keep an eye on things. Since we've been here more, we all agree that one woman shouldn't be here alone. It's not safe," Patsy said. "You know the kind of things that go on these days. If there was a lunch place, we'd need two people here, at least for a few hours a day."

"I'm facing the loss of revenue next door. Mr. Perkins' rent was my cushion." My mind raced. "But ladies, you might have the answer. Let me get back to you on the whole thing. All right?"

Kelly Jo hurried off to her other job. With faded smiles, the sisters moved to the quilt frame. They began stitching together—a rare event. I found perfect fabric matches for a couple of customers. I instructed one of my students on finishing her wall quilt for our quilt show. I scribbled notes as I worked.

Patsy left early. Polly stitched alone for thirty minutes or more, and then gathered her things to leave. She had groceries to pick up since she was fixing dinner. Penny came just before lunch, stitched a few minutes, then left. Pansy was the last of the sisters to appear. A new quilter stabbed and poked for nearly an hour with my encouragement as she worked. Granted, she nearly stood on her head at times—trying to needle a quilt in the frame is a learned skill. She was excited as we inspected her work. She was so enthusiastic she bought a small frame to try hand quilting something of her own. All smiles, she passed Pansy on her way out as the sister came to work on the quilt.

Pansy spared no time in her detailed inspection. Of course, she zoomed in on the beginner's work immediately and began ruthlessly snipping at the irregular stitches. "Mama always said that a good quilt displayed nothing but thirteen stitches to the inch," she mumbled as she dissolved an hour's work in five minutes flat.

I hoped the young woman wouldn't remember exactly where she worked, or she'd get an exaggerated idea of the quality of her work. Oh, well. I wished I'd met the sisters' parents.

I was eager to close the shop that afternoon. Pansy quilted away. I glanced at my watch for the fourth time as Shelby walked into the shop. *What a pleasant surprise. I could use some time with my lovely daughter.* I don't know what gave me the idea it would be pleasant.

CHAPTER

14

"I'm going to Columbia with a bunch of kids Saturday. Payday isn't until next week. So, how about fifty dollars till then?"

"Hello, Shelby," I paused and smiled very deliberately. "I don't have fifty dollars extra right now. I don't have credit cards, and cash is tight. Besides, I thought you were going to help me Saturday. I'm really counting on you. You'll have money after you work."

"Oh, great. Look, I'm just trying to have a little fun. Is there anything wrong with that? I don't want to work here. My life didn't end just because yours did, Mom. At least, I don't go around acting happy and praising the Lord all the time. I'm not a hypocrite acting like everything is just fine and dandy." She glared at me.

"I do my share of struggling, honey. We've had a deep loss. That doesn't excuse your behavior or your attitude. You said you'd work at the shop. Any employer expects advanced notice if you aren't fulfilling your obligation. Don't make this something else."

"Okay, I don't have to answer to you anymore."

"I still pay the bill for your education, you know." I scowled.

"Well, I don't even live with you. You're paying for Carter's education, and I don't see him fussing with fabric for you. Look, if you won't give me any money, I won't be going anywhere Saturday. Does that make you feel good? One of us needs to feel good, and it sure isn't me. I'm giving you notice—I won't be here Saturday." She turned and traipsed out of the store.

Pansy stopped quilting. She smiled as she walked to the front door, locked it, and turned the closed sign to the front. I walked to the office and plopped into the chair, burying my head in my hands.

"We have Shelby's quilt ready to give her. Maybe she'll feel the love put in it. It really is lovely," Pansy said sweetly from the other room.

"By the sounds of it, she may not even want it."

"Don't give up, Abby. Don't ever give up on your child."

On the drive home, I realized I'd purchased a ticket for an event at the college that evening. I couldn't back out. I'd promised to sit with the woman who owned the store down the street. I heard the beeping sound of my answering machine as I scurried into the house to change. It was Rhonda Bell, begging me to call. I'd dropped her a card the other day. It was full of pleasantries—I'm fine, everything is going well. The intent was to stop the calls. I guess it hadn't worked.

Maybe the program would take my mind off my remarks to Shelby. Surely, I could have said something constructive. Why was I at my worst with those I loved the most? I had just enough time to change clothes and run. Even finding my clothes was a challenge in my makeshift room. As I threw my slacks on the bed, my eye caught the bed pillows and an image came to mind. I envisioned an old feather pillow, open at one end; the contents lifted to the wind. Beautiful feathers danced in the air and flew in every direction. *All right, Lord, I remember. The example I used in Sunday school class years ago. If my words to my family were feathers, I couldn't retrieve them all, could I?* I slipped into my clothes. *Why can't I keep my mouth shut or at least speak gentle words to them? Lord, it's hard to live in this skin.*

I slapped fresh makeup on my not-so-fresh face; I raced to the college. To my amazement, I arrived a few minutes early. As I strolled into the dining room, I craned my neck to find my friend above the crowd. Instead, I saw a sea of white hair. I headed for two of the last empty chairs. I slumped into the seat. The woman to my left smiled and greeted me. I took a deep breath. Everything was fine, I could relax. Sure. From the corner of my eye, I saw a man slide from his chair to my friend's awaiting seat.

"Hi there, honey. It's good to see some new blood at the banquet." The words oozed from his mouth as he waved his arm to encompass the large room. I swiveled to get a better look and wished I hadn't. There sat Caesar. The man was pencil-thin and wore a cheap, old suit, but all I really saw was his hair. I'd seen comb-overs before, but nothing like this. He didn't have over an inch of hair growing on one side. On the other side, he'd grown hair to lengths that no one had ever attempted before. He plastered this long hair over the top in a way that would have been hilarious, had he not been smack dab in front of me. Worse yet, he was giving me every pickup line known to the octogenarian set. When my friend finally arrived, we pried the man out of her chair— not literally—that would have been easier.

So much for a good time. *Lord, I get it. It's not so bad being alone.*

That night, I slipped into bed with my notebook and my Bible. I asked God for His wisdom for my business decisions. Could I accomplish the things I'd envisioned for the shop? I took my scribbled notes and put them on my lap. As usual, money was the big issue. I lifted the notes up and asked God to show me what I was to do. Until He did, I wasn't doing anything.

Each day, I saw Dinky's progress. She was alert much of the time. She fussed with the quilt her friends made her. She said she gained strength from knowing so many faithful people were praying for her. I hoped we wouldn't be interrupted. I showed her my notes, jumbled as they were.

"I guess we just can't do it all. I want to put in a kitchen at the shop, finish my house, and get the garage apartment ready for Shelby. But if the business isn't generating revenue, then it doesn't matter how good the house looks. Sterling would know how to get it done, but I feel like giving up the dream."

"You're making good decisions. Don't let this setback stop you. I'll be back to work soon, so those expenses will be back to normal. I love the idea of a kitchen at the shop. I've got some money to invest in it. Mr. Perkins might just have done us a favor by moving out. I know you have to be frazzled, with so much work going on around you. Maybe adding anything to your schedule would be too much. We need to put the whole thing in God's hands."

To my surprise, Dinky reached for the phone. She called the church prayer chain.

"Hi, Pastor Roy." She answered questions about her health, then continued, "I called because Abby and I need clear direction in our business. We want God's wisdom. Would you please ask the others on the chain to pray? Thanks."

Having made the call, Dinky changed the subject. Did I notice the latest flowers Buck brought? Look at all the cards, she cooed. I teased that there couldn't be a single loving card left within a three-mile radius of the hospital.

"He is good for you, isn't he?" I murmured.

She nodded with a sweet smile. She fumbled in the bedside drawer and found her lipstick.

"Let me guess. It must be time for Buck to be here."

I stood at the window, looking at the distant mountains with a haze of bluish purple surrounding them. They never really changed. The weather may have given them an appearance of being further away at times, but I knew they stood firm. They were the marker in our town—with the mountains in sight, you couldn't be lost for long. I wished life were like that. Buck touched my shoulder. I jumped. I was surprised to see Nathan and Shelby with him.

"Must be something big for all of us to be summoned," Nathan said, smiling.

"Dinky's probably ready to go home," I said hopefully. Heart issues had complicated the healing process of the broken bones. I hoped all that was behind us.

Buck cleared his throat as he spoke into his phone, "Dinky and I have something we want to say to all of you." He looked at Shelby and me. "I have the Atlanta clan on the speakerphone. All present and accounted for. Can y'all hear me?"

They said hi. "In case you haven't guessed, Dinky and I have fallen in love over the last months." He beamed as he looked at his lovely Dinky. "We want your blessing on our plans to get married."

Shelby looked horrified. "My Dinky needs our care. She can't be running off getting married. This is crazy. She just needs to come home with us. We'll take care of her." She held back tears out of sheer stubbornness. I wondered where she got that lovely trait.

CHAPTER

15

Shelby couldn't have cut deeper if she'd used a knife. My mind raced; I needed to soften what she said. Surely, she didn't mean to strike out at Dinky.

As I opened my mouth, Dinky cleared her throat. "It can't be a surprise to any of you that Buck has become increasingly important in my life. You've all seen how wonderful he's been in the hospital. We aren't ancient—we have life left in us. If anything, this accident has shown me that I should grab happiness while I can. We've both been in prayer about this for a long time. We just want your blessing, not your permission." Her voice softened as she continued, "Shelby, I will still be your grandmother. I'll always be here for you." She held out her arms to my frail child. Shelby threw herself into the waiting arms. A muffled sob was absorbed into Dinky's shoulder.

"When is the great event, and have you given any thought to who would perform the ceremony?" Nathan asked, jokingly.

"We have someone in mind for that job. We have a place and time picked out, too." Buck looked at me. "Abby, could we please have the wedding at Hollingsworth Hill? We were hoping we could get married on Christmas Day, with all our family around us and you, Nathan, blessing the union before God."

"Of course you can, if the house is ready," I said.

The room exploded with chatter. I could hear Claire's voice as she shouted, "Abby, will you be ready for such a big event? I'll help you."

"I have a great foreman overseeing my project," I said as I looked at Buck. "He's been a little distracted lately." I smiled. "But if he thinks it could happen, I guess it can be done. Let's see, that gives us about six weeks, huh? You must be getting discharged, right?" I looked at Dinky.

"Friday, Dr. Everett says. That gives us time to invite a few friends, but we knew our families would be available that day, so it'll be perfect—nothing fussy. Abby, your home brought us together. Thank you for letting us marry there." Dinky beamed as she held Buck's hand. "God is so good to us. Look at all He has done."

We lingered and said good-bye to the Atlanta group, promising to talk in the following days. I shot a glance at Shelby and started across the room when Nathan suggested walking through the house together. We'd see what needed to be done. Buck hugged me, promising to join us soon. Shelby seized the opportunity and flew from the room. I caught up with her at the elevator. Others pressed in around us in the small space. When the doors opened, Shelby bolted. I tried to keep up with her.

"I can't believe all this. I think I'm going to vomit. Y'all seem to act as if this is a good thing. What do we know about this man? Are you going to just let him move in to my grandfather's house like Papaw never existed?"

"It's impossible to live in the past. I tried. You wouldn't want that for Dinky, either. Spending time with them in the hospital made me see how devoted they are to each other."

"Oh, great, now it's about me not spending time with Dinky. I guess you forgot that I'm going to school and working, too. I have no time." She dropped in her car seat and started her car.

"Meet me in an hour at the pizza place. We can talk...."

She glared at me and was gone; my mouth hung open, my words stuck in my throat. As I drove home, I forced myself to think about the plans that were unfolding before us. Actually, I began questioning my sanity. What had I been thinking—a wedding in my home, in six weeks? Even calling it my home seemed strange. Not only did I have an unfinished house, but the garage was crammed full of possessions. I'd really entertained the idea of not decorating this year. That was before the big announcement. Now things would have to be done, and done well. My stomach began to ache in rhythm with the throbbing of my head as I thought about my Christmas decorations, which were buried in the clutter.

Nathan was waiting in his truck when I arrived at the house. "Well, were you as surprised as I was? I mean, we knew that they cared for each other, but a wedding, this soon?"

"All I want to know is can we do it? I'm beginning to panic. I've been thinking of everything that I need to do. I know it's small stuff compared to the remodeling, but it looks large to me."

"Oh, I think we can accomplish it. I guess I'll be doing some marriage counseling, so I'll be pretty busy." He chuckled. "Somehow, that seems awkward, to say the least. Dad ought to be here in a few minutes."

We stepped into the front hall and flipped on the lights.

"Life is strange, isn't it? It's taken forever to get this far and now we're thinking of finishing in a hurry," I mused.

"Yeah, it can be strange. I mean here we are, nearly related. That never entered my mind a few months ago."

Our eyes met, and my stomach did flip-flops. We chuckled, and I stepped back. I saw glimpses of junior high. I fumbled with my notes to ease the tension.

"A dining room chandelier and finished floors, and we'll be done in that area. It's too bad the old fixture is in a pile in the shed," Nathan said. "I see you've almost finished with stripping the wallpaper. The kitchen is ready for my trim work. I'm glad Dad and I put the cabinets in place before the accident. The ceiling repair in the den looks great. I guess the electrician is okay."

"Yeah, he's working again. He cut a little off his bill, and I absorbed the repair costs. I'm just glad he didn't sue me or anything."

"Always the optimist, aren't you?" He chuckled. "Really, the majority of the work left is in your bedrooms and bath. I have vacation time before the end of the year. I guess I know where I'll be."

"That is what I want to talk to you and your dad about." We heard Buck shout as he came into the house. "We're in the kitchen, Buck."

Buck squeezed me hard. I giggled. "Well, we'll soon be relatives. Do you give a discount to family?" I asked teasingly.

"I usually charge them more. Right, son?" We chuckled.

"Actually, I've wanted to get together ever since Nathan and I talked at the hospital. Buck, how much of the original budget do we have left?"

"You'll have a little left when we finish the bedrooms and bath, but not much. You need to finalize the kitchen appliances, too. Then I can give you a closer figure."

"What if we do just the minimum there? You know, just get done as quick as possible? I'll go conservative on the appliances, too."

"Are you unhappy with the remodel? Are you firing your future family member?" Buck sputtered.

"Not at all. I want to put you to work on the store, but I need money to do it. If I take the rest of my budget and Dinky matches the funds, could we put in a kitchen at the shop? That way we could expand the business with a café and have room for more merchandise as well. The chance of renting out the space Mr. Perkins occupied is slim. We might as well use the area ourselves. Our quilt business has dropped slightly, but a lunch counter might bring revenue back up. People have to eat, right?"

"Are you sure you want to do this?" Buck asked. "I've got a friend in Spartanburg who might have used kitchen appliances—that would cut costs."

"Well, really, at the house, all that has to be finished before the wedding is the front bathroom. Of course, I'd love to have a kitchen and bedrooms, too, but I'm getting used to strange living conditions. So, what do you two think?"

"Nothing like putting on the pressure. If I don't finish everything before the wedding, you'll be living with us afterwards, huh?" Buck said.

"Sounds like great incentive to me, Dad." Nathan laughed.

"Let's walk through with an eye for remaining costs, then go to the shop and see what you have planned. It might be doable, but I don't want to agree too soon." With that, Buck launched his assault, mumbling and scribbling as he walked from the kitchen to the family room.

"Maybe I ought to leave you two to work on this. Just know that my part of the finished carpentry work will be done." Nathan started to exit. "Although I guess some of my work might be eliminated."

"What do you think? I mean, am I crazy?"

"I think you're capable of making good decisions." Nathan grinned.

"Something no one could've said some time ago. I really want your input. You and your dad started me on this journey, you know.

"I'm a spiritual leader and a part-time carpenter. My opinion on your business decisions wouldn't count for much."

"Your opinion as my friend would."

I felt as if we were standing on the edge of an unexpected cliff and leaning toward oblivion.

Buck swooped into the room. "Well, don't just stand there. Let's get a move on. I want to look at the shop and put my pen to paper, so I can get back to my sweetie as soon as possible. Meet me at the store. I'll call Dinky and fill her in while I drive." Buck yelled. It felt like all the air left the room as he rushed out.

"How will two decisive people like Buck and Dinky make it together? They can't both be in charge all the time." I giggled.

"Love is an amazing thing, huh?" I felt him lean closer to me.

"Where are you two? We don't have all day." Buck screamed. He opened the door and stood impatiently, waiting for the two stragglers.

We jumped to attention and bolted toward him.

Nathan said he'd have to see the project later. He had a meeting at church in less than an hour. We lingered at the cars until Buck honked impatiently. I rode to the store in a daze.

"I estimate three weeks to complete the house if we stick to the minimum. After the men refinish your floors, you'll have to give them time to cure before moving in. That still gives you time before the big day," Buck boomed. "The work here has its challenges but barring unforeseen structural problems, the project is within reach. I'll talk to that friend in Spartanburg about used commercial kitchen equipment. I'll get with him before I tell you for sure. Maybe you can do the painting. That could help—I won't have to supervise, and you could work whenever you want."

Buck hurried back to the hospital. I held my paperwork in my hands as I sat in the office. "Okay, Lord. I'm new at this. I ask You to show me if this is what You want me to do. I need to hear from You. I'm trusting."

I locked the door to the shop and grabbed a bag of popcorn. I stuck it in the microwave, plotting my course on paper. The popcorn seemed to lay heavy in my stomach as I finished placing orders.

At home, in the middle of the night, I awoke to the familiar throbbing in my head. The gurgling in my stomach was new. What was I doing, trying to balance all this? Maybe balancing the shop and the house was beyond me. I was putting out fires wherever possible but I still felt as if I was being burned.

With all this going on, I still couldn't ignore the fact that Thanksgiving was approaching with lightning speed. The Hollingsworth family was coming together, whether it was convenient or not.

Claire came Tuesday evening to get a jump-start on Turkey Day. That gave me Tuesday and Wednesday to get ready for the big after-Thanksgiving sale. It was the biggest event of the year for the shop. The revenue it produced had always been significant.

Tuesday night, as I climbed into bed, Buck called to say the kitchen project came in below the budget figures we'd discussed. In fact, he said he was amazed.

"Abby, girl, you must be living right. Every possible problem just vanished as I began figuring the price. My friend nearly gave me the equipment because some of it had minor scratches. Really, all we are doing is tearing out an opening and putting new electrical in. The water hookup is already in place. I'm not figuring a fancy kitchen, just one that will pass inspection. Let's go, girl."

"I don't know, Buck. I'm not sure that I should get started yet."

"That's not everything, Abby. I wasn't sure I could take on this job right now. You know, Mrs. Edmond has been pushing me to start her remodel immediately. Well, she called this evening and said unexpected company was coming. I couldn't work in her house for ten days. Since we're almost finished with the bedrooms and bath, I can tackle the kitchen at the shop."

"Let me call you in the morning, please. I don't want to make a mistake and go ahead of God's leading."

"Well, kiddo, I wouldn't want that, either. I'll pray with you right now. God always shows Himself big to those who seek His direction." He asked God for clear confirmation. After praying, he said he looked forward to hearing from me early tomorrow.

I'd been at home only long enough to let Lexus out at lunch. When I came home after work, I'd laid the mail on the bedside table, thinking I'd deal with it tomorrow. I glanced at the pile, then sifted through the stack until a letter from my Atlanta attorney caught my eye. We'd worked on estate matters by e-mail for some time now, and I couldn't imagine why he'd be corresponding by mail. I tore open the envelope and opened the letter. As I did, a check fluttered onto the bed, revealing a nice sum with my name on it. I clutched the letter and read it quickly. He routinely ran an internet search to see if the decedent had unclaimed money from sources unknown to the family. The enclosed money came from two sources. One was a bank account from a defunct savings and loan. The larger amount was a whole life insurance policy Sterling had taken out years ago at his place of employment. He'd worked there from college graduation until he and Pete started their own business. I read the letter three times. Tears ran down my cheeks. These tears were sheer, unadulterated joy. The money was amazing, but the timing was perfect.

Buck prayed that God would show Himself big.

I picked up the phone and called Buck. He seemed to understand as I screamed into the phone, "He showed Himself big, Buck!"

"Sweet child, you don't know how big. Pastor Roy called to say some men at the church were responding to the prayer request. They called me, and they want to donate their time to finish your home and the shop. They are bringing the wallboard needed. So now, I'll have a large crew to watch after."

"Why would they do that? I mean, that is just too generous."

"Roy said they often helped widows in the church. I told them Dinky would be a married woman soon. He laughed and said they'd better hurry, then, if everyone was to receive the blessing."

"I'll see you tomorrow."

The drive to work in the morning was breathtaking. The hills were ablaze with reds and golds while pines stood in contrast to their brilliance. As I listened to music, I sang along, thinking about the contrasts in life. Life lost made life regained sweeter. God was moving in unexpected ways. The cobwebs in my mind were clearing. I could face anything, I told myself. I'd handled the situation with Rhonda Bell by sending notes whenever I thought of her. That would surely stop the gnawing emotion produced every time I thought of her. I'd forgiven her. Surely, no one—not even God—expected me to do more. I'd think more positively about my relationship with Dad. Maybe a card now and then.

Buck's truck was parked in my spot in the back parking lot as I arrived at work. Apparently, Dinky had given Buck her key. *He must have started early.* As I made my way into the back corridor, I realized that the sound was not coming from next door as I expected. I picked up speed, coming to a huge hole between my store and Mr. Perkins's locksmith shop. I stood there unable to speak as dust swirled around my head.

Buck yelled from deep within the opening, "I see you're surprised. Hey! What do you think?"

"You said you would construct a kitchen, and then connect the two areas later."

"That was the plan at first, but this really makes more sense. I couldn't risk damaging the finished kitchen by putting the opening in later. Don't worry, after we get the entrance done here we'll put plastic up, and you won't know we're even here." He choked as he breathed the dust.

Perfect timing. What was I thinking? I could either go to my office and cry or grab some rags and start mopping up the mess. Kelly Jo arrived as I dropped to my knees and trapped the filth in towels. She gasped as she saw the men scurrying to the back door of Mr. Perkins shop with loads of trash.

Hmmm. Maybe I should've gone over the details a little more carefully with Buck.

I'd just finished swiping the last of the grime off the floors when men from the church traipsed into the shop.

"Thought we'd get a look at the job," Pastor Roy shouted above the pounding.

The men's footprints made an interesting pattern on the damp floor. I pointed the eager philanthropists in the direction of the hole and told them to follow the deafening sound. Buck would show them around the small area. I thanked each man as he maneuvered through the narrow hallway.

I blew hair out of my face and looked at Kelly Jo.

She must have read my mind. "What were you thinking? What will we do? The sale starts Friday!"

Kelly Jo had planned to leave at lunchtime, since it was her day off at the home improvement center. Instead, she took over the cleaning detail. By the end of the day, the men had sealed the area with plastic. We juggled cleaning and helping customers. They waved and left from the other shop. When the kitchen area was finished, they would construct a new opening in the front of the store, so that the two buildings would flow together as one shop in front as well as in the kitchen area. For now, there was little flow. I glanced around one last time, before locking the door and heading for my car.

In the midst of the mayhem of the day, I'd found myself anticipating the fun of dinner with the family. It would be like old times. I'd make a couple of pies after dinner and be ready for bed. When we made the plans for Thanksgiving, Claire had insisted that I sleep at Dinky's house. She said a sleep over, just like the kids used to have, was just what we needed. With the only bathroom in my home partially gutted, it wasn't a hard decision.

Claire and I were on our own as far as the bird went, and we were apprehensive about our first solo turkey performance. Dinky had always gotten up early and put the bird in the oven. We often suggested we'd help, but Dinky would quickly give us the look. We often saw that look when kitchen work was involved. It paid to obey that glare. It was amazing that we had been able to dodge this duty so long.

Dinky was keeping Lexus at her house, since she was at home all day. She said she wanted my puppy's company. Claire tried to dissuade Dinky, saying that Lexus was too energetic; she could get under Dinky's feet. There was no changing Dinky's mind once she decided something. Lexus eagerly greeted me as I came in the door. The dog hair in the air arrived soon after the dog. I wonder if a groomer could shave a lab. The hair is killing me but poor Lexus would be humiliated if hairless. I'd look into that when I had time.

Claire and I stood at the kitchen counter preparing vegetable casseroles. "It's so hard, not having Sterling here with us, but I've sure looked forward to this time together. I sent Rhonda Bell a card last week. I guess you see her in church these days."

"Yeah, I met her parents when they visited from Florida. They were glad Rhonda was in church.

"I would have invited her to dinner tomorrow, but everything seems to agitate Shelby these days. I'm sure Rhonda would be no exception." Didn't I seem magnanimous? *Her presence would bother Shelby. All right, Lord, she would bother me, too.*

"Where is Shelby this evening? I was looking forward to talking with her tonight."

"I don't know where she is most of the time or, for that matter, who she is with these days. I used to know all her friends, but I haven't met any here. She backed out of helping at the store."

"That doesn't seem like Shelby." Claire stopped putting a congealed salad in the refrigerator.

"Nothing seems like the old Shelby, Claire. She's making poor choices and, well, she isn't herself."

When Dinky, Buck, and Pete came into the kitchen, we changed the topic of conversation. We caught up with each of our busy lives, chatting comfortably as we worked. Dinky glowed as Buck held her hand. I wiped a tear away, hoping no one noticed. Carter was coming in late and would sleep on the couch. We'd talk tomorrow. Lexus and I made a loop around the house looking for a good doggy spot. After coming in, I hugged everyone, and headed to the daybed in Dinky's office. I fell asleep instantly. In a fog, I heard an irritating sound that refused to let me continue my dream. *The phone. Oh, please Lord, not an accident.* I hadn't heard Shelby come in. The clock shone brightly next to the phone. It was 3:30. Who could be calling?

I jumped to my feet and put the receiver to my ear; Claire was talking.

"Yes, this is her home. I am her aunt. What has happened?" Claire's voice cracked.

"Aunt Claire, can you come and get me?" Shelby said very softly.

"Where are you, Shelby? Are you all right?"

I listened, unable to connect to what was happening. "Shelby, this is Mom. We'll come get you, just tell us where you are."

With that, a woman came on the line. "This is the Greenville Police Department."

Claire took over the conversation. I shook as I listened to the directions to the station. I threw on clothes and ran to the door. Pete was already in the car; Claire and I rushed to join him. We knew nothing more than the fact that Shelby needed us.

CHAPTER

16

An officer escorted us into a sparse room and closed the door. Shelby sat in a straight-backed chair with her arms crossed, her foot swinging, and a scowl on her face.

Before we could speak, she whined, "I can't believe this is happening to me. Everybody I know drinks. What's the big deal, anyway? I wasn't even driving."

"Shelby, it's a big deal, believe me. I guess we should be grateful that the charge is just underage drinking and public intoxication. I'm thankful you weren't riding in the car with your drunken friend when the police arrested you," Pete sputtered.

Thank You, Lord, for Pete.

"Oh, Justin. I've been with him when he's had a lot more to drink. Get real, Uncle Pete. I bet your kids did the same thing lots of times when they were my age. You just chose not to notice."

"Well, since you brought my kids into this, I'll talk to you as if you were one of them. First, you'd better watch your tone of voice, young lady. I know you've been through a lot, but if you think I'm going to let you give me a line of garbage, or overlook everything you do, you'd better think again. I owe my brother more than that. Second, you have a choice. You can go on feeling sorry for yourself and excusing your behavior, or you can take responsibility for your actions. Own up, Shelby."

"Mom, are you going to let Uncle Pete talk to me like that? My daddy would help me, not yell at me."

"Shelby, for the first time since your father died, I'm glad he isn't here. You don't seem the least bit sorry for what you've done. I'm half-tempted to come back in the morning for you—let you think about what the problem really is here. I love you, but you've gone too far."

"Well, that is just what I could expect from a bunch of self-righteous hypocrites. Where's the love? Huh? You're always talking about love, well, where is it when I need it? Why don't y'all just leave! That'd be better than getting a lecture like I was five."

Claire stepped closer to Shelby and tried to embrace her. She stood up and pushed away. Before we could say another word, she swirled around and rushed out the door. As she left, she yelled she'd rather stay the night in jail than spend one minute with us. She'd find another way home. We watched as the officer led her away. Pete took me by the arm and led me to the nearby chair.

"She made the decision for us, Abby. That's probably the best thing that could happen right now. Let's talk to the officers and see where we go from here." My brother-in-law was ashen and shaking as he spoke.

An officer said Shelby would appear before the judge in the morning, since she refused our involvement. "What you're going through is a regular occurrence these days. Kids think they can handle everything when they're really walking on thin ice. Perhaps she'll be one of the lucky ones who gets the true picture while she sits alone in that cell. We call it a come to Jesus moment. It works for some kids. They realize they never want to come here again."

"Thank you for your concern," I said. We turned to go.

"I'll have one of the police women keep an eye on her. She won't be here long. It'll just seem like an eternity to her," the officer said.

At home, Claire and I slid the turkey into the oven while we were still physically able. I hoped things would look better after a few hours of sleep. They didn't. Blurry-eyed, Claire and I worked around the kitchen, while Pete and Dinky sipped coffee quietly. As I watched

Carter fix himself a bowl of cereal, I heard a car drive up the lane. The front door opened, and I braced myself for a confrontation.

Shelby yelled as she went bounding up the stairs, "A friend came and got me out. I'm going to take a shower—I'm filthy—then go to sleep. I'm not interested in turkey or all that family stuff, so don't bother me. Have fun!" The sarcasm oozed from my daughter's mouth.

I bounded up the stairs. She needed her mama. I'd come to her aid. The door slammed in my face. I was undaunted. I knocked and turned the doorknob. The door was locked.

"Shelby, please, let me in."

"Go away. I don't want to see any of you. Just leave me alone. I don't need another lecture." Her angry response resonated throughout the house.

I tucked my tail and ran, regaining composure as I hit the last step. All eyes were on me as I fussed with my sweater. As if on cue, everyone glanced away and dispersed. Buck and Nathan arrived just before noon. Claire and I were finishing our meal as Dinky came into the kitchen with her walker.

"Girls, I asked Buck to bring the traditional corn kernels since I couldn't get out. Is it time for us to gather at the table? We don't want to get the food on the table before we give thanks."

"Oh, I just thought we'd forget that this year, Dinky, with all that's going on," I said softly, not looking up from my work.

"When the days look dark, that's when the praises should be lifted up, my dear." Dinky came close, put her arm around me, and squeezed. "God is not in the giving up business. You know it. Come on."

Dinky was always right. A praise report was due; I couldn't stand in the way. We headed for the table. Dinky motioned for Buck to sit at the head of the table. She sat next to him as she pointed for all us to sit down. Our tradition had always been to place kernels of corn on each plate.

"Lord, we remember the first Thanksgiving and how thankful the Pilgrims were in the midst of adversity. We want to take this time to give thanks for the gifts You have given us." Dinky prayed and we raised our heads.

We were to pick up one kernel, telling the group a blessing we'd received over the past year. I must admit, thanks didn't tumble out of my mouth. In fact, as I waited my first turn, the image of a little Abby, barefoot and standing in dirt, came to mind. It was as if God was saying to that little girl, "Come on—can't you think of one thing for which to thank Me?"

"Well okay," little Abby said as she kicked her foot in the dirt, "just one."

But after giving thanks for one thing, I seemed to hear God say, "All right now, what else?"

The battle in my mind raged until it was my turn. Slowly, I picked up my first kernel and said, "I am so thankful that Dinky is here with us."

I heard laughter from all around the table. "What is so funny?" I said.

"Where were you, Mom? We've already said that in one way or another all around the table. Now here you are saying it as if you're adding something new. Nice." Carter chuckled.

"Sorry, I was in my own little world. But, since I seem to be repetitive, let me list a few more things." I stood. "I'm so thankful that God has blessed me with wonderful family and friends." I smiled and looked at Nathan and Buck. "I'm thankful for my beautiful home. I'm thankful to be headed in a new direction in my life and not totally frightened to death, frightened a lot at times, but...."

"Okay, Mom, once you got started you really couldn't get stopped, could you?" Carter put his arm around me.

"Group hug," Claire said. She smiled and joined us. Everyone laughed and gathered round. As we stood in a circle, we finished our thanks. Nathan began to sing, "Praise God from whom all blessings flow." We all sang "Praise Him all creatures here below."

We brought heaping dishes to the table. Words flew around the table as shared what had been happening in our lives. At that meal, we were fed more than turkey and dressing. There were ball games and board games in the afternoon. No one mentioned Shelby. Late in the afternoon, Carter said he needed to leave. He had plans with his study partner, Alex.

"Are you sure you can't stay? Studying while on vacation sounds extreme," I said.

"Got to keep the grades up with graduation around the corner. It isn't easy. Do you think it would help if I talk with Shelby?"

"Oh, I'd appreciate it so much, Carter. I don't know where to go from here. Maybe you could get her to come downstairs and join us. She must be starving."

"I doubt she wants to face everyone. She's probably more ashamed of her behavior than hungry. It just isn't like her. She'll be filled with so much regret. I just want to get a handle on the whole thing before I go back."

I put turkey and Shelby's favorite congealed salad on a plate. I handed it to Carter. He was upstairs for quite a while.

As he trudged down the stairs, he sighed. "She really needs help. Find a good counselor, Mom. That person upstairs isn't my sister." He seemed to regret his words. "Keep me informed, Mom. I really do love the nut."

He squeezed my hands and plodded out the door. Nathan left after our second meal of turkey and pumpkin pie. I watched the handsome man leave, and a tinge of longing swept over me. I hated to see him go. It shocked me.

Back inside I struggled to speak. "I can't tell you how sorry I am to have dragged you all into our pain. I...."

"Wait, Abby, you forget that you are our family, and your pain certainly is ours," Claire said. "Pete and I have already decided we're staying the weekend. I'm going to work with you tomorrow, and Pete will be here to help Shelby in case she is ready to talk."

Dinky cleared her throat. "Pete, I need to get some rest. Would you please pray for us all before I go to bed?"

We gathered in a circle and lifted our concerns up to the Father in heaven. I went to the shop that evening with a spring in my step, anticipating God's work in our lives. After an exhausting hour of final preparation for the sale, I hurried home.

The Quilter's Circle sale was always held the Friday and Saturday after Thanksgiving. Claire flew around the shop, answering questions and pointing women to merchandise requested. Kelly Jo spent the day returning bolts of fabric to the rack. As she was leaving, I thanked her for working so hard and asked her to go to church with me Sunday. Without hesitation, she said she'd be there.

Friday was busy; Saturday was hectic. The muffled sound of Buck and his men pounded in my head. I began the day thinking that if this wasn't a good sale, I'd be working until I was eighty years old. With every bang of the hammer, there was a battle. No matter how many times I gave it all over to God, anxiety crept in. My exercise in faith was exhausting.

The "P" sisters, precious sisters as I had begun calling them, all paid me a visit, enthused and ready for the coffee shop to open. News travels fast in Travelers Rest. Polly and Patsy put bolts back in place for me before leaving.

"Dear, do you know that we sisters hardly ever go out to a restaurant? We take our evening meals together, five evenings a week. That is what we've done all of our lives. We have our table set with our wedding china and silver. It is elegant. We eat by candlelight and have good music playing. Our parents raised us that way. Of course, Mama always had servants to do all the work. We do it ourselves. Our late husbands so enjoyed the daily family gatherings," Pansy said with a sigh.

"We are ready to join you for lunch as soon as you open. It will be quite a treat. We might even quilt together afterwards," Penny said with glee.

"I wouldn't count on that," Pansy challenged. "You know what happens when we try to quilt together."

"Why, I have no earthly idea what you are implying. Bless your heart, Pansy." Penny patted her sister on the back. "Someone must have gotten up on the wrong side of the bed. Mama always did scold you for being so negative."

With that, Polly interjected, "As I recall, the last time we quilted together, you came along after us to inspect, and stitches were ripped out. Caused quite a stink, as I recall." She got louder with every word, and the last, as I recall, surely resounded in downtown Greenville.

Patsy yelled from the other side of the store, "We can cooperate when it counts, now, can't we? After all, we are family." All wore broad smiles and headed for the door. *Oh, isn't family fun?*

At the end of the day, I dragged myself to the car. It seemed driving triggered thoughts of Shelby more often than not. I'd given Shelby into

God's hands. My job was to keep joyfully out of His way. I wasn't doing a very good job of the joy part.

It took about ten minutes to get from the shop to the house, first on a four-lane road, then a narrow two lane that twisted up the hill. I slowed as I came to our property. First, there was the familiar white fence that led to Dinky's lovely home. Next, the lake was visible behind the home itself. Looking at the lake with the distant mountains behind it was peaceful. Beyond the lake, I could see my home.

As I went around the curve, I entertained thoughts of a quiet evening at home, working on the house. *Claire and Pete need some time with Dinky by themselves.* Dinky's driveway was still some distance ahead, but there were several cars parked outside. *Hmmm, they look familiar. Wasn't that Betsy's car, and Nathan's? Oh, no, I hope nothing is wrong.*

In the faint light of early evening, I saw Nathan and Shelby strolling down the sidewalk together. Shelby waved to Betsy. What was going on? By the time I pulled over on the other side of the lane and began to walk to the house, Shelby was approaching her car. She put her hand on the door, then turned and skipped back along the walk. I knew she hadn't seen me, so I started to yell. Luckily, I hadn't yet made a sound when I saw her throw her arms around Nathan and kiss him on the cheek. Quickly, she swiveled and returned to the car. She acted as if she hadn't seen me as she backed out of the drive and flew down the lane. Nathan turned and went back inside, with Betsy by his side.

CHAPTER

17

I froze. Was I upset seeing Shelby flirt with an older man, or was it the older man she was flirting with who evoked this odd sensation? I tramped up to the house. As I entered, Nathan greeted me. I felt my stomach flutter. I started to speak, but Dinky yelled from the next room.

"I hear you two. I may be hobbling around, but my hearing is perfect. Come in here with Betsy and me."

"Hey, sis. I decided to visit. I was driving home from Thanksgiving at Eleanor's," Betsy said casually. "I called Dinky, and she said to come ahead." She gestured with her arms.

"Thanks, Betsy, that was sweet. We know your real motive is just to be with us sane people for a change, right?"

"I'm leaving—have an appointment," Nathan said rather abruptly. "Abby, be sure and check out the house this evening." He quickly turned and departed.

"What was that about?" I asked. "And what was Shelby doing kissing Nathan anyway?"

"Wow, sounds like someone is edgy, or maybe even jealous," Betsy teased.

"Just what I need right now—a snotty sister," I retorted.

"Hey, watch out, or you could be in that pink feathered boa," Betsy giggled as she wagged her finger at me.

"What's this about a pink boa? It doesn't sound like you, Abby." Dinky raised her eyebrow.

"Didn't I ever tell you about our Aunt Ada's funeral?" I smiled at Dinky.

"Aunt Ada was Mother's aunt by marriage," Betsy interjected. "Our Uncle John died long before her. Anyway, she always dressed in a housedress with her nylons rolled up at her ankles. She wore old lady's black shoes—you know the kind. Her hair was pulled back in a bun, and she never wore makeup."

"Let me tell the story," I teased. "When she died, we went to the funeral home for the viewing. Well, we were hardly in the room when we saw the pink feather boa. Her niece was responsible for her affairs. There Aunt Ada was in a pink negligee and makeup an inch thick. To top it off, curly hair framed her face. We tried to behave, but in the end we excused ourselves and ran to the bathroom and laughed till we cried."

"Come on, we were mortified for poor Aunt Ada," Betsy added. "Well, anyway, I told Abby right then that we might end up like Aunt Ada. You know, we might end up with no one to select appropriate clothes to do us up right. So, we made a pact that the first one to die would definitely look good. The other one was on her own." Betsy chuckled.

"Yeah, so now every time I displease my sweet sister, she threatens to dress me in a pink feather boa when I die. I guess that means I just have to outlive her, don't you think?"

"You two are too much." Dinky laughed. "I haven't heard anything so funny in a long while." She sighed. "Abby, I know you are tired, but Betsy wants a tour of the house. I thought I'd come with you. You get Betsy settled here. Put her suitcase in the office and put clean sheets on the daybed. Claire and Pete went out to pick up dinner, so we have just enough time to see the progress on the house and be back here for dinner. There's plenty of room for both of you in that office," Dinky said in her most authoritative voice. I knew better than to object.

"Yes, ma'am." I promptly did as I was told, then helped Dinky settle into the seat for the short drive to Hollingsworth Hill.

"Abby, I'm worried about Shelby's drinking problem," Dinky said.

"What do you mean, drinking problem? I think she is just a teenager making a few bad choices, don't you?"

"Betsy reminded me about your dad," she said.

"What does my dad's horrible behavior have to do with Shelby?"

"It's worth thinking about, don't you think, Abby?"

"I'm thinking that my daughter shouldn't even be mentioned in the same sentence as my father. It's not the same at all. She's just adjusting to her dad's death, that's all."

"Wasn't your dad an alcoholic? Don't they say that the tendency runs in families?"

"Look, Dinky, I just don't want to discuss this, all right?" We pulled in front of the house. I noticed that Betsy said nothing as she sat in the back seat. *Where is my talkative sister when I need her? I guess she did all her talking before I got to Dinky's house.*

Betsy assisted Dinky with her walker while I went ahead, turning on lights. *Great, now they're talking about Shelby behind my back. They just need to give her a break.* Off the entry, the three rooms were now two. The tile men would soon be finished with the enlarged bathroom. Thanks to Kelly Jo, the area was painted. She had surprised me by working while I was at the hospital. As we went into the living room, Dinky walked past us and into the dining room.

"I will turn on the lights in here, dear," Dinky shouted.

"Oh, there isn't one there yet, Dinky. I haven't had time to buy a new one. Remember, the old one was in shambles? We found it on the floor when we started the project."

"I remember," Dinky whispered as she flipped the switch and a beautiful soft glow came flowing from the room.

"Oh, what on earth? How can this be?" I gasped.

"This must be what Nathan wanted you to see," Betsy said.

"Abby, Nathan assembled the old fixture in his spare time. Isn't it beautiful?" Dinky grinned.

"Wow, there must be something going on between you two. I mean, I think this guy is trying to impress you!" Betsy giggled.

"I don't think I'm the one he is trying to impress. I saw him with Shelby a little while ago."

"I better get my paperwork started."

"Paperwork, what paperwork?"

"My three documents—the physical, psychological, and financial statements, that's what. You could need those soon, don't you think?"

I stood in the dining room, basking in the glow of the gorgeous chandelier. The wonderful work Nathan had put into the job was mind-boggling. I felt like a giddy schoolgirl. Was it possible that Nathan had more in mind than simply helping a friend finish her home? Maybe he was nervous when I saw him at Dinky's. He did seem different. If it weren't important, he would've just shown it to me himself. No, I wasn't good at reading any man but Sterling. This was beyond me. It was probably a simple gesture of very kind friend. *Listening to Betsy and her spin on life got me in trouble when I was twelve. I can't go there now.* I followed the sounds of laughter echoing from the den.

CHAPTER

18

Sunday morning, I walked down the aisle and slipped into the pew. Just as the music began, Kelly Jo slid in next to me. Buddy followed her.

"I'm so glad you're here," I whispered.

"I wasn't sure Buddy would come, but he's here." Kelly Jo squeezed my hand.

Following church, we went to our favorite restaurant. I looked around the table. Dinky and Buck talked softly at the far end. Kelly Jo and Buddy no longer had the panicky look they both wore at church. Betsy and I sat with an empty chair next to me.

Kelly Jo smiled. "Maybe Shelby will come yet."

"Maybe," I said.

"She told me she'd meet us for lunch as we left this morning," Betsy said.

Everyone dispersed after the meal, leaving Dinky, Betsy and me to drive home. As we pulled out of the restaurant parking lot, Dinky suggested a drive to the cemetery. Betsy hadn't seen the grave marker or the new flower arrangement. Betsy and I assisted Dinky on the uneven ground after parking the car.

We stood over the marker. "The Cherokee say, 'when you were born, you cried and the world rejoiced. Live your life so that when you die, the world cries and you rejoice,'" Betsy said and squeezed my hand. "I know Sterling is rejoicing. It's just hard to understand his joy when it brings such grief to us, isn't it, sis?" She hugged me. "Abby, I miss his kind gentle ways and his keen insights. I sought his advice often for the man's point of view. I enjoyed being with the two of you. You always kept me balanced. The whole world might have been messed up, but the two of you made sense in the midst of it."

I remained motionless, eyes swollen and a chill running through me, as I felt a breeze gently touch my cheeks. I let what Betsy said saturate my soul. I knew that Sterling was in a better place but, until this moment, I hadn't allowed myself to think that he rejoiced as he left this earth. I wanted him to miss being with me. It sounded stupid and selfish, but sometimes the truth is like that. Everything became clear. Sterling was rejoicing with the King, and I'd never see him again in this lifetime. How could this be a new revelation, after all this time? I had certainly experienced the aloneness first hand every day since his death. However, as far as the heart goes, I had never permitted myself to let the realization of being without him for the rest of my life settle in.

After Sterling's death, a strange thing started happening. At church, as I sang worship songs, an image would pop into my mind. It was always the same. A huge door opened just enough for me to see my husband kneeling at the steps and praying. This happened the first week after his death and just about every Sunday after that. I didn't think about it Sunday to Sunday. I didn't anticipate it occurring—it just did. As I stood over his grave, I thought back to that morning.

I worshipped just like always, singing praises and enjoying that sweet time in God's presence. However, for once the image was different. In my mind, I saw the large door again and I saw Sterling kneeling and praying. This time, however, the door swung slowly open. I was unaware of anything else but my Sterling. I seemed to move closer to him. Then, as if I was really experiencing it, a large pane of glass stopped me. I saw Sterling, but I couldn't be with him. I couldn't kneel with him as I had done so many times in this life. I couldn't be a part of what he was experiencing. A thick, gray curtain closed across the glass. I not only couldn't be with him, I could no longer see him. In the cemetery, a few hours later, I struggled to understand what had happened. I finally asked Dinky and Betsy to sit with me on the nearby bench. I cleared my throat and told them what I had experienced, hoping that they wouldn't think I was losing my mind.

"Sweetheart." Dinky put her arm around me," Our Father seems to be preparing you to go into another phase of your life. You've found comfort in the familiar scene of worshipping with Sterling. Now, I think, God is telling you to leave Sterling there and move on. He can't go with you." She breathed deeply, regaining her composure. She sniffed into her tissue. "You aren't alone. You are so loved by Sterling and by Your Father. You just can't stay in that loving, secure past, my dear. We all must live today. You see, God has assured me that Elliot and Sterling and all those believers that I've loved are my deposits in heaven, lovingly cared for by my Father. They won't age. They feel no pain. They are rejoicing. One day, we'll join them. In fact, the older I get the more God reminds me that moving toward heaven is my main objective. Having Elliot and Sterling already there keeps me moving in that direction with joy. It is less and less about what I'll be leaving behind. It's more and more about what I'll someday experience. God doesn't want us to fear the future. It isn't unknown when we know Him." She used her tissue to wipe her tears and began singing, "Jesus loves me, this I know." We joined her. There was a sweet release in the simple song.

CHAPTER

19

Excitement shot through me as I opened the store on Monday morning. I hummed "I'll be home for Christmas" as I hung red and green quilts on the walls. Buck's workers arrived and moved display racks, assembled the large artificial tree, and helped me lug heavy decorations from the storage area. The work went quickly with Dinky's supervision. Just before lunch, I unpacked antique Christmas decorations and placed them in the shop window. Laughter resonated from Dinky's class in the back of the store. This was her first class since the accident—a simple Christmas wall hanging. It sounded as if the women were enjoying themselves. I moved a miniature sleigh filled with packages closer to a small fir tree at the window. I settled into a comfort zone while hammering floated from the adjoining space. I heard the buzzer, turned to see L.J. coming toward me, and smiled.

He suggested that we go to a wonderful bistro for lunch. I was about to tell him I couldn't leave the shop when he ushered me over to one of the new tables. Chuckling, he said Dinky told him about our changes one day when he checked on her progress. I protested, telling him we weren't open yet. He turned abruptly, left the shop, and returned, pulling a large cooler. I looked around me. The two tables made the area snug, to say the least, but Buck had assured me that he wanted to finish the new space by Christmas more than I did, so snug was temporary. Add all the Christmas decorations, and snug was bumped up to a new level. We sat down at the crowded table in its temporary spot close to the front door.

The sun streamed in from the front window of the shop. I relaxed as we talked. I'd just asked about his children when I glanced out the window. Nathan walked up the sidewalk and stepped into the shop. I raised my arm slightly, waving him to come near, when L.J. put his hand on mine. He said something that ended in, "So I bought tickets for us to see the play Friday night." I was at a loss. Nathan smiled; he looked at us—the smile faded. He swiveled and headed for the back of the store. I jumped up and followed him, talking as I flew. I nearly overtook him. He reached the new doors to the construction site and went through them, leaving my face in the door. I stopped in mid-sentence.

It took a minute to compose myself. I opened the door and summoned my confidence as I joined Buck and Nathan. "Hi, Nathan, I'm sorry I couldn't catch up with you. I can't thank you enough for the wonderful chandelier," I stuttered as my heart fluttered.

"Oh, that's all right. I just thought it'd be a shame to throw such a beautiful old light fixture away. I just came to talk to Dad. I really didn't need to speak with you," Nathan curtly dismissed me as he glanced at his dad.

"All right then, I'll go back to work." I turned to go.

"Didn't look much like work to me," Nathan mumbled as I retreated, bruised and bleeding, from the room. I walked slowly back to the front of the store, picking up my dignity and dragging it along behind me.

"I'm so sorry, L.J., that was Buck's son. I wanted to make sure I didn't miss anything going on with the remodeling back there." I plopped down.

"I'd love for you to show me what you are doing. Maybe after we eat, I could have a tour. Now, what about the theater tickets?"

I stumbled through lunch, half-listening and half waiting for Nathan to come back through the store. By the end of the meal, I realized that I had inadvertently accepted an invitation to attend a play on Friday with L.J.. It was sweet of an old friend to want to spend an evening with me. A casual and uncomplicated evening sounded wonderful.

I thanked L.J. for coming, telling him work was calling. Dinky's class had ended, and the students were scurrying around the store. I assumed he was leaving, but instead he leaned over and kissed me. That took me by surprise, but I wasn't the only one who seemed surprised. Nathan was squeezing his way through the bolts of fabric. He stood near me as L.J. planted the kiss on my cheek. He brushed past me as bolts of fabric fell on the floor. I couldn't utter a word. L.J. smiled and left behind Nathan.

"My goodness, dear, what was that all about?" Dinky said as I shoved the bolts back on the display rack.

"I'm as clueless as anyone could be." Before we could comment further on Nathan and L.J., the precious sisters arrived. Patsy and Polly were excited about the shop and their possible role in it. Chatter filled the space as they noticed the transformation and perused our sample menu. They couldn't wait for the lunch area to open. Until then, they were content to check out the Christmas fabrics. Patsy bought a quarter of a yard of fabric, and Pansy stayed to quilt. The theatrics of the afternoon fought for attention. I battled against them.

"Did I hear Patsy mention working in the kitchen?" Dinky asked.

"Oh, yes, you know, Patsy and Polly came with Kelly Jo to talk about it while you were in the hospital. Did I forgot to mention it to you? I'm sorry."

"Abby! You forgot more than that. You forgot the stigma surrounding the women and their food."

"Their food? Oh, you mean the oleander stuff? Surely no one believes that."

"I guess we'll see when we open the café, won't we?"

CHAPTER

20

I watched as Dinky walked into the kitchen without the aid of a walker. She and I admired the new commercial kitchen.

"It will be convenient, even if it is small," Buck said.

"It'll meet our needs. The used equipment you found looks brand new. Doesn't it, Abby?" Dinky said as she took his hand.

"It's great. Are we still on track to take over next week? How is the money situation?" I inquired.

Buck bellowed, "We're right on course. We'll be out of here as soon as the men from church finish painting and the inspections are complete. In fact, with all the help the church contributed, you'll have some money left over."

"Sterling would be so proud of you, my dear. Look how you've changed Hollingsworth Hill, the business, and our lives," Dinky said, taking my hands. "Without the remodeling work, Buck and I might never have met."

"It's a God thing. He amazes me more each day," I said as we hugged. "Now we can get Shelby settled in her apartment. Can we start working on that soon?"

"The men from church are scheduled to construct the interior while we are on our honeymoon. I knew how important it was to finish, it so Nathan volunteered to supervise. It'll be a snap." Buck hugged us both.

"Oh, Abby. You didn't tell me that you were planning to do the apartment," Dinky said. "I'm so thrilled. I'm sure that will give Shelby balance."

"We're finishing the space, except for a stove. She'll probably just use a microwave, anyway. The stove will have to come later."

"It will be her own little world. Cute as a bug in a rug," Dinky said. "I keep praying."

"Me, too." I hugged Dinky hard.

My head swirled. With all that was going on, I would have been in a frenzy some time ago, rolling up my sleeves to do it all. These days, I spent more time on my knees and less time scurrying.

I headed home. Buck had given the okay to move into Hollingsworth Hill. I rushed through the cold garage and opened the door to the house. The floors were finished. The smell of varnish tickled my nose and the luster of the wood excited me. I'd been living out of a suitcase at Dinky's during the bedroom and bath remodel, so I was more than ready to get into the house but as I surveyed my domain, I knew I was home.

I checked the paper runners on the floors to make sure they were secure. Kelly Jo, Buddy, and two men from the home improvement store were coming. We'd move my things out of the garage, no small task. The three men labored until nearly midnight. Kelly Jo and I pointed the men to designated rooms and helped them place the furniture. We unpacked boxes, as we had time. At the end of the night, a curious mix of unopened boxes and homeless items remained.

Kelly Jo insisted on breaking down the emptied boxes before anyone left. The men complied, but grumbled. As the last collapsed box was stacked in the garage, I handed them cash. They nodded their thanks, and scrambled to their awaiting vehicles. Kelly Jo cheered as we looked over the area. I jumped up and down.

Once they had gone, I studied the mess alone. Strangely, even though Kelly Jo and I had unwrapped and put away things all evening, the boxes seemed to have multiplied. I couldn't see the floor from the front hall to the den. The clutter was everywhere. How could I accomplish this monumental task? My aching body shouted that the answer to that question would have to come tomorrow. My thoughts turned to my Shelby and the day we had first moved things into the old place. Her laughter echoed in my mind. "The boxes almost reach to the stars", she had said. Maybe once we finished the apartment, things would settle down for my dear child. Maybe she'd reach for the stars. *Thank you, God.* I drove to Dinky's for a hot bath.

I heard Buck come to the front door the next morning. I listened to Dinky's sweet greeting, and I drifted back to sleep, hoping to catch up on much needed rest. The happy couple pounded on the door. I groaned as I stumbled across the room.

"We've already whipped through the house. There is still a bunch of stuff lying around!" Buck declared. *As if I didn't know.*

"Sweetie, don't depress the girl. The furniture and the rugs look exquisite," Dinky exclaimed, smiling sweetly at me.

I threw clothes on my throbbing body and followed them to the house. Coffee, tea, and bagels awaited us in the kitchen.

"You were still working when Buck left last night. We thought it must've been a long evening, and we knew you'd want to get started early. So, we brought a treat over this morning," Dinky said softly.

"I don't know what to do with some of these things. They fit into my Atlanta home and I thought I purged everything unnecessary before moving. I should've left most of it in the garage and dealt with it when I had time. I guess Carter and Shelby will want some of this someday, but not now." I threw my hands in the air in sheer exhaustion. "I can just shove them back into the garage, but my Christmas decorations are in here somewhere."

"That's why we're here. Kelly Jo called on her way to work this morning and made a suggestion. I contacted everyone I could this morning. Friends from church are coming here tonight. We can make these piles disappear, my dear." Dinky smiled.

"It'll come together. We know that without our wedding, you could've taken your time and not been pressured. We appreciate all your hard work." Buck leaned over and hugged me, planting a kiss on my cheek. "Would you mind if I put shelves up in the garage? I'll use some leftover lumber and finish it today. How about it?"

"You are both wonderful." I sniffed.

In the middle of the conversation, I remembered L.J.'s theater invitation. I desperately needed to unpack, but I certainly didn't want to be rude to my friend. Realizing how late it was, I raced to dress for work.

I called L.J. the minute I got to work, explaining the cancellation to him. He shot back a reply. He preferred assisting in unpacking. He'd give the tickets to neighbors and join the crew. *What a relief.*

Kelly Jo and L.J. came early. They started putting like items in stacks and then directed the whole effort as others arrived. Buck furnished pizza and laughter filled the house. By the end of the evening, I stood in an empty foyer. I was amazed at the number of things we crammed into closets, cabinets, and garage shelving. Dinky directed furnishing my bedroom.

"Compared to your large bedroom in Atlanta, you're going to be cramped here," Dinky said, "but it really turned out larger than I thought."

"Are you kidding? I see the debt-free expansion of our business in this room. Everything will fall into place at the right time." We hugged long and hard.

Kelly Jo and L.J. were the last to leave. They called me into my den to show me my office. L.J. opened a file drawer and displayed its order. Satisfaction showed on his face. It looked good on him.

"You have a great view from your desk," Kelly Jo said.

"I really don't mind giving up an office. I need a guest bedroom and this area is really nice, isn't it?"

Kelly Jo hugged me and went to her car. L.J. helped her to her vehicle, always the gentleman. We waved as she drove away, and he returned to the porch.

"Did you say you weren't working tomorrow?" he inquired.

"I'm working here until noon. I have the shop covered until then."

"Well, why don't we have breakfast at the closest restaurant, and I'll help here for a couple of hours? There might still be a few things requiring strength." He raised his arms, showing muscles. "I'm still struggling with boxes in my condo, and I've been there a while. I can't imagine having a deadline on organizing it all."

I regretted the theater fiasco, so I asked him to bring fast food to the house. *A strong friend who is willing to help can't create a problem.*

L.J. arrived at eight, and I felt pumped as we started working. L.J. amazed me yet again with a cooler of goodies. *What an organized man.* After a couple of hours of work, he suggested Cokes, which he produced from under the ice.

"Abby, I've wanted to talk with you for some time." He sat down next to me on the couch. "I've been so lonely since Fran died. I know that you're struggling with grief, too." He paused, looking away. "I'm sure that you and Sterling cared deeply for each other. Fran and I were in love to the end." He paused. I fidgeted. "I wouldn't ever hope to have that lifelong love again, but I know how much my sweet Fran cared for you, and it just seems natural for us to…."

"Wait, L.J.," I protested. Before I could say anything else, he kissed me. There was passion in the kiss—I could feel it and I responded—but it was passion for our loss, not for each other. I pulled away. "There's been a huge misunderstanding. I'm grateful to have you as a friend, but I'm not interested in anything more right now."

"Well, I can wait. I think spending time together will prove to you that we could have a comfortable life together."

"You don't understand. I'm not interested in just a comfortable life. Sterling and I adored each other. I can't settle for anything less in another relationship. Actually, there is a new person emerging inside me, and I'm okay, whether I'm single or married."

"Obviously, I've handled this all wrong. I haven't dated in so long, I just didn't know how to go about it."

"That is the whole point. I'm not interested in dating. I'm interested in your friendship, but I want bells and whistles before I commit to another relationship. I want God to be in it."

As we talked about the pain of loss and the confusion of singleness, I said, "I wouldn't have chosen this life, but I've pushed my skills at work and here at home. I've found the strength to strip wallpaper and paint this house. In fact, I really enjoy looking at the ceilings Kelly Jo and I fixed." He looked disinterested. I continued, "I attend Sunday school and church. I'm studying the Bible. That was always hit or miss before, but my relationship with God is growing more intimate all the time. My desperate need has brought me to a very special place. It's exciting to see how He meets those needs."

L.J. interrupted me. "Well, maybe God sent me to take care of those needs. Did you ever think of that? You know, I have a dream of doing all the traveling Fran and I planned. We are still young, Abby. We could see the world together. I'm financially comfortable and you wouldn't have to struggle anymore. I know how hard it's been for you."

I couldn't think of a response. His comments slashed at my heart. He wanted a replacement for Fran, nothing more. *O Lord, I know You have good things planned for me. Help me to see things the way You see them."*

The sound of my phone pierced the air. Kelly Jo called to remind me of our plans after work. I jumped at the chance to end my conversation with L.J.. He left, still eager to get together again. I wasn't so eager. I put in time at work, then headed for the theater. The movie was a great way to end the day. After all, a dark theater, a Coke, and a bag of buttered popcorn were the best prescriptions I knew to relax and escape, even if it was a short-term fix. It was a chick flick; everything ended happily. I slipped into my car, eager to go home to my awaiting bed. I looked at my phone, ready to take it off vibrate. I'd felt a call just before the end of the movie but ignored it. Now I saw that Dinky had called. I pushed her number, and she wanted me to stop at her home. I mumbled my compliance.

"Abby," she said, placing her hand squarely on my shoulder as I entered her home, "come, let's sit down for a moment. I have something I need to say."

After making sure that Dinky was comfortable in the chair, I sat on the footstool and faced her. "Is there something we need to do for the wedding?" I asked.

"Oh, no, sweetheart, nothing more. You've done so much already." She grimaced. "There is no easy way to say this, so I will just get on with it. Shelby came home while Buck and I were watching TV. I was excited to see her, until I got a glimpse of the rough-looking young man accompanying her. Abby, she just came for some of her things— she moved out of the house. I pleaded with her to sit down and talk. I begged her to call you. Nothing helped. I'm so thankful that Buck was here with me."

"Oh, no. No." I sobbed. "I should've known. I just can't...."

"I was hoping Nathan could get through to her. He talked to her several times and then recommended a counselor. She kept at least one appointment with the woman but her actions tonight said it all—moving out like that."

"I didn't even know Nathan was counseling her. What did she say?" I began squirming in my seat as I thought about my daughter and the scruffy young man Dinky described.

"She said she was an inconvenience to us all. She wasn't about to live in my home when Buck took her grandfather's place. I explained that you were working as quickly as possible to get the apartment ready for her. I begged her to hold on just a little while, and everything would work out. Buck even told her we would postpone the wedding until she could move to the apartment if that would ease the situation for her."

"I explained the apartment timetable to her a couple of days ago. I said we could get her up there right after Christmas."

"Well, she said she isn't attending the wedding, Abby. It's as if she wants to cut us all off."

"Her emotions are running wild, Dinky," I said." Why...?"

"Nathan tried to help. He understands the sorrow of a youngster who has suffered loss. His Andrew has dealt with his share of anger and pain, with the death of his mother."

"I know if Sterling were here, things would be different, but what would he do?" I asked.

"I don't know. She wouldn't even tell us where they were going. We didn't get the boy's name. Buck says that the bottom line is, if she wants to separate herself from us, she's old enough that we can't prevent it from happening," Dinky said.

I took her hand, and we cried.

CHAPTER

21

As I opened the door, I heard a loud "Surprise!" Buck held gigantic boughs of greenery. Behind Dinky, Kelly Jo, and Buddy carried the perfectly shaped Christmas tree. Women from my Sunday school group came, carrying goodies. They placed them in the kitchen.

"What on earth...?" I gasped.

Dinky scrambled nimbly on her walker from behind the group. "We're having an old-fashioned Christmas party—a hanging of the greens."

"Wow. What a treat." I giggled.

They sang "We Wish You A Merry Christmas" as they came into the house. Buddy worked quickly, setting up the tree in minutes. Dinky spotted the box she wanted and retrieved the antique quilt I always placed under my tree.

"Would you be a dear, Kelly Jo, and put this under the tree. If I go down, I might not get back up." Dinky laughed.

Kelly Jo dropped to her knees and arranged the red and green stars under the evergreen.

Dinky was busy arranging the extra greenery on the mantle. "Abby, I think this foliage and your beautiful crystal candlesticks will be exquisite here. I'll purchase all new candles this week," Dinky said.

We grabbed ornaments and chatted as we trimmed the tree. As I placed a silver bell on a limb, I heard Christmas music.

Buck peeked from around the corner and smiled. "How do you like your sound system? Merry Christmas from your builder and his future bride."

"When did you do this?"

"It was easy to do while the electrical was being installed. It wasn't labor-intensive at all."

I shot a questioning look at Dinky.

She laughed. "Don't look at me. He surprised me, too. Remember the evening you found us dancing? We were trying out the new system as well as the floors. It sounds great, doesn't it?"

"Ah, you distracted me that evening with your waltz. Thanks again."

The final task was to place the manger scene on the entry table. The familiar pang of heartache hit. Sterling and I had always assembled the pieces together each year. But, I was detecting something new this year. Now it was more a sweet memory than a tremendous pain. *This is the season for joy, and that is what I choose to feel.* In the glow of holiday laughter, it didn't seem like an insurmountable task.

"Wow, does my home look amazing! Thank you for filling the rooms with love and laughter. I really needed the reminder that y'all are family," I said with tears in my eyes. Kelly Jo put her arm around my shoulder and squeezed.

Buck cleared his throat. "Could we have a house blessing while we're all here?"

"Oh, yes, that would be wonderful." I sighed as we formed a circle, holding hands.

"Father, we ask that You would dwell here. And because You reside here, those who come into these rooms will be aware of Your presence, assured of Your love, and thankful for Your many blessings. You are Our Strength, Our All-Sufficient One. Thank You for providing this lovely home for Abby. We see Your hand in all that has been done. We love You. Amen," Buck said.

We began singing Christmas carols, and the sound permeated my home with warmth that had nothing to do with the temperature of the room.

For days, we'd been hunting Shelby. We knew she was too old to be considered a runaway by law, so we were on our own. We all scoured the surrounding area. Our efforts produced nothing but more anxiety. Shelby and her car had disappeared into thin air. I spent time just sitting in her room at Dinky's and praying through my tears.

The school semester was over. She'd quit her part-time job and vanished. When I'd exhausted every possibility, Dinky called a friend who was the retired police chief. He called back saying there was no trail. She hadn't used her credit card or her cell phone. He'd made calls but turned up nothing. Three days before Christmas, Carter and I followed my well-worn path in the area, looking for Shelby's car. We'd decided to head for home when I spotted a beat-up blue Toyota ahead of us. We followed for a couple of blocks, but then traffic slowed right in front of us. The clunker turned the corner while we waited to proceed. Carter gunned my car, and we turned as quickly as we could. There were no cars on the side street. We toured the surrounding streets, but the car had disappeared. We headed home, exhausted.

Dinky and I decided not to open the store on Christmas Eve, so Kelly Jo and I started cleaning before eight that morning. Carter was staying in the garage apartment. He said he wanted to be at home with me rather than at Dinky's already crowded home. I thought he wanted to avoid as much chatter as possible. As we carried Shelby's mattress to the empty apartment, I cried.

"If Shelby had only waited." I lamented with a heavy sigh.

"Maybe she'll change her mind and show up for the wedding," Carter said as he took Lexus upstairs for the night.

I was glad to see him relate to my little girl. Mercedes and Lexus were not easing gracefully into their new environment. My cat was old, but still playful. In addition, she was tremendously opinionated. Her original survey of her new territory produced copious sounds, none of which were happy. I couldn't take the chance of her messing with the tree this year. In years past, she'd made her way up the tree and then tried to exit by a limber branch, which had never ended well—for the tree or my ornaments. Fortunately, the pocket doors to the den and kitchen area kept her from any thrill-seeking this year. The dog was always a disaster waiting to happen. I had taken her to obedience school for a short course in September. Although she had passed with excellence and received a trophy, she remained a bull in a china shop. Her tail alone could level a coffee table. She would be relegated to the garage until after the wedding, poor baby.

Carter jumped into the details of the day with gusto. While we cleaned, he ran an errand for me. He'd finished the last minute assignment in town when he came into the house via the garage. Lexus bolted down the stairs and flew into the house before he could get a free hand to shut the door.

Kelly Jo and I stood in the hall, admiring all we had accomplished when we heard Carter yell. A second later, we saw the reason for the shouting. Carter's last stop for the day had been at The China Garden. Lexus wore a generous portion of Chinese noodles, which she distributed as she flew through the house. We were on the run. Kelly Jo tried to cut her off by going into the living room as the pup headed to the dining room. I scurried behind my dog commanding her to stop, to sit, to do whatever—nothing worked. Carter raced into the skirmish as we circled the dining table, trying to grab the slippery baby. Lexus slid under the table. I clutched her back legs as Kelly Jo grasped her collar. She finally stopped in her tracks, wagging her tail with glee. Still adorned with noodles, her tail stung my face, but I shut my eyes and held on for dear life. What a dog. The thought of the money wasted on obedience training hurt more than the whacks of her tail. Carter and I held Lexus as Kelly Jo opened the doors to the patio. We ushered her outside while Carter apologized for the dilemma.

"I guess the door to the apartment wasn't shut all the way when I left this morning. I didn't have the heart to put her in the crate. She was asleep on my bed when I left. I'm so sorry, Mom," he said.

We stood on the patio, holding the stinky dog. Our lunch was distributed all over the now dirty floors. Panting, I collapsed on the ground as the dog licked me. Lexus then shook hard, causing debris to hit me square in the face. We laughed. It took us nearly an hour to put things back in order. Luckily, the dog had only traipsed through a couple of rooms, or we'd have been scrubbing until January.

I was relieved that Lexus missed my bedroom. Buck had delivered the wedding apparel the day before, and it was hanging everywhere possible in the room.

On Christmas Eve, we were exchanging gifts at Dinky's house— without Shelby. Strangely enough, I remained at peace about the matter as I got into Carter's car for the short drive to Dinky's house. I couldn't force her to be with us. I concentrated, instead, on those who would be there.

I hadn't asked Dinky if Nathan would be coming, but as we entered the front hall, I heard his laughter. I experienced a strange flutter as I helped carry gifts to the tree. Dinky and Buck had decorated every inch of space, so it was difficult to get to the corner of the crowded room. I brushed past Nathan and smiled. He quickly smiled back. It occurred to me that I hadn't seen him in some time. Well, we'd be together Christmas Eve and Christmas Day. "Abby, Carter, let me introduce you to my son, Andrew," Nathan said.

We shook hands, and Andrew quickly took the packages from my arms and put them under the tree. He was a handsome young man, but something about him reminded me of my Shelby. I guess it was the sad, faraway look in his eyes.

"Glad to meet you," I said. "Exciting, isn't it? The wedding and all."

No answer. A little smile appeared on his lips and it disappeared quickly. Awkward moment.

I turned to Nathan. "I guess you've had lots going on, with the holidays and all."

"It's a busy time of year at the church," he responded. I felt strange, and he acted uncomfortable as well. "How's your friend?"

"Friend?" I asked.

"The one you were having lunch with at the shop."

"Oh, L.J.—fine, I guess."

"Time to eat! Come and get it!" Buck called. "Dinky and I worked in the kitchen together to give y'all a feast."

We seemed to move beyond the original awkwardness of two blended families exchanging gifts. Dinky had suggested drawing names as soon as we knew the two were marrying Christmas Day. Of course, after admiring gifts, the conversation turned to the wedding.

"Are you ready?" Nathan asked.

"Well, now that we have the marriage license, we are. We had no idea that the fee had to be paid in cash. Can you imagine, in this day and age?" Buck chuckled.

"Probably so it can't be traced. I'll bet somebody in the system takes part of it, don't you think?" Andrew said. No one responded.

"Well, what did you do?" Pete asked.

"It was nearly closing time. We pooled our money, and between us we had one dollar more than needed. Can you believe it?" Dinky laughed.

"We need to have another counseling session," Nathan said. "We'll discuss finances. If it took nearly your last dollar to get the license, you two are headed for money problems. Say, since everyone is here, maybe we should include a discussion on how to get along with the relatives?" We all laughed.

"Let's pass on that dialogue," Carter suggested.

We ended the evening early. Dinky and Buck had invited twenty people besides the family to the wedding.

We were discussing the invitation list when Carter spoke up. "Say, Mom, I invited Alex to the wedding. I hope that's all right."

"Your study partner, sure," I said. *Strange. Since when did Carter hang out with a guy all the time?*

The ceremony was to begin at 10:30 in the morning. Carter was responsible for the music. I was in charge of distributing fresh roses throughout the house. That would be easy enough.

CHAPTER

22

Tossing from one side to the other side, I fluffed my pillow. Shelby, intense and angry, burst into my thoughts. What could I have done to stop her from spiraling out of control? Where was she? Was she safe? I prayed a pitiful, whiny prayer. I stretched, yawned, and fumbled with my sheets. Sleep finally came around three in the morning. At seven, I heard Carter in the kitchen. With plenty of caffeine flowing through my veins, I faced the day.

The sisters were the first to arrive. Their huge sedan roared up an hour before we had asked them to come. We planned to leave four tables and their chairs in the guest bedroom until after the service then place them in the living room and hall for lunch. The buffet-style luncheon would be placed in the dining room. We were setting up the last chair in the den when the sisters, like a gaggle of hostile geese, swooped into the room.

"We must have chairs in the living room. Where are they?" Pansy gasped.

"We thought everyone would stand during the short ceremony," I mumbled.

"That will never do," Penny said, putting her gloved hand to her cheek.

"Mom, why don't we place the chairs for the living room and hall in rows like in church? It'll be easier later on to just bring the tables out," Carter suggested.

We shoved the furniture against the walls and formed rows of chairs. With the plan and the chairs in place, the women fanned out for further inspection. Patsy was in charge of the registry. She turned up her nose as she saw the small table I'd placed in the entry hall to accommodate the book.

Pointing to the manger scene, she barked the command, "Baby Jesus will have to be put away early this year. This table is stable and tall enough for people to use comfortably. It will do nicely."

I wanted to dig my heels in—it was a tradition worth fighting for—but Carter retrieved the box from the garage and began wrapping. Baby Jesus was gone in minutes. With Patsy appeased, we followed the gaggle into the dining room, where the sisters repositioned serving dishes and fussed over flowers. They had insisted on working. Now Carter and I knew the reason. Things must be done properly, and we couldn't be trusted to do the job.

Dinky rescued us, as she floated into the house and promptly directed us to our stations. Carter headed to the kitchen to check the sound system, and I followed Dinky. Claire joined us in my bedroom to dress. I heard Nathan and Buck greeting people at the door. Soon, beautiful music and excited chatter floated in the air from the other side of the door. Then sounds came from further away, and there was a knock at the door. We giggled, and the bride opened the door. She laced her arm in Pete's and motioned for us to lead the way.

Claire smiled and we strolled slowly to the living room, and once inside we awaited the arrival of the bride. She wore her simple taupe dress, displaying the pearls Buck gave her the night before, and carrying a rose bouquet in her arms. Pete beamed as he ushered his mother into the room. The plantation shutters reduced the sunlight, allowing the soft glow of the candles to illuminate the space. The sparkle of the Christmas tree's white lights dimmed next to Buck's shining face. Andrew stood straight and tall at his side.

I wished my Sterling could have been part of it all. He would've relished the joy of the day. If only. I shoved the thought to the back of my mind as tears formed. My eyes moved about the room and rested on the handsome pastor. Suddenly, I was aware of a stranger in our midst. It was supposed to be an intimate ceremony for family and friends. Who was this girl? Carter said his study partner, Alex, was coming. Maybe Alex brought a girlfriend. *Oh, great, there's L.J. Who asked him to come?* This was becoming a three-ring circus instead of a cozy gathering.

I focused on Dinky as she and Pete came near. Pete extended his mother's arm to Buck as Claire put the walker in front of Dinky for support. She'd insisted she wouldn't need it. Claire got the look. *Slick move, Claire.*

The muffled comments stopped as Nathan began the ceremony. He read the Genesis passage recounting Adam receiving his treasured wife as a gift from God.

He paused and talked to the bride and groom as if no one else existed. "You are embarking on a journey together that is extremely significant in God's eyes. It is a covenant relationship designed to last the rest of your lives. That relationship will bring blessings to you and those whose lives you touch. In this passage, God said it is good. Those of us who have watched as you met, courted, and fell in love, know it is good. You are to nurture and encourage each other, and cling to each other, as you grow closer to your heavenly Father. You've prepared vows that you would like to give each other today."

Buck began, "Jane Ann, you are the light of my life. I promise to hold you above all others for the rest of my life. I'll cherish you and adore you until God takes me home."

Dinky cleared her throat and looked sweetly at him, saying, "God has been so good to me. He has blessed me with a man of integrity and godly wisdom in you. I promise to love you, cherish you, and respect you as long as I live. You are my dearest friend and my joy."

It was hard for me to see through blurry eyes. They stood, telling each other and the world that the years might be few but the joys would be plentiful. I heard the rest of the ceremony, but more than that, I saw it and felt it. *Lord, life is worth the risk, isn't it? Please give them an abundance of time together. I know You have numbered their days, but please give them quality time.*

I was brought back into my surroundings as Nathan pronounced them man and wife. Everyone cheered, and the photo op began.

I glanced again at the mysterious stranger. She stood next to L.J. while everyone posed for pictures. Regal, with thick raven hair that contrasted her creamy skin, she seemed comfortable in this setting. Who on earth was she? *Maybe she is L.J.'s date. Maybe he brought her to make me jealous. Not working, big boy.* As I encouraged the guests to head to the dining room for lunch, Carter came up with the mystery girl.

CHAPTER

23

"Mom, I'm sorry I didn't have time to introduce you two before the wedding. This is my study partner, Alex."

"Ahhhh. Now I see why the boy is spending so much time studying." I laughed. "I guess you just forgot to give me any details about Alex—is it Alexandra?"

"Yes, but I've always been called Alex. My dad desperately wanted a son, thus the name. I guess that is why I chose engineering—he's an engineer. I'm sorry I got lost and almost missed the beautiful ceremony."

"I'm thrilled to meet you, but does that mean you sacrificed Christmas with family? I'm so sorry."

"No, please, don't be. We don't celebrate holidays anymore. My parents divorced years ago and well, holidays are...."

"I understand how things change, Alex. I'm just sorry Carter hasn't brought you with him before now. We can always include one more. We're slightly dysfunctional, but we do have fun." I introduced her to everyone as we moved into the den.

By late afternoon, my footsteps echoed in the hallway. Everyone had scattered, and my house was back in order. Pete and Buck had loaded the rental tables and chairs in Buck's truck. Buck had insisted that he return them before they left on their honeymoon. My furniture was in the den for the first time. I tried to stay focused on the furniture placement but I knew what had to come next. I couldn't postpone seeing my family any longer. I was committed. I had emailed Eleanor some time ago, saying that I'd come the Friday after Christmas if that was convenient. Her brisk reply stated she would rearrange her busy schedule to suit me, since Daddy was beside himself at my absence during the holidays. Betsy took pity on me and agreed to meet me there. Daddy hadn't replied to my email or my voicemail. *Another terrific time with family.*

I hadn't been to Atlanta since a quick trip in September. Claire called often, encouraging me to visit them. When I told her I'd be in Augusta after Christmas, she suggested that I make a huge loop and come to Atlanta after seeing my family. She called back to say several friends were coming to an open house to see me. The remodeling was finished at the shop, and Dinky was gone on a honeymoon, so I'd decided to close the shop for a couple of days. Quilters would need a trip to the shop on New Year's Day while husbands watched football. Until then, I was free.

The drive to Augusta was wonderful. Eleanor lived on a palatial estate outside the city. The rolling hills were picturesque, as were the gorgeous horses grazing in the pastures. The house was a quarter of a mile from the road and stood majestically on the highest part of the property, making the mansion visible for miles around. Eleanor's husband had been a United States Senator for the past ten years so they were accustomed to dividing their time between Washington and their home in Augusta. They'd never invited my family to their home in D.C., but I heard about it in glowing detail from Daddy. I called and told Eleanor when I would arrive. She quickly informed me that Daddy and Katherine, our stepmother, would be there before noon, so she hoped I would be prompt. So much for a warm reception, but at least it didn't take me by surprise—nothing did, where my family was concerned.

I managed to arrive with time to spare, and the maid escorted me to my room—no sister in sight. I quickly dressed for lunch, or luncheon, as Eleanor had said. I went downstairs, hoping to say hello to my distant sister, when my father drove up.

I felt very vulnerable without Sterling to watch over me, so during the drive to Augusta, I'd rehearsed my responses to the obvious questions. "Where are the kids? Why haven't we seen you?" I determined to be as unemotional as possible. I couldn't let my guard down. There would be landmines in every direction. *Keep alert, Abby. There could be a blowup at the slightest hint of vulnerability.* I watched from the window as my father helped his ailing wife from the car.

The maid promptly appeared and invited them into the study where she had brought me moments before. *Okay, show time.* I tugged at my clothes as I stood up and plastered a smile on my face.

"Hello, Katherine, how good to see you. And you are looking good, Daddy."

"Well, you certainly look like you were rode hard and put away wet," Daddy said loudly. "Those dark circles under your eyes don't become you."

"Now, darling, that's not a nice thing to say. Come here, child, and give your mother a hug. My, it's been so long since we've seen you." Katherine smiled her typical insincere smile and held out her arms, motioning me to her as if I were a child.

I responded with a hug and then walked over to my dad. "Daddy, you do look good," I cooed.

"Well, the doctor is amazed I'm still alive. I'm on seven different medications and still in constant pain. You'd think I was going to be around forever, as seldom as I see you."

"I'm doing very well, Daddy, thank you for asking." I smiled and sat down.

"Don't get smart with me, little girl," Daddy said.

Luckily, before he could say more, Eleanor made her grand appearance. "Well, my goodness, how could there be harsh words already? Y'all just got here!"

Eleanor's three daughters, Augusta, Madison, and Savannah, wouldn't be joining us. Eleanor ushered us into the spacious dining room. She asked about Carter and Shelby, but was content with vague responses. That, of course, gave Daddy and Eleanor more time to center the conversation on their activities. She was gearing up for the campaign trail for the next run for reelection. Daddy told all about his latest doctor's appointments. I inquired about Betsy. She was to arrive around four and would leave after brunch tomorrow. *Who could blame her?*

The table was adorned with fresh flowers and greenery. The candles flickered as I watched Daddy at the other end of the table. He was full of himself even nearing the end of his life. All the memories of my childhood came roaring back. Even now, I wanted to ask him how anyone could send a tiny girl away each summer. I was sure he blamed me for Mother's health problems. She'd been ill all my life. *Watch it, Abby. Think about good things, and don't take this whole thing on again. Remember, you have forgiven.* In the background of the self-talk, I heard my sister gloating about her many accomplishments. *Oh, yeah, you seldom went with me to South Carolina, and when you did, Grandmother didn't pour her petty anger on you.*

The maid set a beautiful salad before me with lettuce, Mandarin oranges, and celery seed dressing. Mandarin oranges.... I poked at the salad, and my memories went back to childhood. Traveler's Rest was a small town. I lived for those times when I would be released from the deep freeze of Grandmother Carter's front porch and into the warmth Dinky poured on me.

At home, my mother was gentle, kind, and tender, but never active. As Betsy and Eleanor grew older and had outside interests, I got Mama's full attention—at least, during the school year. She'd sing to me while she combed my unruly hair. My hair was a bone of contention with anyone but my Mama. She prayed with me and told me how much Jesus loved me. I remember as a girl of six or seven looking at my mother's face as she called God her All-Sufficient One. Even at that age, the idea of this delicate woman telling me God would take care of all my needs, and He was all I needed, seemed odd. He hadn't taken care of all her needs, had He? I determined then that being with her was all I needed or wanted. I could bury my head in her chest, hear her heartbeat and her gentle breathing, and know that I was loved and cared for—by my mother and, if she said so, by my Heavenly Father.

Mama died the summer after I graduated from high school. Eleanor was in Washington D.C., working during her summer break from college. Betsy was married and living in Asheville. Grandmother Carter's health had declined and Daddy was determined to send me to take care of her that summer. He announced his decision as I sat holding Mama's hand. Mama asked me to get something from the next room, and I heard her tell Daddy I was staying home that summer. I'd never known her to stand up to Daddy before. So that summer, I spent every moment with Mama. No food appealed to her, and she couldn't keep anything in her delicate stomach. I tried everything, until one day I offered her Mandarin oranges. She loved them and ate them constantly from then on. I remember one day close to the end, I put an orange in her mouth. She chewed and whispered how thankful she was that she still loved Mandarin oranges. Thankful.

Now, the Mandarin orange stuck in my throat. I knew my mother loved me with her dying breath. My earthly father's love was certainly questionable. Daddy brought home a new wife five months after Mama died. I was in Traveler's Rest in college. Wife number two walked out after a few very long years. Katherine was number three, and obviously a survivor. Betsy and I had made a pact long ago to keep her around. Otherwise, we'd have to take care of Daddy, and neither of us wanted to be put on death row for strangling the old buzzard. All of these thoughts rattled around in my brain while my face wore the obligatory smile. *Ah, yes, and they wonder why they don't see more of me.*

The long cool afternoon dragged on. The tall ceilings produced a draft on my neck, and the company produced a similar feeling deep within my heart. The surroundings excited my eye with the beauty, the meal excited my taste buds with rich flavor, and the company excited my memory of times past. In the end, I experienced indigestion and bad dreams in the middle of the afternoon. It sounded vaguely like a song.

Betsy finally made an entrance, with some excuse for being late. She and I both knew she was a brave soldier to do so many tours of duty with family this holiday. We were released from detention around noon the next day, when it became clear that Eleanor and her girls had other things to do. Her husband had already gone back to Washington, and Eleanor needed to get the house in order before catching her plane.

The girls, who had been too busy to spend more than a few minutes with me, were staying in Augusta until the New Year's Eve parties. Betsy and I arranged to meet at the fast food place on the highway. After comparing notes on the stay, we did our traditional good-bye. We stood in the parking lot, hugged, shook the dust off our feet, and got into our vehicles. For a brief moment, I wished I could shake off the emotional baggage. I chuckled, then dropped into the seat of my car and headed to Atlanta. *What a mess. What a mess indeed.*

With the horrendous traffic, I arrived at Claire's just in time for the party. The number of friends who were there surprised me. I brought pictures of the house and the wedding; it was exhilarating to relive fun times. I avoided discussing Shelby.

When the others left, Claire brought out a beautifully wrapped gift. It was a scrapbook filled with pictures of our families through the years. Claire and Pete's two girls had husbands in the military and were stationed in Europe. They had planned a trip to see their children before Sterling's death, but the trip had been put on hold.

"Oh, Claire, this is wonderful. Look at the kids—this must have been when they went camping with their dads. Wow, the girls were so tiny here. What an enormous work of love. Thank you."

"I copied all the pages, so I have a set too. Read this." Claire pointed to a letter in the back. I pulled it out and giggled as I read. She titled the page "the rest of the story," our name for child-centered discussions. Claire wrote that each child, of course, gave a different spin on any event in question. We learned the truth was often in there, somewhere between the individual twists and turns. It was our job to ferret it out of all the information.

I dropped the album into my lap. "Oh, Claire, I've put off doing something, and this letter makes it so clear. I have a spin on Sterling's death, but Rhonda Bell has her side as well. I've extracted a pound of flesh from the woman, and it still doesn't seem enough. I need to forgive her once and for all so I can be at peace. It really isn't about her, after all. That's the real truth."

"Pete's working at the office tonight. Why not give her a call before you change your mind, and we'll visit her? She goes to our church so she can't live too far away."

I made the call and got directions. We drove to our favorite Mexican restaurant for dinner. My stomach didn't appreciate the basket of chips I consumed. I washed it down with Coke. By the time the meal arrived, I was no longer capable of eating another bite. I found it difficult to talk as Claire drove into a modest subdivision of well-kept homes. As we stopped the car, I had a sudden urge to cry.

"Claire, this was a bad idea. I don't know what to say to her. Maybe we should just say I'm sick and let it go at that."

Rhonda appeared at the door and came down the steps. Claire lowered the car window and asked her to give us a minute. Rhonda anxiously went back inside.

"It's your call. How much do you want to put this behind you?" Claire said.

"Enough to get out and face Rhonda, I guess."

Claire grabbed my hand and asked God to be in our midst and to give me the words I needed to say. As I climbed out of the car, I noticed a green Honda in the carport. *Hmmm. I wonder where the flashy yellow sports car is.* I hesitated, then walked to meet Rhonda. Claire greeted her. We entered the tiny living room. As we stood in the middle of the room, I was aware of ice dropping down into its container in the freezer in the next room and a dog barking outside. I didn't hear the words exchanged between the two women. I wondered how quickly I could bolt for a bathroom; my stomach rumbled at my dinner choice.

Claire handled small talk brilliantly. When she stopped and no one said a word, I knew I needed to speak.

"Rhonda, I'm here to apologize." As the words tumbled out of my mouth, I wished I could retrieve them. What was I thinking? Suddenly, it was clear. "I have given you the impression that you had to earn my forgiveness, that there was some unknown thing out there for you to do to make everything right. There isn't. God has freely forgiven me, and now I freely forgive you."

Rhonda jumped to her feet and raced to the couch where we sat. "Abby, thank you. I'm so sorry for the pain I've caused."

"It's time for both of us to move on with our lives. I really mean it this time—car or no car."

"Did you see the green car outside?" I tilted my head. She continued, "I sold my sports car. Neither of us needs it around. I'm going to church, too."

"I'm glad," I said.

Rhonda served ice cream and coffee. As we drove to Claire's house, I felt a huge burden fly off my shoulders. Claire spoiled the moment by asking me about Dad. Even I had to admit that the night had been miraculous, but it would take something really gigantic to get me to deal with Daddy.

CHAPTER

24

On New Year's Eve, my cell phone rang. I glanced at the incoming number, but I couldn't identify it.

"Happy New Year, Mom."

"Shelby? Are you all right? Where are you?"

"I'm in the mountains. I... just... wanted to hear your voice. I love you, Mama."

"Honey, please come home. We all need you. Please...."

There was no response. I pulled to the side of the road and called Dinky's police connection. I gave him the telephone number on my cell phone, and he said he'd look into it. Kelly Jo and I were taking in a late afternoon movie, and Buddy was joining us at my house later. I waited until after dinner to divulge my news.

"I think it's a good sign, her calling and all," Kelly Jo said as we started playing a board game.

"Let me see the number." Buddy glanced at my cell phone. "That's a North Carolina area code."

"Abby, she's not far away. Maybe she'll come home soon," Kelly Jo said hopefully.

Sweet potato skins and bones were all that remained on our plates as we scraped dishes and loaded the dishwasher. We'd watched a thriller on the large screen, and we began sketching our own plot as we plunged into a board game.

"I bet your police friend can tell us what town the call came from," Buddy stated.

"I think we ought to pile in the car and go after her," Kelly Jo volunteered.

"I think we're getting ahead of ourselves. It's taken me a while to get to this point, but I don't want to force her to come home if she isn't ready. God has got to be in charge, not me," I blurted.

Kelly Jo stared at me as she pressed her lips tightly together and squinted. Buddy shifted his feet under the table.

"Okay, I know I sound crazy, but I've prayed a lot about this. I have to leave room for God to work. I have to have faith."

"I don't know much about the Bible, but I recall something about faith without works being dead," Kelly Jo sputtered. "I think we ought to work on getting her to come to her senses. Let's find her and bring her home."

"What if we do find her? If she doesn't want to be here, she'll just disappear again."

They threw out more possibilities for Shelby as I took my turn on the board. *Lord, I give the situation to You. I've handled enough things the wrong way. Not this time.*

By ten o'clock, we finished our game, hugged, and went our separate ways. Dinky called to wish me a Happy New Year. We prayed for Shelby's safety. Slipping into my bed before eleven, Bible in hand, I prayed in the New Year.

Dinky and Buck honeymooned in St. Augustine, Florida. They'd planned to cruise the Caribbean, but realized the ship offered little stability for Dinky's already unsteady gait. After three weeks away, the pair returned with pictures and souvenirs. I received my orders immediately upon their arrival. We'd meet for dinner that evening. Nathan was coming, too. As I spoke with her, the shop phone rang. L.J. was on the line, suggesting dinner and a movie. What a shame, I already had plans, I said. His voice seemed edgy—I'd been busy for some time now.

"One day you'll quit playing your silly little game, Abby. You'll see I'm the man for you." L.J. sounded more than edgy now.

"I don't like the tone of your voice, L.J. Have you been drinking?"

"What are you, a girl scout or my mother?" I heard the line go dead.

After work, I flew home and dressed in a black top and black slacks. I put on a multicolored jacket. Black to slim, and color to give my pale skin a glow. I lingered in front of the mirror, checking out the effects of my new wrinkle cream. *Oh, well, I can only hope the restaurant is dark—very dark.*

As Buck, Dinky and I glanced at the menu, Nathan called, saying he couldn't join us. I felt disappointment mixed with relief as Buck explained, "Nathan has a parishioner who is near death and his wife wants the pastor to be there tonight. The children are all going to visit, and they don't get along."

"How sad," Dinky said.

"Oh, there is plenty of dysfunctional stuff going around," I said. "You two were just spared all that. It must have something to do with the hard work you put into raising your kids." I smiled at the two lovebirds.

"Abby, Dinky and I are from totally opposite sides of the spectrum. She and Elliot did everything right, and my first wife and I did everything wrong. It hurts to see the seeds that I sowed continue to sprout," Buck muttered as he studied the menu. After placing our order, he continued, "Nathan's mother and I were way too immature when we married, and we never grew up, at least not emotionally. I handled the problems by working constantly. She went from doctor to doctor with every symptom known to man. She got medication for it all. Added to the mix, my success allowed her to consume major amounts of alcohol. All in the name of advancing my career. The worst thing was that I just stood by and watched. I guess I felt I was off the hook as long as she was busy. It wasn't until our only child became hard to handle that I got involved. Finally, Nathan and I started going to church. Unfortunately, his mother didn't want to change her lifestyle. If you drink all night, it's hard to get up and go to church the next morning." He paused.

"Nathan and I both became Christians just weeks before my wife died. I talk about it nonchalantly now, but it took years to work through the guilt and pain. I relived our life together and agonized over it all. I could've done more—I should've done more."

I winced. "I'm so sorry."

"The sad thing is that Nathan married a woman as needy as his mother. Nothing he did was good enough for her. She came from a very influential family and was accustomed to a pampered lifestyle. The only productive thing to come from their union was Andrew."

"Oh, my. With all that behind you, I can't believe that you would even think of getting married again."

"I didn't think of it. I was just going along when God gave me Dinky—a gift from heaven. It was as clear as day that she was the one I was to spend the rest of my life with."

Dinky patted his arm. Her eyes glistened as she looked at me.

"Say, let me see those pictures," I said in a high-pitched voice that surprised even me.

We looked at all the snapshots, then decided to go to Quilter's Circle. I was eager to show them what had been done while they were away. I opened the door and Dinky gasped. The area had come alive while they were gone. Nothing was the same. Kelly Jo, Buddy, and I had varnished the floors and woodwork, and we'd moved things from one area to the other. The Christmas decorations made way for spring inventory and spring class displays. Kelly Jo was teaching some evening classes, which would help lighten the load. Her samples for the classes hung on display. Patsy and Polly had commandeered the kitchen. Dinky hadn't seen the work at the front of the building. Buck and his men finished the opening between Mr. Perkins's old space and ours just before Christmas. There was now plenty of room for the café tables, with additional room for inventory expansion. The redesigned space was stimulating customer response. Overall, it seemed to be a huge success already.

I watched Dinky walk through the enlarged space. She touched each bolt of fabric, each new display, finally sitting down at a table, visibly moved.

"This is better than I ever imagined it could be." She lowered herself into a waiting chair.

"We opened the café last week."

"I have one huge question. Didn't anyone balk at eating the sister's cooking?"

"Oh. You won't believe what happened!" I sputtered. "I wrestled with how to bring the matter up to the sisters. When I went into the shop the day before we were to open, I was prepared to talk with them about the whole thing. I didn't have to. There was a huge paper banner hanging there, big as you please." I pointed to the spot on the wall.

"A banner? Come on, out with it," Dinky prodded.

"Café open—all food prepared oleander free. I couldn't believe it. Patsy and Polly had Kelly Jo make the sign, and they climbed up on the ladder themselves to hang it. It caused quite a stir, let me tell you."

"And…?"

"The café is a hit. One customer took a picture of the banner and put it on some website. People have been flocking in. Kelly Jo even printed an explanation. Here." I handed a copy to Dinky.

An urban legend has it that four sisters plotted the demise of their husbands by using deadly oleander powder in their food. Nothing could be further from the truth. Aware of the gossip surrounding their proud family, the sisters have used fictitious names each year for many years when submitting their baked goods at the county fair and have always received first place ribbons. No one ever complained of feeling sick afterward.

Statistics show that it is not uncommon to succumb to death during the months of January through March, when viral infections are rampant.

Buck read the information out loud and then began laughing. His belly shook, and he stomped his feet. He finally wiped his eyes with a handkerchief and took a deep breath.

"I can't believe it. I mean, which is funnier—the legend or this explanation?" Buck shook his head.

"Well, it has made us famous. There are people in here every day checking out the food. Kelly Jo is thinking of printing up tee shirts to sell—I ate the sisters' food and survived."

"How are Penny and Pansy taking it?" Dinky asked.

"With true grace, how else? They are working on compiling a cookbook with all the family recipes in it, because everyone in the area knew Mama was a wonderful cook."

"I can't believe it. Some ugly gossip turned into good."

"Well, with all this going on, are you coming back to work any time soon?" I prodded.

"I wouldn't miss it. I'll be here next week. The doctor dismissed me from therapy before our wedding. Anyway, it sounds like I better get into the flow of things before you decide you can do it without me."

"Oh, yeah, sure. It's a piece of cake." I stopped and we all laughed. "Seriously, I'm glad you'll be here. I go to Quilt Market pretty soon, you know. Hey, I have a suggestion I want to go over with you, but it can wait," I announced as we closed the door to the shop.

The Market had been my project each year. Since it was held in Atlanta, I'd accompanied Dinky from the start. Her partner wouldn't go to Atlanta.

"People are killed every day in that big city," she'd said.

Dinky had quickly decided it was too much for her, too, leaving it solely on my willing shoulders. It had always been a highlight of my year. The sights and smells invigorated me. The main hall had fabric from one end to the other. There was hardly room to breathe when the crowds pushed in.

Over the years, many of the vendors had become friends. After Sterling's death, Dinky had gone in my place. This year, I recruited Kelly Jo to make the drive. With her aunt nearby, she'd help me at the show and then visit her family. My adrenaline pumped as we pointed the car toward my hometown. We dropped our luggage off at the hotel—a new experience. I'd always just driven into town for the day and gone straight home to Sterling. We hurried to the floor of the large hall.

"We can't possible cover this huge place! I've never seen anything like it!" Kelly Jo gasped as we entered.

"Watch out. Touching fabric can become addictive." I chuckled as my friend stood silent. There is a first time for everything.

After five hours of walking, I was ready for dinner and a comfy bed. I jotted down locations for vendors I wanted to talk with the next day, and we made our way to the restaurant to have dinner with business friends—another new thing. I was surprised that my friends were seated in the bar when we arrived. We sat down, and the server quickly came to take our order. Kelly Jo and I ordered Cokes. There was a gasp and snickers as the others ordered a second round of cocktails.

"Why come to Market if you don't plan to have some after-hours fun?"

"Yeah, the night is young. At least get a glass of wine. Oh, look, I think the handsome guy at the bar is looking our way."

"Loosen up, Abby. You're single. We're going from here to a club and meet some of the salesmen from the booth next to ours. There are plenty of them to go around. We'll show you how to have a good time."

Kelly Jo jumped in like a pro. "Oh, I'm sorry. We've got plans. We just have time for a Coke, and we're off. Right, Abby?"

"Right. Sorry for the mix-up," I babbled. Kelly Jo excused herself. She returned a few minutes later, saying it was time to catch our cab. We assured the girls we'd see them tomorrow, then squeezed through the crowded bar. Our coats were too thin for the strong wind, so I huddled on the curb as Kelly Jo whistled for a cab. We got one immediately, and Kelly Jo gave the driver instructions.

"That was amazingly smooth. What just went on in there?" I scooted across the seat.

"I'm an old hand at that kind of awkward situation. Next to getting away from pushy men, my specialty is getting away from women who are looking for a good time."

"Slick. I'm amazed. You seem comfortable in the city. I thought you were a country girl." I offered my hand. "Give me five." We slapped hands. Two blocks down the street, we slid out of the cab and back onto the sidewalk.

"I remembered your saying this was your favorite restaurant in town, so I made reservations while I was away from the table."

"Kelly Jo, I think there is a lot I don't know about you. I've got a lot to learn about this single stuff."

"I'll tell all over a great dinner."

"I've seen it all. Women lose their heads when the prospect of love comes along." She made quotes in the air to emphasize love. "I learned years ago that I march to the beat of a different drummer. There was a verbal abuser in my sordid past. It wasn't until he cheated on me that I got the courage to leave. Believe me, it took guts. The girls were little, and I'd left my dad's place to live with the guy. I was afraid Dad wouldn't take me back."

"Oh, Kelly Jo, you are always so cheerful. I didn't know."

"Hey, it took a long time for me to figure things out. I know it sounds crazy, but it was like I was part of a cocoon. His skin stretched over me until there was nothing of me left. I ran home to my dad. I'd been bouncing from one bum to another. I told myself that I was worth more than that and so were my girls. I was going to make a better life for them than I'd had. It wasn't until I met you that I got another piece of my puzzle. I've been praying. I never did that before."

"I didn't see that coming tonight. Thanks. I sure see how needy I am on a regular basis. It's a big world out there, and I have lots to learn."

"Give it time. You'll see what I mean. Just don't run from yourself."

"Or run ahead of God," I said.

Our food arrived, and I pulled out my notes from the day. Kelly Jo was a knitter, and I planned to bring knitting supplies into the shop. We discussed the merchandise displayed that day and made our plan for tomorrow. She'd go back to the Market first thing in the morning, help me order yarn and accessories, and then visit with her family the rest of the weekend.

"As much as I pray, I still feel like half of me is missing," I sighed.

"I'd say get used to it, but that's too depressing."

"Well, you are a great guide through the maze of singleness."

Friday, I called Dinky after I knew what the preliminary costs would be to add a small knit section to the shop. I explained the benefits of enlarging our revenue base and the profitability of the new line.

"I think we start small, Abby," she said. "We don't know where the economy is going. I was hoping to sell quilted pieces the customers make on consignment. Would we still have room for that?" I assured her we would.

I escorted Kelly Jo to the nearest Marta station just before noon, feeling like a tourist in my hometown. Traveler's Rest was comfortable. I wondered if Kelly Jo was up to riding the subway twice in one weekend as she disappeared into the mouth of the Marta terminal. I knew I wasn't ready for that much adventure.

I didn't leave the Market until ten that night. I gulped a Sub and Coke and kept going, making all the necessary stops to complete the shop's orders. I'd planned to relax the next day since I was having dinner with my boy. I couldn't remember the last time we'd spent time together, just the two of us.

Saturday, I watched demonstrations and asked questions. I went back to the hotel and did some paperwork. Surprised that I still had more than an hour to kill before Carter picked me up, I slipped on comfortable shoes and hit the streets. I caught my breath as a blast of cold air tugged at my coat. A belligerent piece of trash whipped by me. I picked up my walking pace and resolved to toss some mental baggage on the street with the litter. I gawked at the once-familiar buildings and the curious people. I scurried down the sidewalk reliving the failures of the past. When I thought of Shelby, phrases like *I should have and I could have* came to mind. As a large man scurried by me, wearing the same smirk Daddy often displayed, my father demanded my attention. I stopped and looked into a department store window. My reflection jumped back at me. *As a mature, fully-grown individual, Daddy can only get to me if I let him.* I vowed I wouldn't let him anymore. I visualized my father being lighter than air and floating into the brisk wind. He dropped back into my thoughts like a lead balloon.

A couple walked past me, swinging their arms as they held hands. She gazed at him in a cozy way, eyes sparkling, a slight smile displayed on her lips. *Sterling and I were in love like that. Could I ever be that happy again?* I knew Sterling. I knew everything about him. I knew his favorite foods, I knew what the twitch in his neck meant, and I knew what pleased him. I knew about him. I didn't have a clue about men in general. I walked back into the hotel lobby, not sure I wanted to risk learning about someone else again. The risk of someone knowing me seemed too scary to trade my newfound freedom for a possibility of love. A woman barked at an older man as I walked into the hotel lobby. *Obviously, she knows him and doesn't like what she knows. Ah, the single life.*

The ride in the elevator brought thoughts of Nathan. *Play it safe, Abby. What would happen if you went with your emotions, told him you were interested in him, and he rejected you? Clumsy holiday gatherings, that's for sure.*

My cell phone rang as I slipped my black pumps on my feet. Carter suggested I come down to the car, since he couldn't find a parking space. I bounded out of the revolving door and strode to his awaiting car.

Through puffy eyes, Carter peered at me. "It's over."

"What's over, honey?" I asked as I climbed into his car.

"Alex, Allllex. It's over." His voice quivered.

"Carter, what are you saying?"

"I'm saying she's out of my life. Mom, I thought she was the woman for me."

As a car behind us honked impatiently, I tried to grasp what he was saying. "I don't understand."

Carter had asked Alex to marry him. She'd said yes. They'd planned a fall wedding. Last week, she told him she didn't love him; in fact, she'd moved out of her apartment with her girlfriends and in with her old boyfriend. Apparently, she'd been seeing the guy for some time without Carter knowing it. She said she didn't want to be stuck in an archaic institution like marriage—being with one man for the rest of her life wouldn't work for her.

"You were planning on marrying this girl, and you hadn't talked to any of the family? If not me, your uncle lives in the same house as you."

"There never seemed to be a good time to talk to anyone. I'm sorry."

It wounded me to see his red eyes. How could this woman do this to my son? My default mode kicked in—I should have been there to guide my son through this. I could have had them to the house more, gotten to know the girl. I would have warned Carter. Me, me, me. This was about Carter; he needed understanding and support. *Oh, Lord, help.* I hadn't figured out how to comfort my grown daughter, but here was an opportunity to be the mother my adult son needed.

As we ate, I listened. I just listened. Carter poured out his loneliness, his despair, and his fears. It was a privilege to be a part of his life.

"Mom, remember Stephanie?"

"Stephanie Kitredge?"

"Yeah, I loved her from kindergarten till fifth grade."

"I thought you didn't like her at all."

"Yeah, that's how great I am with women."

We laughed and talked about the past. Finally, after finishing dessert, we approached the subject of the future.

"Women seem to like the bad guy these days, Mom."

"Well, you stay the good guy, okay? I've been praying for your mate since you were born. She's out there."

"Wow. Maybe I should get back in church and start seriously looking."

"You haven't been going to church? There's your problem. You know that Aunt Claire and all our friends will be doing the looking for you if you just cooperate." We laughed.

"Great—as if I didn't have enough problems. That thought will produce nightmares." My son straightened his back.

"Listen, young man, you could do worse."

"I've already proven that."

Carter dropped me off at the hotel. I spent a fretful night, as I suspect my son did. Kelly Jo arrived the next day just as I was cramming the last item into my suitcase. We claimed my car and hit the road. We met Claire and Pete at church. I couldn't take my eyes off the empty seats up in front, where Sterling and I always sat. Empty. We were nearly finished singing when I felt a bump on my shoulder. Carter. *Thank you, Lord.*

After a quick lunch together, Kelly Jo and I headed toward the mountains. She buzzed with excitement as she told me about her family. She listened intently as I talked about Carter.

She tilted her head. "So, how does Mom feel?"

The question caught me by surprise. How did I feel? "Well, since you asked…." We had a counseling session driving up the road.

It ended with laughter as Kelly Jo hummed, "If you're happy and you know it…." I joined in and clapped with her. The people in the car next to us on the highway didn't seem amused. *Oh, well.*

I dropped Kelly Jo off at home and pulled into Dinky's drive. She'd called inviting me to dinner. Lexus had enjoyed her deluxe accommodations at Dinky's while I was in Atlanta. After dinner, I steered my pup to the far side of the driveway to do her business, put her in the car and drove home. Once inside, Mercedes greeted me with an attitude.

"I know, old girl. Dinky just checked on you. I bet she didn't pet you and cuddle you like you're used to being treated."

It occurred to me that Mercedes was the one constant in my ever-changing world. She must've read my mind. As I plopped down in the chair to review the mail, she jumped on the footstool and began purring. I relished the sound. The telephone rang.

"Mama."

"Shelby. I'm so glad you called."

"When I called before, you said you were going to Atlanta? Did you go by our old house? Did you see anybody I know?" Nearly thirty minutes later, I trudged to bed. Each time she called, I begged her to come. Each time, she said she couldn't yet.

The store was doing more business than ever. New people came because of the oleander controversy and stayed to eat. Often, they bought thread or fabric. The sisters' baking skills stood on their own merit. Despite hard financial times, the cakes flew out the door. The older sisters ate lunch in the shop at least once a week. It all made heading to work exciting. We created a knitting section, which sparked additional interest. The citywide quilt show was in June, and I had lots loose ends that kept me busy.

By the time we attended Carter's graduation at the end of May, I was thanking God for saving him from more heartache. If Alex wasn't the woman Carter had believed she was, better that he found out now. I just wished Carter could see through his pain.

Dinky insisted on having a party at her home for our graduate. She stated that people in Traveler's Rest had known him all his life. They'd want to celebrate his victories with him. He agreed only to please his grandmother. Fresh flowers from the yard spilled over in vase after vase. The dining table brimmed with finger foods and greenery. Kelly Jo and Buddy were the first to arrive. The sisters followed right behind them, but left quickly. Penny felt frail, Polly said. Several friends from Atlanta came to celebrate with Carter. I was in the dining room, placing a tray of pimento cheese sandwiches on the table, when L.J. appeared in the hall. I smiled faintly. He entered the room and hugged me a little harder than I expected. I blushed. I didn't invite him. Dinky must have. The last time we'd eaten together, I'd told him plainly—we were friends, nothing more. I knew it; he seemed to settle for it. He was persistent; I persistently prayed.

There was a reason his presence bugged me. I was looking forward to seeing Nathan. L.J. complicated things. Nathan had been strangely busy for months. True to his nature, L.J. seemed a little pushy. He insisted that I sit with him, telling anyone who'd listen about all the things we did together. Just what I needed. I spent as much time as possible in the kitchen, nervously looking for Nathan to make an entrance. As I walked back and forth, I watched Carter laughing and enjoying his friends. How I wished Shelby could be there with him. She'd been away nearly six months now.

People came and went. The party was winding down as Nathan appeared. Luckily, I was refilling the dessert tray as I saw him walk into the room. Handsome and poised as ever, he seemed perfectly at ease talking to everyone as he worked his way across the room. He looked over at me and smiled. He asked Carter about his plans for the future.

L.J. kissed me on the cheek, said something to the kids, thanked Dinky, and left. I glanced over to see Nathan staring at me. I blushed, and took the empty dessert tray back to the kitchen. I fussed with my hair then walked back into the room.

"Is something wrong, Mom?" Carter asked.

Nathan looked up and stared. "Why, nothing at all, Carter," I said. "Nathan, thanks for coming."

"I wouldn't miss it." He rubbed his chin and looked at me. "It's a shame your friend left so early. I didn't get a chance to talk to him."

"Who, L.J.? He is just a friend of the family," I said. *Oh, that sounded weird. Maybe no one will notice.*

Not so easy. Dinky and Buck stopped their conversation. "Abby, you and Nathan come over here. We haven't gotten to see either of you all evening," Buck boomed from across the room.

"Abby, dear, I just got a call from Patsy. Penny is on the way to the hospital. Buck and I are going to meet them there. Would you stay and lock up when everyone leaves?"

"Of course. What happened?"

"She didn't feel well when they were here, so Patsy took her home to stay with her for awhile. She collapsed, and they called for help."

"I'll stay and help. It looks like things are coming to a close here, anyway," Nathan said, touching the small of my back as he leaned in to assist Dinky to her feet. I straightened my back, and Nathan took Dinky's hand. He walked her to the door.

CHAPTER

26

"If we're done cleaning up, I've got to go," Nathan said.

"Church comes early in the morning, huh?" I quipped.

"Yeah. So what's with you and L.J.?"

"He's a friend. Why do you ask?"

"What kind of a friend is he?"

"Why do you want to know?"

"You drive me crazy, Abby. I have to go. All I want to know is if you are seeing him, or not? He seems to be around you all the time."

I tried to hide my pleasure. "Are you asking as a family member? Worried about me?"

"Forget I asked." He was gone in a second.

I was astonished. I had acted like a schoolgirl. *Really, Abby.* I played the conversation over in mind, taking in every nuance, every body movement. *I could of, I should of...* In the end, I realized I couldn't process the information. I had no basis for comparison to this man. I concluded he was from an unknown planet. I locked the house and drove home. When Shelby called, she told me Justin needed her. She was helping him get his life straightened out. I begged her to come home. As always, she concluded it wasn't time yet. What did that mean?

I wasn't surprised to see Kelly Jo walk into the shop Friday morning. What did surprise me was the look on her face. Her puffy eyes and scowl were totally out of character.

"Kelly Jo, what happened?" I placed the fabric I'd been holding on the counter and scrutinized her face.

"Yesterday, Buddy and I met with Pastor Roy and then went to supper. I told him I can't live with him any longer. I know that isn't what God wants. He didn't want to get married, so I asked him to move out."

"Obviously, it didn't go well."

"No, he was fine with it. We finished dinner, went home, and he packed his things and left. He's staying with his brother till he finds a place."

I put my hand on hers and looked into her eyes. "You having second thoughts?"

"I know what Pastor Roy says is right. I'm a new creature, and I need to live the way God wants me to live."

We moved over to the table and sat down. "It's scary, taking a step of faith like that," I said.

"I didn't want it to turn out like this. I really thought Buddy would just say he'd change his life and commit to God. Then we could ride off into the sunset together. Instead, he said church stuff wasn't for him. He's been there and done that, and wasn't going to do that again. He liked things the way they were. When this religion stuff got old, he said I should give him a call." She wept.

Dinky spent time with the sisters at the hospital that morning. Penny was alert and begging to go home. When she arrived at work, she saw Kelly Jo's tears and went to the kitchen, bringing out three slices of the best chocolate cake ever made. We sat together, lingering over the indulgence. When the world feels like it's spinning out of control, chocolate makes you want to hang on for the ride. Kelly Jo left around noon. As I watched her leave, I wished that things were different for my friend.

Claire and Pete came for a weekend visit. She brought her latest scrapbook project, and I admired it as we relaxed on the patio. As the sun set, it became difficult to see the lovely memories laid out on the page. I asked if she wanted to go inside.

"I really like it out here. How about a cup of tea?" she said as she set the book aside.

As we sipped our tea, I said, "I seem to have clear thinking when we are together. I've been deluding myself in the last few months about the past. So many struggles have assaulted Shelby, Carter, Kelly Jo, and even Penny. With the struggles, I've allowed myself to think that before Sterling died everything was perfect and now everything is chaos. That isn't really the case." I took a sip of green tea. "We certainly had our struggles through the years, especially just before..."

"Do you remember telling me once that you were glad they didn't put epitaphs on graves anymore?"

I laughed. "Yeah, because I was afraid they'd write, 'She never got it,' on mine."

"Well, I now know the truth. Your epitaph would read, 'She had it all the time.'"

"I guess it really depends on what 'it' is, right? I'm so fortunate to have you as a friend, dear sister-in-law. You make life gentler—you know what I mean?"

"You mean I can calmly look at what you go through and reassure you. You know, I don't always apply the same gentleness to my own situations."

"Don't see the forest for the trees, huh? That's what I'm here for," I said. We both laughed as darkness surrounded us. It's strange, how sometimes darkness can illuminate our path. I'm glad we can't see the future. If we could, the thrill of surprise would be gone.

On Monday, I'd worked all day and was fixing dinner for Mercedes and Lexus when the phone rang.

"Hi," Nathan said.

"Hi, is everything okay—Dinky, Buck?"

"Yeah, everything is great. I was just wondering if you would go to the opening Concert on the Green with me."

I didn't wait to hear the details. I just blurted out my acceptance. I thought the conversation was finished, when he mentioned that over the last year, three people had asked him to call me. First, my electrician told him that we would make a nice couple. That was quite some time ago. He ignored the idea. One of the women in his church took a quilt class from me. She not only mentioned how much she enjoyed the class, but she told him she had a nice widow lady he should call. After seeing me with L.J. numerous times, he felt the issue was closed. Then, last week at the party, Kelly Jo approached him and told him what a wonderful friend I was. When Nathan mentioned L.J., she smiled. She wrote my number down, handed it to him, and suggested he make the call.

Sounds like a God-thing.

I dropped the phone onto the receiver and sat quietly as the evening sun cast a glow over the room. I'd known Nathan for a long time; I'd even felt drawn to him some time ago. Was this a date? A relationship? What would Buck and Dinky think? What would my kids say? Most of all, what would Sterling think? Was I delusional? Sterling, of all people, would want me to be happy. Going to a concert with a man would not make him think I hadn't adored him for all those years. It was dark when I fixed my dinner. I'm not sure what I ate.

I fussed around the house. I finally turned on the television. I couldn't remember the last time I'd watched it. I needed noise to drown out my thoughts. I finally faced the problem. What really agitated me was not the one date; it was the possibility that one date could lead to commitment. I told God I wasn't interested in the dating scene. I knew Nathan well enough to know the call was anything but casual to him.

I avoided talking much to anyone the next few days. It was my secret. I enjoyed the wave of excitement that came over me as I cut fabric for customers or sat with Penny at the hospital. I spent Tuesday evening going through my closet. Was I ready for this? Was God in this? Every time my thoughts wandered to the big event, I'd come back with the thought that it was just an evening with a friend. I'd spent the evening with L.J. many times. This was different. How different remained to be seen.

CHAPTER

27

I fidgeted at the front door, anticipating Nathan's arrival. As I heard the truck roar up, then stop, I strengthened my resolve to wait for the knock on the door. He'd think I was too eager if I threw it open right away. After all, I was a Southern woman—I needed to control my behavior. Reason took wind; I opened the door to greet him as he jumped from his truck. I invited him into the house. I asked if he'd like to sit down, extending my arm toward the living room. He fidgeted. We had a reservation, he said. He opened the front door. I started for the passenger side of his truck when I realized Nathan was following me. I jerked to a stop as he opened the truck door, and helped me up the tall step.

At the restaurant, a man ushered us to a quiet corner of the very dark restaurant. I scooted into the booth, thinking Nathan would slide into the seat opposite me. When I felt him sink into the bench next to me, I slipped over a few inches further.

"I thought we could talk better this way." His crooked smile disarmed me.

"Hmmm," I said. My stomach did flip-flops as I peered at the menu.

"How's the house? How's the café going? Was it a good decision?"

"Whoa, I'm just trying to adjust to the two of us being here alone. Give me a minute."

"Are you saying I'm taking your breath away—you know, being this close?" He paused. "Cause you're making me act pretty silly."

"It's my fault, huh? The business is going well. It was a good decision. I'm seeing new faces and more money coming in every day."

"Okay, then. That's all I had prepared for us to talk about the whole evening. What now?" We both chuckled as the server came to the table and we ordered.

"I don't know much about you, really. Tell me why you chose to go into the ministry?"

"I had a rocky childhood, and my relationship with God got me through the tough times. Actually, I was finishing my business degree when I felt the call."

"What exactly was the call?"

"I looked around at my friends and family and saw that those who had the kind of life I wanted also had a deep faith. Things happen to us all, but some people function at a crisis mode most of the time. I wanted to be one who was on solid ground."

"Did you have to be a preacher to do that?"

The girl brought rolls and our salads. Nathan took my hand and blessed the food. He didn't let go of my hand.

He looked at me for a moment then said, "I knew that my life's purpose was to comfort and encourage others. I could've done that in the business world. It just would've been more complicated. To be honest, I'm not sure the lure of success wouldn't have been too much for me. Bottom line, God nudged me and nudged me till I said yes."

"Buck told me a little about your childhood...."

"You mean, he didn't fill you in on my whole life story? I thought he'd tell you I married the wrong woman, and that is why my life was a mess. Nuts."

"Nuts, what?"

"If he'd said that, I might have been tempted to leave you with that impression. The truth is, we were both at fault, and we didn't try hard enough to make our marriage work."

"You really don't have to explain."

"Look, I don't want this to be a casual relationship. I don't think you do, either. I want you to know where I'm coming from. My wife and I started our marriage arguing. We had Andrew nine months later, and the arguments got worse. I tried to be a good husband and father, but it was never enough. I had just started seminary when we met and married. Her parents were wealthy, and they continued to indulge their only child. She thought the extra years of education would mean glamour or prestige some way. The ministry isn't a job. It's a lifestyle. I made the choice, but she couldn't. By the time I finished seminary, I wasn't even sure I was cut out to be a preacher."

"Why?"

"I already served a small church. Every minute was absorbed in other people's needs. That left no time for a self-centered wife and a colicky baby. The time I did give her didn't seem to matter so I threw myself into my work. She looked for good times elsewhere and found them. With all the moves, she had no base of friends, so she spent more and more time with her doting parents and more and more time away from me."

"Wow, it sounds wild."

"When rumors of affairs became undeniable facts, I gave up. She was in the process of divorcing me when she was in a boating accident. They never recovered the body. There was always lots of drinking on the high seas, but that evening she and her boyfriend were speeding and didn't see a boat dock. There was a huge explosion."

"What about Andrew?"

"He was with me. He's always lived with me. There was no place for a kid in her world. He still has lots of issues stemming from his relationship with his mother. For a long time, he kept thinking he saw her."

"Saw her? After she died?"

"Yeah. For a while he was okay. Then he tried going to college but the sightings got worse. He said he was either going crazy or his mother was watching him."

"Does he still see her?"

"When he dropped out of college, we went on a long camping trip. I wanted to get him back on the path I thought he should go. But, on that trip, I saw he loved the outdoors and the rugged lifestyle. That made him comfortable. He has a large trust fund from his mother, so we found a company up in the mountains for sale. He now runs a campground and boating company. He seems really content with his choices."

"You don't sound convinced that all is well."

"I'm concerned about him. He lives on the top of a mountain on a dirt road. It's really rugged. I can't always reach him by phone—no cell towers in the mountains. I don't know, it just wouldn't be my choice for my only child."

"Makes my life look simple."

"From where I sit, you do look simply wonderful." We chuckled.

We drove to the amphitheater and chose a good vantage point for the performance. The area was a grassy slope with the large stage at the bottom and layers of deep rows going in horseshoe form. We pulled our folding chairs out of the carriers and placed the seats close together. I watched children playing in front of us, as couples chatted. The violinists began tuning their instruments, then the rest joined them. The orchestra played pops, starting with music from the thirties to more current melodies. I felt Nathan's hand on mine. I welcomed the touch. The evening ended with fireworks. We oohed and aahed as the explosives filled the skies with sparkles and the music increased in intensity. The last explosions flashed into the air—blast after blast of vivid color, each blast more spectacular than the one before. Boom after boom shook me to the core. The music ended with the clash of cymbals echoing in my ears. The show had begun with children playing nearby, couples setting up their chairs and chatting, and the sound of cars in the background. Now, as the program ended, I was aware of Nathan and the fireworks, nothing more. We sat there long after others scurried to their vehicles. We looked at the stars and then each other. We stood. The amphitheater was nearly empty.

"I guess we'd better be going," he said.

"I guess."

We stared at each other as if we had no clue what to do next. He took my hand, and we walked to the parking lot. The ride home seemed short. At my door, there was an awkward pause. Nathan said a friend was having a party next Friday night and asked if I'd go with him.

"What time?" I asked. As I finished speaking, he leaned over and kissed me. I melted.

The answering machine was making that annoying little beep when I entered the house. I pushed the button. L.J.'s voice was loud as he demanded I call him. *That won't happen.* The second call was Dinky.

"Abby, give me a call in the morning. It's the sisters. No emergency, but call me." Dinky sounded tired; I knew I was. I'd definitely wait until tomorrow to talk to her.

CHAPTER

28

The sisters were distraught by the discharge process and flatly refused the hospital staff's recommendation of an extended care facility.

We found Polly and Patsy pacing in the hall. "All Pansy will say is that we never subjected Mama and Poppa to such care, and they would not approve of it for our Penny. She says Penny is going home," Patsy said.

Nathan became the mediator between hospital and flustered, but stubborn, sisters. In the end, Penny moved to Polly's home, where the main floor study became the perfect space for the ailing woman. Home healthcare providers would visit often. Crisis averted, or so we thought.

It soon became clear that Patsy and Polly were in over their heads, trying to work at the café and do everything needed for their siblings. Dinky and I called a meeting at the shop with the three sisters while the visiting nurse was with Penny. We suggested Meals for Seniors, a community program, but the older sisters would not hear of it. "Mama and Daddy would roll over in their grave if we took such assistance."

We met at the shop to discuss the issue. Kelly Jo was working on a display as we talked.

"Girls, I know you are doing too much. Maybe you shouldn't work here. It's selfish of us, when we know your older sisters need you," Dinky said.

"This place keeps us sane. Maybe we could get help at home."

"What would Mama and Poppa think?" We said in unison.

Kelly Jo jumped in. "Why don't I help some? I have some time. That way, you two could care for your sister and get out some, too."

The sisters were ecstatic. After Kelly Jo walked away, Pansy said it would be just like their childhood to have a servant in the house.

"We'll need to talk to Kelly Jo about what she will charge, but she is doing this as a favor. Please treat her with the dignity she deserves. She isn't coming as a maid. In other words, mind your manners," Dinky said.

"Of course, we will conduct ourselves appropriately. We do realize that times have changed. I guess for a moment we hoped they hadn't changed that much," Pansy stated.

Penny would have lunch from the shop each day. Kelly Jo would make dinner on her day off. Dinky told Kelly Jo not to plan to dine with them. Their traditions ran deep.

"So, are they expecting me to wear a white apron and curtsy?"

"Oh, I hope not. You don't have to commit to anything after the one meal, if it doesn't go well. We're just thrilled you are trying."

"I've been praying about how I could help others. In our new member's class at church, Pastor Roy has been talking about being a servant. It sort of goes against my grain to give a handout—I work hard for everything I have—but these women are different. They can't do it all for themselves anymore. Maybe it'll work, who knows?"

On Friday afternoon, the doorbell rang. *Who would be coming here? Probably Dinky. I'll have to get her to leave quickly.* I glanced outside; Kelly Jo's car sat in the drive. I opened the door, and she scrambled inside.

"Abby, that new restaurant opened and I have the evening off. I raced over the minute I heard the ad on the radio."

"Oh Kelly Jo, I wished you had called first. I have plans," I said too quickly. *Oh great, not very casual. She has her antenna up.* "Why don't you see if Dinky and Buck want to do something? I'm sure they would love dinner at the new place."

"Sure. It'd be great for the four of us to go. They're fun. How about it?"

"Well, I'm not going anywhere with them this evening," I said as I steered her into the den.

Kelly Jo narrowed her eyes, zeroing in she began pressing me with questions. Who was I seeing and where was I going? *Rats.*

"Nathan and I are going to little gathering together. That is all. It's no big deal."

She howled. "That's awesome. What are you wearing? When are you leaving? I want to stay and see you off."

"Really, I've gone to dinner with L.J. several times, and you never carried on this way."

"No sparks with him. I could tell. But Nathan, well…!" She raised her eyebrow, then squinted at me. "Have you two been dating for long?"

"Dating? I didn't say we are dating."

"Oh, you should see your face. Hmmm."

"Call Dinky if you want to do something this evening."

"Hey, do they know about this dating stuff?"

"Kelly Jo, you are killing me." I groaned.

"Sure, sure. You haven't told them either, have you? Just your little secret, huh?"

I urged and nudged my friend to leave. I did everything but bribe her. She giggled as she sauntered from my den to the front door. She was enjoying this immensely. I had little time to dress, and she was probably busy blabbing everything she knew and more. She couldn't keep a secret like this. I was painfully curious about Dinky and Buck's reaction.

I didn't have to agonize for long. As Nathan and I climbed in to his truck, my phone vibrated. At almost the same second, Nathan's phone rang. *Nuts!* Buck and Dinky. We pulled the truck over at their house. The three of them appeared at the door, looking ridiculous, each sporting a grin that went from ear to ear. *Spare me.*

I could tell Dinky wanted details. I gave her none. Nathan seemed amusingly quiet as well. We were enemy combatants interrogated by very skillful interviewers. We knew this would not be the last such session. The fewer words uttered, the fewer words to be reexamined later. Where were we going? Why hadn't they been told before now? They stopped short of asking our intentions, but the implications were there. Kelly Jo stood back and watched the pros at work. I had the distinct impression that she was gathering skills she would use on her daughters at some later date. We scrambled back to the vehicle and drove off.

We arrived a little late, but there were no visible marks to show the torture we'd endured. Nathan's friends wasted no time in launching their own inquiries. Maybe it was just that my defenses were down after the earlier battle. We drove home laughing and exchanging glances as we discussed the evening's events. Nathan's truck clanged to a halt, and he turned off the engine.

"Even with all the hubbub, I can't remember when I felt so relaxed with my friends. Thanks." He played with his keys as they hung in the ignition.

"They're really nice. Thank you for including me in your evening."

"I hope to include you in many more evenings. Is that a possibility, or will I suffer the same fate as L.J.?"

"I've never thought about L.J. day and night. He's just a friend."

"So, you think about me as much as I dream about you? That sounds promising." He squeezed my hand, then jumped out of the vehicle and escorted me to the door.

CHAPTER

29

A couple of weeks later, Dinky and Buck invited Nathan and me to a Sunday school class gathering at their home. Afterward, we drove back to my house and sat on the porch.

"Did I hear you and Dinky talking about setting up for a quilt show?"

"Yeah. It's at the high school. I set up on Thursday after work."

"Well, I guess if I'm going to see you this week, I'll be forced to help."

"My best guy is helping me. You'd have to see if he needs an assistant." I poked his arm and smiled.

"Oh, no. I'm in competition with my dad. Right?" His relief showed as I nodded yes.

After work on Thursday, Buck and Nathan loaded everything needed and we drove to the school. Buck began setting up the tables provided in the lunchroom. Dinky met us there and unpacked the boxes as we brought them to her. She arranged our merchandise on the tables while Nathan and I assembled the giant quilt racks. These would display the show quilts. Several guild members were there to help display the quilts. Later, a panel of judges would evaluate the 110 quilts in the show, giving awards according to design, color use, and workmanship. The guild ran the event. Our job was to set up and then work in our booth once everything was organized.

We had been working for a couple of hours when I secured the last quilt to its rack. As I started down the ladder, my foot slipped. I screamed as I plummeted toward the floor, but Nathan grabbed me midair and pulled me close. I wiggled to release his grip. Buck raced to help, and Dinky followed. Nathan seemed oblivious to any help offered and continued holding me.

"Let me see you move those legs. No broken bones. That's good. Your bruises are going to be doozies. You must've hit every rung of the ladder. Are you sure you are all right?" Buck said.

With my arms around Nathan's neck, I sighed. "I am now."

"Hey. Excuse me, children, there are other people here," Buck boomed loudly.

"My goodness, Nathan, you saved our Abby from disaster. What would we have done without you?" Dinky swooned.

"Give us a break," I said.

Nathan's phone rang. *There is no getting away from his parishioners.* He waved as he walked away from us, and he lowered his voice. The large lunchroom resonated, making his footsteps echo as he moved. I thought I heard Shelby come from his lips. Dinky asked me to look at the display she had just finished. At first, I strained to hear Nathan's conversation, then dismissed what I heard as my active imagination. As Dinky pointed to our book display, I glanced back at Nathan. He'd leaned against the doorway, his head down; he was rubbing his leg as he spoke. We waved to the judges as they came into the hall. Dinky and I were discussing the layout of the material when Nathan grabbed my arm and pulled me away from the booth.

"That was Shelby. I've got everything set up for her rescue."

"What are you saying?" A pain shot through my jaw. "Rescue, what rescue?"

He tried to hug me; I pushed him away.

"Abby, listen. I didn't have Shelby's permission to tell you this until now. We've been talking for some time, and we've got a plan to get her out of her situation."

"She told me she didn't want to be found. She could take care of herself. What about her car? Couldn't she just get in it and drive home? What's going on?"

"We've got to focus on getting her out of the situation. She hasn't had access to her car or a phone for the last several weeks." Nathan hugged me, no doubt trying to comfort me. I shoved him away, frustrated.

"Why am I just hearing about this now? She's called several times, but never said she was in trouble. Why…?"

"She didn't have her phone. She called from payphones. Remember, the policeman said he couldn't trace her cell. Lately, she hasn't had access to her phone or the car. She didn't want you to know how bad things were, but we're set now. It won't be long until you can ask her all the questions you want." I melted into his arms and cried.

He said Shelby had been watching Justin's actions and found a pattern. She'd leave the next time he started bingeing with his friends. Nathan had mailed a cell phone to her latest place of employment, a bar and grill in the North Carolina mountains. Since they moved often, she didn't know how long they'd be at this location. She'd call us when the time was right.

"Why send a phone? Why didn't we just go pick her up? Tell me. I don't understand," I said.

Nathan said we needed a block of time to get her to safety before Justin knew she was gone and came looking for her. Dinky and Buck came closer, and Nathan told them the situation. Dinky began sobbing with me. We stepped into the hall and petitioned God for protection and courage.

"What are we dealing with, son?" Buck asked.

Nathan pulled a large box close to Dinky, and she sank down onto the sturdy seat. I leaned against the wall and simply slid to the ground next to her. Buck leaned in and patted Dinky's shoulder. Nathan said Shelby's counselor found a safe house here in the upstate. She'd stay there for a while to avoid further contact with Justin. Anything else would be decided after the rescue.

"All right, son, we're taking elaborate steps for a reason, right? What is this kid like anyway? I take it there has been abuse."

I gasped; Dinky's sobs grew louder.

Looking at me, Nathan shrugged. "Let's just stay focused on getting her out of the immediate situation."

I cringed. Nathan helped us finish our work and took me home. We were to wait. We would go after Shelby the moment she called. There were millions of unanswered questions; the look on Nathan's face told me not to ask them.

We sat on the front porch swing in the dark. The fireflies lit up the yard. Nathan tapped his foot to the floor, and we swung back and forth. He put his arm around my shoulder, and I leaned in to his chest. The world stopped spinning for those few minutes.

"I better leave. We're both too needy right now." Nathan moved away from me.

"Yeah, we better talk on the phone." I stood up. We held each other then kissed. Everything in me wanted to beg him to stay. I needed him.

"I'll call you when I get home." He turned, and moved toward the truck. I walked behind him and leaned in the window for a final kiss.

I stood in the lane watching his truck disappear and turned to go inside. As I stepped onto the porch, L.J. blocked my way.

"What are you doing here?" I said.

"More to the point, what do you think you're doing?" he sneered.

"What on earth do you mean?"

His speech slurred as he said, "you haven't been returning my calls. I've got a right to find out what you're up to."

"A right? You don't have a claim on me."

He grabbed for me. His nails dug into my skins. I tried to push him away. Instead, he pushed me against the door. He dropped one of my arms and grabbed at the door. I slapped wildly at him, hitting him in the jaw. He released me and put his hand on his face. That was my moment. I pushed him with all my strength. He stumbled backwards.

"Look, L.J., I told you I wanted to be your friend and nothing else. I know you're lonely. I have been, too."

"Not so lonely anymore, right? I heard about you and Nathan from Dinky. She sounded real happy about the whole thing. You strung me along. Abby, you and my wife were friends. We can have a nice life together. That's what she would've wanted."

"L.J., grow up. You can't just decide we should get married, and it'll happen. Life doesn't work that way, and you know it. You're too drunk to drive, especially on the windy roads around here. I'm calling Buck, and he can take you home."

He sat on the steps mumbling, until Buck drove up. I walked him to the truck. Putting his arm around L.J., Buck helped him in and slammed the door.

"L.J., give Abby your car keys, and she will follow us to your house. That way there will be no need for you to revisit our property, without an invitation. Do you understand?"

L.J. mumbled something and handed me his car keys.

For two days, Dinky and I took turns working at the quilt show and the shop. My students brought their ribbons by the booth to show me. One student won second prize. Four beginning students won ribbons, as well. They discussed their next project, as they bought books and fabrics. Kelly Jo was all smiles as she displayed her ribbon for best of show.

While I was genuinely excited for my students, Shelby was always on my mind. What had she experienced? When would she call? I fidgeted. I fumbled. I couldn't eat. Dinky kept her phone close to her, something she seldom did. Buck seemed to have nothing to do but pace up and down the rows of quilts and fabrics. I could imagine quilts tumbling down over him, and everyone near him as he lumbered through the aisles. Luckily, Dinky's list of household chores mounted, taking Buck to their home as often as possible. The displays remained intact.

The show was a blessing in disguise. I forced myself to go through the motions of the business of the event. By Saturday night, my jaw throbbed from my clenched teeth, and the back of my neck ached as I carried the weight of my child's future squarely on it. Taking the exhibit down had gone well, and Buck took our weary Dinky home.

Nathan and I lingered over a late dinner. We sat in the back booth of our favorite Italian restaurant as Giorgio served pizza to nearby families and the smell of lasagna tickled our noses and delighted our taste buds. We chatted about the sales at the show and about Shelby. As we finished our meals and pushed the plates away, Nathan asked me to come to his church the next day. I fidgeted with my napkin. We had skirted the issue of church attendance for some time. We both knew things could accelerate out of control once our relationship was public knowledge within his church. He had been careful around the women from the congregation—several had made obvious attempts to catch his attention. I stared at my napkin. What would everyone think of his dating? What would they think of me? What would it mean to his ministry?

"Is this really the right time for me to visit?" I asked.

"If this isn't a good time, when will that right time be?" he retorted. "Life is always changing, and I'm not entering into this relationship in hopes that everything will calm down and be easy. I tell my parishioners that normal is just a setting on the dryer. I think I read that years ago, and it's kept me from a lot of worry."

"I'll keep that in mind," I mused, "especially tomorrow."

"They won't bite. Now, they have been known to swallow people whole." I squinted at him. "Come on, lighten up. It'll be fine."

I arrived just before the service was to start, and panic set in. My plan had been to come late and slip into the back row. Unfortunately, the back seemed popular. The sound of a piano and organ filled the sanctuary, as I found a spot halfway down the aisle. Relieved, I strolled to the seat. Every eye was on me, the stranger. Even though it was nearly time for the service to begin, several people came over to shake my hand and ask me questions. I was vague in my answers. My stomach flittered and flopped unmercifully as the service began. Nathan came down the aisle dressed in his black robe. I'd forgotten that this was his traditional service. The contemporary one was too early for me to face right now. It'd been years since I'd attended a service like this. I was uncomfortable singing from the hymnal. *I guess reading glasses will be part of my not-too-distant future.* I wasn't used to such a defined order of worship. However, as the choir sang, I relaxed. I listened intently to every word Nathan spoke. What a morning. I'd never thought of a preacher the way I thought of this preacher.

I bowed my head as he pronounced the blessing over the congregation and began planning my strategy for a quick exit. No luck. The only way out seemed to be through the foyer, and I was in the middle of the mob as I exited the aisle. My palms began to sweat as I felt people press in around me. A cloud of perfume floated around me. I fumbled in my purse for a tissue as I approached the exit. The area was crowded, and no one seemed to be moving. As I looked at Nathan, the contents of my bag spilled onto the hardwood floor, clanging as it hit the ground. Everyone stared; in fact, they seemed to step aside to watch the whole catastrophe. I felt like Moses; the seas parted. *Good one, Abby.* Well, at least there was now a clear path to Nathan and then the open door. I grabbed the contents of my purse and extended my hand to Nathan. My heart pounded as I saw the door was almost within reach. I'd never wanted anything more than a quick escape. I could almost feel the fresh air from the other side of the door. Maybe my dignity would pick itself up and run.

Nathan wasn't in tune to my anxiety; he was in his comfort zone. He took my hand and held it. The sun streamed into the room from behind him. Was it just me, or was the room getting warmer by the minute? He smiled and lit up the room. He was wonderful. I knew it, and so did those women who glared at me. The hair on the back of my neck felt scorched by their gaze. Beads of perspiration formed above my lip. After an eternity, Nathan leaned over and whispered an invitation to lunch. He smiled softly as I said I'd meet him at a nearby restaurant.

Luckily, none of his congregation followed us to the restaurant. We talked long after we finished lunch. As we walked to our cars, he stopped. "Do you love me as much as I love you?"

"Well...." My knees shook. The word "love" had never entered our conversations until that moment. "I do love you. How much do you love me?"

"Enough to ask you to marry me."

"I love you enough to say yes."

"Rest-of-our-lives kind of love?" He shot back.

"Until I die, stick a needle in my eye."

We stood gazing at each other as people came and went. Reluctantly, we said good-bye.

I turned music up as loud as possible and opened the sunroof of the car. I sang with the music, until I reached Dinky's house. I saw Buck and Andrew in the garage. They were building a bookshelf, so I waved and hurried inside. I grabbed a Coke from the fridge and plopped into a chair. Dinky was humming as she put a cookie sheet in the oven and turned on the timer.

"Dinky, are you as happy as you sound?"

"Why yes, child. Why would you ask?" She put her hands on hips and moved in close.

"No, I mean, do you ever regret getting married again?"

"I've never regretted one minute with Buck. I thank God continually for all that we have together. Why are you asking me that now? Did something happen with Nathan? Having second thoughts about seeing him? Spit it out, girl."

"In the midst of the stuff with Shelby, I'm feeling like I'm twenty again. It's strange. Ecstasy on one hand and sadness on the other." I held my hands out to show my confusion.

"You're trying to tell yourself you don't deserve to be happy. You shouldn't. I had strange feelings when Buck and I fell in love." Dinky sat down next to me and patted my arm. "Abby, our men are in heaven. God gave them to us for a season. They wouldn't come back if they could. I know God sent Buck to me ,and I'm going to enjoy every minute I can with my wonderful husband."

"Thank you, my sweet Dinky," I said with tears in my eyes as we embraced. The oven buzzer rang. The men seemed to sense their cookies were done and came into the kitchen. Buck peered at me and cocked his head in a questioning way. When I didn't volunteer information, he said nothing. *Smart man.*

I floated home with my secret.

Katherine called as Nathan and I ate at a Mexican restaurant the next evening. Daddy had made yet another trip to the emergency room. They had been there for hours, but now, after taking his new prescription, he was feeling better. I thanked her for the call and slipped the phone back in my pocket. *Why now, Lord? I don't have time to deal with him now.*

I poked at my food. Nathan rambled. I watched his wonderful mouth move, but I had no idea what he was saying.

"Did you hear a thing I just said?" Nathan inquired.

"I'm so sorry. It's the call about Dad. It wasn't that the call surprised me—Daddy's always sick one way or another. I was just trying to figure out why he always pushes my buttons. You know what I mean?"

"Is he in serious condition?"

"Didn't seem to be. The call's the same as always. Not important. It's just that nagging feeling I get when something new comes up with him."

"Maybe your relationship with your dad is what's important."

"Not hardly. You and I've been there before. I've just got to get over it."

"Over what?"

"Oh, you know. I'm sure he did the best he could as a dad. I don't want to judge him."

"Maybe we need to go see him. I could ask him for your hand."

"Ask for my hand? Nathan, please. My dad isn't that kind of loving, interested father. That will just put pressure on me. I buried my feelings for him years ago."

"How's that working for you?"

"Well, maybe after we know Shelby is safe and sound…."

"Maybe he won't be alive then. Did you ever think about that?"

"Why do you insist on being so irritating?"

"Maybe that's what you need right now."

"All right. What do we do?"

"We go to see your dad tomorrow. You call and tell them we're coming. I'll rearrange my schedule, and Dinky can handle the store."

"I don't think…."

"You'll thank me later. You just wait and see."

"Sure." I dialed Daddy's number.

Dad said he hoped I didn't expect them to go out of their way and prepare anything for our arrival. They were too old for such things. I assured him we would bring some pastries from the shop.

As we drove to Augusta, I told Nathan how ironic it was that we were driving all this way just to ask Daddy's blessing on our marriage. Anxiety swept over me as I shared memories of my first wedding. Sterling and I had planned our day carefully to include my dad and wife number two—what's her name. They were mysteriously absent from the showers to which they'd been invited. As the rehearsal evening approached, my fears increased. They whined about the location and the attire expected. They grumped that none of their friends were invited to the rehearsal dinner—just family and relatives from out of town, we explained. They were late getting to the church. We'd already gone to the restaurant. When Daddy learned that Elliot stood in for him at the rehearsal, he let me have a piece of his mind, a commodity he shouldn't have given away so freely. After his tirade, his wife expressed her displeasure about things in general and then stated they were leaving.

My queasiness mounted as we neared Dad's house. I explained to Nathan that wife number two left Dad that night. Of course, since the world revolves around Daddy, he didn't show up for the wedding the next day. When Betsy finally found him, he'd gone fishing.

After hearing this, Nathan stopped at a fast food place. I used the restroom, and we got Cokes. He insisted on praying one last time before we faced my dad and wife number three. *Poor Nathan. Maybe now he realizes what we're up against.*

"Abby, God is pleased with you. He's pleased with your openness to forgiving and loving your dad. We both know that he is a tough guy but he may not soften even now. You have so many people who love you. Think of them."

"Thanks for going into the lion's den with me. That takes guts."

"I face a tough crowd every Sunday," he said with a smile.

We pulled up to the house and I straightened my rumpled clothing. Katherine met us at the door and guided us through a maze of furniture into the small kitchen, where Daddy sat drinking coffee and watching a ball game.

"Hi, Daddy."

"Hmm. Hi. What have you got in the box?"

"Sweets from our shop. How are you, Daddy?" The television roared in the background.

"I'm still breathing."

Katherine took the box, turned off the television and offered us seats at the table. "Abby, I see this box is marked sugarless. That's so thoughtful of you. Isn't it, hon?" she said.

"Great. I was looking forward to good ole sugar. How can they be called sweets with no sugar? Ugh."

"Daddy, we came to visit to tell you our news. Nathan and I are getting married."

"Oh, how lovely, dear," Katherine said from behind the counter. She brought two plates to the table—one with sugary goodies, one without. She placed napkins in front of each of us and offered us coffee and tea.

"Daddy, we're planning a March wedding."

"My! My! Sterling's hardly cold, and you're marrying again."

"That's enough, Daddy." I stood up, feeling Nathan's hand on mine. I looked at Daddy, forced a smile, and took a breath. "Whatever it is that you hold against me, I'd like to know. I've buried all the hurts and affronts you've hurled at me over the years, but I can't carry them around any longer. Daddy, I don't have to put up with your rude behavior either. I would like you to walk me down the aisle, but if you can't, I'll get over it. I guess this trip has been a mistake. Let's go, Nathan."

"Wait, Abby." Katherine rushed forward. "You grumpy old man, act your age and show your daughter you love her. Somebody deserves to know you love them. And while you're at it, tell her the truth you've hidden for years." She tromped out of the room. A door slammed in the distance.

Dad's shoulders began to shake. He put his hand over his eyes. I heard a sob come from down deep within him.

"Daddy, do you love me? Have you ever cared for me?"

"You're my child. Of course I do." He seemed to choose his words carefully—something brand new for my dad. "I just have a hard time showing affection. Eleanor never seemed to require it. You and Betsy never wanted me around. I knew you didn't need me. I tried to keep you at home. It just seemed easier to send you away. I just can't...." His body shaking, he stood supporting his weight on the table. He breathed heavily as he reached for me and hugged me.

"Thank you, Daddy." I stood, melting into the embrace.

"You won't love me when I tell you the awful truth. I don't deserve it."

"What do you mean?" I cocked my head and leaned toward my dad.

"Your Mama told me never to tell you girls...." He slid back into his chair.

"Tell us what?"

"The reason your mother suffered all those years was because I was driving drunk and caused the wreck."

I felt Nathan's arm touch me as I shot out of my chair.

"Let him explain, sweetie," Nathan whispered.

I lowered my voice. "Please, Daddy, tell me about it." I dropped back into the chair.

"You were just a few weeks old. We lived next door to Gail's parents. I came home drunk. I rummaged around for more money. I found some and headed out the door. Gail had run next door and gotten her mother to watch you kids, and she ran after me. She begged me not to go back to the bar. I wouldn't listen. She grabbed the car door and jumped in and I gunned the car. I ran the light. I can still see your mother, Abby. I never drank another drop...."

"Oh, no." I rocked uncontrollably in my chair, my head down.

"It's a lot for Abby to take in right now. Let us go outside for some air." Nathan pulled me out of the chair and guided me outside. I heard Daddy yell that he wouldn't blame us if we just kept going.

"Mama loved him, Nathan. All those years of pain, and she loved him. She couldn't have faked that. How did she do it?"

"God gave her the grace to do it. He will for you, too."

I crumbled into his arms on the front porch. After a very long time, Nathan disappeared and returned with Katherine. Her tears flowed. My tears mingled with hers as we embraced.

I followed Katherine down the hall and back into the kitchen. My daddy sat with his head buried in his hands.

"Daddy, I forgive you. I'm so sorry you've carried the secret this long."

He stood slowly and hugged me. "I took your mother from you. I took your childhood from you. I wasn't there for you. It's all my fault. Will you forgive me?"

"Oh, yes."

Nathan stretched out his hand. Daddy took it, then dropped his hand and hugged Nathan hard. Katherine and I joined the men in a sobbing hug.

CHAPTER

30

Betsy called me on the cell phone as we pulled up in front of my home. Daddy called and asked her to forgive him.

"Sis, would you mind asking Nathan if he could give me a few minutes next time I visit. I'm not sure how to process the whole thing alone."

"He's right here. I'll give you the phone and you can set a time to talk. Don't tell him how wonderful he is. He might get a big head." I smiled at Nathan, handed him the phone and got out of the car.

I fixed ham sandwiches and salad for dinner. Dinky and Buck joined us to go over our rescue mission. Nathan made the master list and assigned us responsibilities. I'd located the spare key for Shelby's car and the title, which was in my name. Knowing that Justin didn't have a car of his own, we hoped buying a different car for Shelby would help. At least, he wouldn't spot her car around Traveler's Rest. James Frye, a friend from Nathan's church, owned a car dealership. He'd trade her auto for one of similar value. Her car would be taken to auction to sell. We spent some time at the lot and picked out a suitable trade.

A black economy car would blend in with all the other vehicles on the road.

Buck and Dinky had gone for a ride to the small town and found the Watering Hole where Shelby worked. They took note of the parking lot and everything around it. She'd said that Justin drank most of her paycheck there so she would call the first night he started drinking heavily. With him distracted, her absence would go unnoticed.

"Buck and I will drive Shelby's car, right? We're to put Shelby's car on James Frye's lot and pick up the new car. I've got the key to it," I said.

Buck pulled out maps and put them on the table. "I bought this GPS the other day. The young man said it was the best on the market but the mountains could get tricky even with it. So, I have maps as a backup. I've planned an escape route going through the mountains for a long time before heading back this way." Buck pointed to a well-marked map.

"You are right, Dad. I heard the GPS won't work where your cell phone doesn't. Reception in the mountains is patchy," Nathan warned.

"We'll be fine, son. You can count on me. Abby, you want me to keep the keys in my briefcase? That way you won't have to worry about them."

The call came ten days later. Nathan called me. I called Buck and Dinky. Thirty minutes later, I pulled Dinky's car into the convenience store. I jumped out and slid into the back with Buck, then Nathan took the wheel. Nathan gunned the car into reverse so quickly we all jerked.

"Sorry," Nathan muttered. "Pent-up energy. I've been waiting for this moment for a while."

Buck reached up and patted his son's shoulder. "Father, we ask for safety for all of us, especially Shelby. We don't know what is ahead of us, but we know You do. So, please guide and direct every aspect of this trip. Amen."

No one said a word. Dinky gripped the overhead door pull for dear life in the front seat while Buck shifted his big body in the small space in back.

Nathan slowed as we came into town, and he looked in the rearview mirror. "How are you doing, hon?"

"Could we pull into that all-night station for a pit stop?" I asked as I pointed to the lights ahead.

"Thank goodness," Dinky said. "I need to move around some before this whole thing gets started."

We climbed out and Buck hugged Dinky. "We'll look back on this as a great adventure, my dear. You just wait and see. God is in it. He is Good."

"All the time," Dinky concurred.

"I just wish it was over and Shelby was home with us." I said as we climbed back into the car some minutes later.

"It will be shortly. Abby, do you have the keys? Dad, do you have your GPS?"

"All systems are go, Captain. I have everything in my briefcase," Buck said as he handed me the keys.

We circled the parking lot. No Shelby.

On the second loop around the block, Dinky pointed. "There she is, in the shadows. Do you see the car?"

"I do. Tell her I love her and I'll see her soon," I said as Buck and I leaped from the back of the car and headed for Shelby's vehicle. We jumped in and waved as we pulled out onto the street. I saw Shelby throw herself into the back seat of Dinky's car. They sped off in the opposite direction.

I think both Buck and I were just a little disappointed that no one followed us. We said little. I listened for directions from Buck as we wound around the tiny town and headed north into the surrounding mountains.

After looping around the long way back to Traveler's Rest, we dropped the car off at four in the morning in the dealership parking lot. We drove to the back of the building and dropped the key in the box designated for the service department. We jumped into the waiting black car and headed home.

Nathan called while we were on the road. I talked briefly to Shelby, but our reception was sketchy. Her voice was shaky. She was vague in her responses. Nathan assured me they were on track with no problems. Kelly Jo had left her old clunker truck at her brother's business when we first made our plans. Dinky and Shelby drove on to the safe house. Nathan followed at a distance in Kelly Jo's truck. He called again to say no one had followed them.

We'd agreed to go about our usual routine as much as possible after our wild night's ride. I forced myself out of bed and went to work the next morning on a couple of hours sleep. One of our part-time workers was at the shop until noon; I worked the rest of the day. Dinky called to say she was aching all over after the long ordeal. Nathan called after talking with the counselor. Shelby needed a couple of days to rest before talking with us.

I couldn't wait to see Nathan that evening. We decided to meet at the pizza place, have a quick bite, and head to our respective homes. The whole sexual tension thing had led to fewer times alone. Neither of us wanted intimacy to play a part in our courtship, so we invited others to do most things with us. That night, no one was available to tag along.

The restaurant was empty when we ambled to our usual table. We scooted close to each other, held hands, and giggled as the waiter brought our sweet tea.

"I can't get over all you accomplished in getting Shelby out of that horrible situation. I was always used to thinking about what Sterling and I would do in any situation. Now, I think about you and me making decisions together. This whole thing has given me a comfort level about us—the couple—you know what I mean?"

"This situation has made things move quickly. If my counseling classes taught me anything, I know healing from loss takes time. You can't put grief in a box and compartmentalize it. You're still in the process of handling your loss and will be for a while yet. I don't feel challenged by that. I've been a friend for a long while now, and I love the way you loved Sterling."

"I feel odd talking about him with you. It seems that so many things remind me of him. He's my point of reference on most everything. It can be awkward, though."

"You don't get it, do you?"

"Get what?"

"Sterling is my hero."

"You mean you're amazed that he put up with me for all those years?"

He laughed with me but turned serious again. "No, Abby, I mean I love hearing about your past. Sterling is a huge part of it. Your relationship with him has made you the person you are today." Nathan paused as the server placed the food on the table then left us alone. "You have to remember, too, that my past has made me the man I am. I bet you interact with me in the same way you did with Sterling. I sometimes fall into old patterns, expecting you to act or say what my wife would. Remember, you come from happiness; I come from pain."

"Oh, Nathan, I'm so sorry."

"I've worked through it with God's help, but I'm not perfect by any means. I just want to please you, honey. You know, I fell in love with you long ago—while we worked on the house together."

"Really? I had the feeling you didn't even like me some of the time."

"Well, at first I didn't want to love you. I was just fine being single. I had a wonderful ministry, and that was all I needed. Or at least that is what I thought. God finally convinced me that it was right to pursue a relationship with you. I needed to make sure that pursuing you wouldn't threaten my relationship with God or with my church. Those three people telling me to call you finally made it clear to me."

"You are so wonderful."

"I know we've talked about the ministry before, but I'm concerned about the toll it could take on our relationship. It isn't just the long hours away from home that begin to wear on a marriage. It's the hours of sermon preparation, the calls at all hours of the day and night, the disappointments." He paused. "I can get emotionally withdrawn when I'm dealing with heavy matters."

"I guess I can't know all that is in front of us. You do know that I can be mighty needy."

"I don't want to make too much of this, but it'll be your ministry too, not just mine, whether you are ready or not. It invades everything. You know I sold that beautiful old home of mine. I got a good price for it, and the money was a consideration, but that wasn't the most important reason for selling. In my denomination, each preacher is itinerant."

"I don't know much about moving. Sterling and I were fortunate to stay in Atlanta all our married lives."

"This isn't just a transfer like other people have in their profession. We move when told to move and with little time to prepare. I've been at this church seven years. That is a long-time appointment. I'll probably be reassigned next year. We've worked so hard to make your home beautiful, but it may not be convenient to live there if I'm assigned to a church in another part of the state. What then? I don't want you resenting me for taking you from your home. What about Shelby? What about your business? There are all sorts of things to consider."

I sighed. "I can't think beyond my love for you and my concern for Shelby. I know that she loves you. I'm just not sure whether she'll see our marriage as a rejection of her dad. How will she function if we aren't living near here? It's just strange, isn't it?"

"Lots of adjustments, huh?"

"Sometimes I think I'm flexible. But most of the time, I feel like I'm being twisted so much I could snap."

"Don't do it, Abby! Don't snap!" He bellowed.

We laughed and sipped our sweet tea.

CHAPTER
31

Nathan placed his hand on my back and ushered me into the office. Shelby sat with a tissue in her hand, her eyes moist. The counselor sat next to her and motioned us to chairs across from Shelby. My daughter acknowledged Nathan and then stood. She was beyond thin. The veins in her arms were prominent. She had a cast on her left arm and bruises on her neck and face. Her once long strawberry-blonde hair was now chopped pruning-shear style. I sprinted to her. My instinct was to inspect those bruises and touch her face, but instead I opened my arms and she crumbled into them.

"Mom, I'm so glad you're here. I'm soooo sorry."

"Sweetheart, I'm thrilled you're back."

"I need to tell you what's happened to me. I don't mean about Justin. I need you to know I turned to God in the middle of the mess. The girl who worked at the grill gave me a Bible, and I started reading it. I prayed, and God worked in everything. I still feel angry sometimes when I think about Justin, but Nathan and I talked while I was away. I know I can't keep blaming other people."

"Oh, Shelby, I love you." I squeezed her hand. "I made mistakes, too. Will you forgive me?" We held each other close and sobbed.

We sat down across from each other. The counselor guided the conversation as Nathan sat quietly next to me. When we stood to leave, I knew there was one more thing I needed to say.

"Shelby, I don't want to hide anything from you. I want you to know that Nathan and I love each other. I'm not sure you're ready to be happy for us. We want to be sensitive to your needs, but I don't want to hide our relationship, either."

Shelby shot a look at Nathan. I couldn't read her face. Her lips squeezed together, and she stared at him for what seemed like minutes. *Lord, what if she says she never wants to see him again—or both of us again?* We waited for Shelby to speak.

"Boy, have I been gone a long time. This will take some getting used to." She smiled a quick smile. "All I can say is I already love Nathan. I just thought it was in an uncle kind of way." The tension eased, and we all laughed.

The counselor called me at work the next day. She reported that her sessions with Shelby were going well.

"Shelby's eager to have dinner with her family. I thought that tomorrow might be good, if it is with you all. There's a quiet place not far from where Shelby's staying." We made the arrangements.

On the way home from work, I imagined Shelby's furniture in her finished apartment. I pictured my daughter whole and healthy, ready to take on the rest of her life with excitement. All this in a ten-minute drive home. As I turned into our property, I saw a police car parked in front of Dinky's home. I wouldn't let myself think why police would be there—I raced inside.

I ran down the hall and into the den. Dinky sat on the couch, staring at the floor. She didn't seem to know I was in the room. I listened to the police officer.

"There're a lot of places easier to hit. Typically, this kind of perpetrator doesn't break in where there is just one way in and out. He must've passed two dozen easier places on his way here from town."

"We called all our neighbors, and they haven't experienced any trouble. Luckily, my guns were untouched," Buck said.

"If you are going to have them, an old gun safe like that can't be beat," he said as he pointed to the garage. "You say that all they took was your electronics and your change jar?"

"I can't figure out why they left all of my valuable tools just sitting in the garage. Doesn't that seem strange?"

"I stopped trying to figure out the criminal mind about the third day on the job," the officer said. "Sometimes, it's an addict looking for quick cash. Sometimes the thieves know what they can get rid of quickly, and that's all they take."

"Well, I've been saving those coins for years. The jar was heavy. Just the other day I said we'd need help to pick it up before we could start rolling the money. I hope it gave the varmint back problems," Dinky said almost to herself.

"I guess they just saved us the trouble of lifting it. The TV was old. We've been talking about a new set, anyway. I just thank God you weren't home, honey. Everything they took can be replaced. You just wait. Everything we replace will be bigger and better," Buck said.

"I can't get over the feeling of being violated." Dinky began to sob. "They dumped the things out of our drawers and walked on my underwear—you can see the dirty footprints! They even pilfered Shelby's old room upstairs. It just seemed like they spent a lot of time here. I'm not sure I can sleep, knowing they've been here and could come again."

"Thank goodness you put in a security system in my house, Buck. Dinky, throw a few things in a bag, and you two are spending the night with me. Hey, Buck, maybe we can read the manual and really use that security system. I've looked at the keypad a couple of times, but never thought I needed to bother."

"Get ready for guests for a few days, then. I'll start on an alarm system here tomorrow. The new wireless ones will be easy enough to install, but I'll want to research my options before then. It's obvious the sensors at the entrance aren't enough."

While Dinky was in the hospital, Buck had installed pressure sensors at the entrance to our property that rang into both homes. He didn't want her surprised by visitors while she recuperated. He had insisted on the measure at the time. Now that I know the man, I'm sure he paid for the whole thing.

"We can't impose on Abby like that," Dinky said as I started out of the room.

"Dinky, it's all set. Just get moving. Buck, you finish answering any questions the officer has, and I'll bring the car to the front door. Dinky, don't forget your medicine," I yelled and kept walking. *I could get used to being in charge.*

With the Christophers settled in the guest bedroom, we all felt temporary relief. It didn't take Buck long to begin talking about surveillance cameras and more paraphernalia by the front entrance.

"You're going to have us secure in no time," I said. "It'll be a fortress—unless, of course they come on foot! I suppose a tall fence is next in your considerations." We all laughed.

"Don't go there, Abby." Dinky hugged Buck.

"How did you know I was thinking about that? I envision a brick wall near the entrance, and then a privacy fence with brick columns every eight feet," he said, waving his arms in the air to give us the picture. "We'll have a remote to activate the gate. It'll be great."

"I was just kidding. We have an enormous frontage on our road, and none of it is level terrain," I said.

"Yeah. If my men and I start soon, we could finish by winter. I only plan to work on it a couple of days a week, since we have other contracts to finish, too."

I looked at Dinky. "He is serious, isn't he?" She shook her head yes.

"Well, it isn't a rash decision, Abby. We've been talking about it for a while. It'd be practical when Shelby comes back home to live, but you know there has always been deer-hunting traffic. It might slow them down some," Buck said. "Besides, we have Lexus to consider. I wouldn't want her hurt by hunters."

"I keep telling him that those men have hunted in our woods all their lives. They aren't about to stop now. Besides, they seldom do any damage—other than the time when they cut a fence to get a carcass out. We just have to watch that Lexus doesn't get loose during the season and hope Bambi can run fast," Dinky added.

"Who knows, Dinky and I may want to build a new house on the property one day. You know, energy-efficient, no stairs to climb, handicap accessible, and all the bells and whistles in the kitchen for my darling. If we do that, then we will need the entire complex to be more secure. As we get older, we get vulnerable. Hey, we could have ourselves a compound. At any rate, we might as well have a fancy entrance."

"There is just no stopping you and your wonderful imagination, sweetie," Dinky cooed.

"Should we change those plans for dinner with Shelby tomorrow night?" I asked.

"No. She has to know about the break-in eventually. If it was Justin, he saw that she isn't living here. I checked your house and it was touched. What do you think, honey. Do we go to dinner tomorrow night?" Buck said.

"We can't let that young man rule our lives," Dinky said. "If it was just a thief, they've already got what they wanted."

"That settles it. I'm getting supplies to make this area a fortress, before they come back for my tools and guns," Buck said, more to himself than to us.

The next evening, we drove to the restaurant. It was a long way for a meal, certainly out of our normal pattern. That was what the counselor wanted. I watched Nathan and Shelby come in the front door, and I moved to make room for them at the table. Nathan slipped into the seat next to me, but Shelby disappeared.

"Where's Shelby?"

"She's in the restroom. Try to act casual. She's really uptight," Nathan said.

We wiggled around in the booth, rehearsing "casual."

"I saw her broken arm. She looked really fragile." Dinky grimaced.

"She's home now. That's the answer to our prayers," Buck said.

Shelby trudged to the table with her head down. "Come, sit down here and talk to us." Buck stood and motioned with his huge arm as he escorted her to the bench.

Shelby poked at the silverware wrapped neatly in the napkin as she sketched out her life over the past few months. Nathan assured us we weren't ready for the details. We allowed her to say what she wanted without questions.

"Let's give Shelby a minute to relax. Want some chips and salsa?" Nathan asked.

Grateful for a distracting activity, we dove into the chip bowl. We consumed the enchiladas put before us.

"You are making amazing progress walking, Dinky. It won't be long before you are accompanying Lexus and me on our morning walks," I said.

"What? Lexus has finally figured out the whole leash issue?" Shelby asked.

"Well, she seldom twists me up in her leash anymore. Now, small trees can still be difficult for her, but she does stay next to me if I insist on it."

"Yeah, Abby gets better trained by the minute," Dinky said, triggering laughter from around the table. "Right?" she looked to Buck for agreement.

"Okay, maybe so," I conceded.

"Shelby, are you not feeling well? You have hardly touched your meal," Dinky said.

"You do look pale. It's a lot to deal with, isn't it?" I said.

"You two mother hens, leave the girl alone. She is too polite to say that she isn't consuming massive amounts of carbs these days, right, Shelby?" Buck said as he leaned back and patted his tummy. "My handsome body has scared the girl. She doesn't want to end up looking like this."

"Are you okay?" I patted her arm.

"I don't know. I just feel a little tired. So much going on, I guess," Shelby said softly.

After dinner, I pulled yarn catalogues out of my bag. I hoped I'd get Shelby interested in a project. Shelby leafed through them. "Mom, you know how much I love to knit. Well, I was thinking, I'd like to teach some classes and work at the shop."

"It's just so wonderful to hear you talking like that. I know you'll be a good instructor in the future. Right now, Kelly Jo has started teaching classes. Let's be careful for a while. What would you like me to bring to you? Do you have a project in mind?"

Shelby sighed and dropped her shoulders. "You are right. I may never have a life."

Nathan said, "Shelby, you'll have a life soon enough. We want it to be a safe one."

Shelby asked me to bring supplies for a scarf the next time we met. We discussed paint colors for her apartment as we made our way to the restroom. "The place looks huge now that it's empty. It'll be a great place for you, when the time is right."

"I'd love to move back right now," Shelby said.

"The men of the church helped finish the apartment. Right now, the place Nathan found for you seems good. We just need to give it all some time. Promise me you'll take some vitamins and rest. I'll get the paint for the apartment."

"I promise. How about this soft green?" Shelby said pointing to the samples I brought.

Thank You, Father. Thank you for bringing my Shelby back.

As we came back into the room, Buck smiled. "This is my lucky day. I dined with the three prettiest women in town." His smile was a mile wide as he bowed and graciously extended his arm to his awaiting ladies. He ushered Dinky and Shelby outside. Nathan and I followed.

After assisting Shelby into his truck—no easy task with her wounded arm and the height of the step—Nathan turned to me. I hugged him and gave him a kiss.

"Kissing in front of the child, huh? You want our conversation on the way home to be interesting," he whispered.

"Good luck," I murmured.

During dinner, Shelby had outlined the areas she was working on with the counselor and asked us to hold her accountable. She said the small Christian college nearby had accepted her on probation. She'd take two summer classes. They'd hired her at the bookstore on campus since the counselor recommended her. Nothing transferred from Foothills University, so she would budget her money in order to repay me for the semester spent there.

Next morning, Buck insisted on cleaning up their home, so he left quickly after breakfast. I left Dinky bustling around my kitchen. I noticed her wince and rub her back. That couldn't be good. She gave me the look so I decided to say nothing. I called to Lexus and grabbed her leash. We strolled toward the path, waving at Dinky, who watched from the window. My Lab was less cooperative this morning than she had been in some days. She barked and pulled on her leash.

"You'll have to chase that critter some other time. You're learning to be an obedient young lady. Now, heel."

With that, she stopped barking. She did what she could to cooperate although I could tell her heart wasn't in it. She wanted to run through the woods. *We're staying on the path this morning, I need a good workout.* I picked up the pace.

Lexus finally focused on the work at hand, and we moved quickly along the trail. I was close to Dinky's house when I heard a vehicle racing toward my house. I wasn't expecting anyone, and from the path, I couldn't see who it was. As I stood, debating which direction to go, I heard Shelby calling to me. *What is Shelby doing here?*

As I turned and began walking back to my house, Lexus pulled against the leash. Shelby's screams pierced the air. Lexus jolted forward and began barking furiously. More screaming. I pulled my phone out of my pocket, called Dinky at my house, and yelled for Buck. In the ensuing seconds, I loosened my grip on Lexus. She was off, digging her paws into the soft path, and disappearing up the incline before me. I continued to hear Shelby, but now I heard a man's voice. I grappled with fear as my body shook. I pushed forward. As I got to the top of the hill, I saw a young man—it must have been Justin. He struggled to hold onto Shelby. Lexus reached him as I scrambled toward the two. I gasped. As he looked at the dog, Shelby hit him hard with her cast. The punch seemed to daze him for a second, but then he lunged at her with his fists swinging. I winced as her tiny body absorbed the blow once, then twice. As I screamed, Justin paused and began again with more venom. He pulled her toward the car as Lexus leaped at him. With the hair standing up on her back, my dog grabbed hold of his arm. He tried first to shake Lexus away. When that didn't work, he turned all his attention on the dog, thrusting Shelby to the ground. He struck my pup and kicked her. Lexus squealed. As Lexus hit the ground, I heard Shelby moan. He turned from his victory over the animal, who whimpered as she tried to get up. He turned his attention to Shelby. She was on all fours struggling to stand, when he delivered a blow with his foot. I heard her wince with pain. Lunging forward, I dove on his back with my arms gripped around his neck. A snarl exploded from his mouth. The savage man grabbed me and threw me to the ground. Just as he raised his foot to kick me, a shot rang out. He lowered his leg, and

I crawled to Shelby. The shot had missed him. He laughed and leaped for us. I heard another shot and felt blood hit my skin. Red liquid gushed from his arm, and he jerked back in shock. He grabbed Shelby and pulled her in front of him.

"Whoever you are, drop the gun or I will finish her off! I can, you know." He put his good arm around Shelby's neck. As he did so, Lexus flew at him, this time throwing him off balance. He fell back and hit the ground hard. The dog sunk her teeth into his bloody arm and stood over the now-still body. Buck ran up, huffing and puffing. He pointed his gun at Justin.

"Are you both okay? Dinky called the police. Hey, big guy, just give me an excuse to use this now. As close as I am, I think I could really do some damage. Lexus, go to Mom. I wouldn't want to hit you by mistake. Give me a clear shot." His voice trembled as he breathed hard. Sweat ran down his face.

Lexus crawled to me. We scrambled to Shelby. She sobbed and rolled in the dirt, her legs pressed against her stomach. Lexus came close and licked her. Buck yelled for Dinky to stay in the house. The woods closed in around us. I heard groans and heavy breathing as a siren in the distance pierced the air. Justin moved his feet slightly. Buck yelled for me to get closer to the lane and wave the patrol car in. I limped to the road.

In a fog, I heard Buck talking to one of the officers. "I think we now know who broke into our home the other day. This sad excuse for a human being was beating up on our granddaughter before we rescued her. I guess he was planning on going through our daughter's house today. He must've been trying to find Shelby's address or something. I don't know. Thank goodness, no one was in our house the other day. Yes, uhh, yes, officer I'm fine. Shaking, yes, I do need to sit down. Please just make sure someone takes care of my girls."

Shelby and I sobbed. I cuddled her in my arms as I leaned against a tree. The police officer requested ambulances and assured us they were en route. Buck called Dinky and calmly told her everything was under control out here. He asked her to take care of herself. I took the phone and told Dinky I'd go to the hospital with Shelby. She'd be examined. I was sure it was routine.

The first ambulance on the scene took Justin, accompanied by an officer. Shelby was still shaking uncontrollably when they loaded her into the second vehicle. The driver escorted me to the front and assisted me into the awkward seat. Buck took my arm as I got in the ambulance and assured me he'd take care of Lexus. They'd head to the veterinarian right away.

The medic questioned Shelby as I settled into my seat. I put my head back and shut my eyes. I'd never experienced violence. First, L.J. and now this. The physical pain subsided, but then sheer panic came over me in waves. As I relived the incident in my mind, my heart raced, I felt woozy. I needed to concentrate on Shelby. The attendant asked her what medicines she took routinely. Then he asked her doctor's name. Next, he asked if she was pregnant. It seemed normal procedure, but the answer broke my heart.

"Yes, I am. I just found out this morning. You know, one of those home tests. That's why I came to Mom's house."

I pushed my body into the seat and commanded my emotions to stop screaming from inside me.

CHAPTER

32

As the ambulance convulsed over the windy road, I clutched the armrest. The erratic motion reminded me of an amusement park ride. I hate those rides and I was terrified of this one. We survived the trip down the mountain, but my tension mounted when we hit flat ground. Cars loomed on all sides, threatening to pull in front of us. The roar of the siren was constant. It was impossible to hear conversation from the rear of the vehicle.

As we screeched to a halt at the emergency room doors, I allowed the full force of Shelby's statement to sink into my heart. My child was pregnant. That fact should bring celebration. It didn't. I watched as the skillful attendants removed Shelby from the vehicle. Unfamiliar activity consumed the next moments. A uniformed woman pointed me to a room and ordered me to wait, assuring me that the staff would assist me soon. I stayed glued to my chair until Dinky and Kelly Jo appeared in the doorway. I sobbed as I rushed into Dinky's arms. They talked in vague generalities. I watched them speaking. I concentrated on what they were saying, but I just didn't understand a word of it. My body screamed for attention. Fear paralyzed my thoughts. I'd waited in a room similar to this one for news of Sterling. Next, I waited for news of Dinky. This time, I waited for news of my baby and her baby. *Lord, I know You will meet our needs.*

"Isn't that great, Abby?" Dinky shook me. "Abby, did you hear me?" Dinky said loudly. "Buck said that Lexus will be fine. They are keeping her overnight for observation. They taped her up and administered drugs, but they assured Buck she'll move around fine soon. The vet was very impressed with your little gal. Everyone asked about you and Shelby. Buck and Nathan are on the way."

"Okay." I mumbled. *Nathan, Nathan.* The word "pregnant" echoed in my mind. It was private information my daughter would share when she chose. Would nurses and doctors think her pregnancy was common knowledge in her family? Nausea swept over me. What if someone came in and told us Shelby lost her baby? Dinky didn't even know there <u>was</u> a baby. Did I believe God to be capable of handling this or not? Could even this situation be in God's hands? Would He be in this situation with us? I fell asleep in that awful chair, in that awful room, in the middle of wonderful thoughts—*He is indeed capable.*

A nurse woke me, asking me to follow her. The doctor would examine me. The police officer wanted information for the report. I found myself in a small cubicle, where a nameless doctor poked and prodded. In the end, he wrote prescriptions for pain medication and a muscle relaxant. The nurse took me back to the waiting room and assured me someone would come for us shortly. Kelly Jo left just before Nathan and Buck burst into the waiting room. Nathan and I collided in the middle of the room, clinging to each other for comfort. Two hours later, another uniformed woman ushered us into Shelby's room. She didn't respond as we gathered beside her bed. I thanked Buck repeatedly for saving my daughter and me. I laughed as he said that Lexus was being given the hero status she deserved.

"You know, I thought about getting rid of my guns when I got ready to move that big safe into Dinky's garage. I haven't been hunting since Nathan was a boy. On most days, my vision isn't good enough to hit the broad side of a barn. That dog and I make a pretty good team, huh?"

"Who would have thought? As Shelby would say." I smiled.

"Yeah. Who would have thought?" Dinky sighed.

After hours of watching our sleeping Shelby, Buck grabbed hold of his last bit of energy. He fussed over the chair next to the hospital bed, put sheets on it, and then said he was taking Dinky home. "If I have my way, I'll be coming to the hospital by myself tomorrow while my bride recuperates."

"Dinky, please sleep in. Kelly Jo said she would open the shop tomorrow. Let the sisters help there, and I'll keep you posted here. Please."

"I'm too exhausted to argue. Now, tomorrow might be a different story." She patted my shoulder and smiled.

Nathan made a trip to a pharmacy for my prescriptions. When he returned, I took the pills. We sat scrunched in the chair for some moments before I became drowsy. I heard him leave the room, and sleep engulfed me.

The next morning, I woke up when the nurse made her rounds. I took a shower and slid back into yesterday's dirty clothes. I ran my fingers through my hair and wished for a toothbrush. The nurse supplied me with one and said Nathan had gone to the cafeteria a while ago.

"Your daughter might be asleep for some time yet," the nurse said.

"How is she?" I asked.

"Her doctor will be in on his rounds. The hospital notified him yesterday when Shelby arrived in the emergency room. Didn't he come by and talk to you? The chart shows he was here at 5:30 last night."

"That must have been when they examined me."

"I'm sure he'll be in this morning. She had a peaceful night."

Nathan brought hot tea and muffins from the cafeteria. We said little as we ate. He lingered as he kissed me, promising he'd return as quickly as possible. I paced, at first in the room, then down the hall and back. Our doctor came in. He seemed to have all the time in the world as he checked the chart and spoke to me. Then the nurse pulled the curtain and I stepped into the hall. She left the door open slightly. I heard the nurse gently telling Shelby to wake up, the doctor was here.

The nurse opened the door as Shelby called, "Mama."

I rushed in and hugged her. Telling me she was pregnant, Shelby sobbed. Dinky's concern about her health had prompted her to buy a pregnancy test.

"Mama, I'm so sorry I drove home without calling you. I couldn't wait. I needed to tell you. I never thought about Justin being there. I'm so sorry. I've messed everything up."

"Sweetie, you couldn't have known he was there. None of us knew. The nurse says it's crucial for you to rest for the next few days. That's what's important right now."

Dinky and Buck arrived. "What if you hadn't come into our lives? Where would we be now?" Shelby cried. "I'm sorry I've put y'all through so much. Please forgive me. I even got Lexus hurt. How is the little pup? Please tell me she is alright."

We assured her that Lexus would be up to her old mischief soon. Shelby cried as she told Dinky about the baby. Dinky and Buck reassured her that they would be there for her.

"Is Nathan here? I need to talk to him."

Buck said Nathan was just a phone call away. He pulled up his number and dialed the phone. He held the phone out to her, and the three of us left the room.

"We'll be back," I said as I shut the door. It was time for privacy for her and a Coke for me.

"The hardest thing about the last several months is I knew my daughter was hurting and I couldn't make it better. Here it is again."

"Children grow up, Abby. I just wish she'd taken her time doing it," Dinky said.

"She told me she knew abortion wasn't an option, but she wasn't sure it was best for her to raise the baby. Dinky, I couldn't jump in and tell her what to do. I prayed. Whatever the decision, it will set the course of her life and the baby's life. Ultimately, it'll affect all of us. I feel so helpless."

"Nathan can listen better than anyone I know," Dinky said as she sipped coffee. "He was so wonderful with me while I was in that hospital bed."

When Nathan joined us in the cafeteria, he said little. In fact, during the next two days, none of us said anything about her pregnancy. We focused on her immediate future. She and Buck discussed what was happening with Justin. Buck said the legal system was slow, but things looked encouraging for us. Apparently, there were many other charges against Justin in North Carolina. We'd just wait and see. When the doctor talked about dismissing Shelby, she asked if she could come home.

"I hear you have a great alarm system, Mom, and more gadgets to come."

"You're more than welcome. Everyone agrees it's time. You haven't stayed in my new home. It's a pleasure we can enjoy together."

Dinky chimed in. "Well, what about Great grandma Dinky? You two don't think you're going to have a hen party without this old chicken, do you?"

While Shelby recuperated in the hospital, Buck and I had been busy. He finished the apartment bathroom. I painted the area. Shelby would use the guest bedroom until the doctor released her to climb stairs. If Justin was safe behind bars, then we were safe, even if it was temporary.

When the doctor gave the orders to discharge Shelby, Dinky and I gathered her belongings. Buck was the chauffeur, so he scurried out to the parking garage. A woman appeared in the doorway of the room. She was in her fifties, her dark hair showing a few streaks of gray. She wore a white hospital coat. She paused in the doorway.

"Can I help you?" I asked. *Surely, it's not someone else to draw blood.*

"I hope so. May I come in?"

"Yes. We are waiting for the wheelchair to take us home, but come in."

"I asked the attendant to give us a few minutes. I'm Dr. Farris. I work in the emergency room here. I was here when you came in, Miss Hollingsworth. I've been putting some things together in the hours since then. I wonder if you would mind telling me if I'm right in my assumptions."

"Right about what?" Shelby asked.

"Well, I know that you were a victim of domestic violence. I know your medical condition as well."

"You mean my pregnancy?"

"Yes, and I'm assuming that the man who attacked you is also the father of your child."

"What difference does it make to you? Why are you asking my daughter such things? This can't be a question that the hospital needs to know." I jumped up to show the woman out.

CHAPTER

33

"Just a minute, please. I know this sounds strange. It's awkward for me as well. You see, I have two sons. One is a wonderful young man. He is working on his doctorate in biochemistry. We never experienced a bad day in raising him. The other son was in the news the other day for assault on an unnamed young woman."

"Justin is your son?" Dinky said.

"Yes," she said. She struggled for breath. We offered her a seat, and she continued, "I'm so sorry for all he has put you through. I know what he's done is unforgivable. He's harmed your whole family, terrorizing you all. I'm not trying to excuse his behavior, but he's been troubled since he was a youngster. It was little things at first. Later, we sought help for his addictions, and things seemed better until college. Two colleges expelled him, and with each failure, his attitude became more hateful and aggressive toward us. So I can only imagine what he's done to you."

"I can't blame you. I made my choices, and now I am paying for them." Shelby looked at her hands. "I don't know what to do now."

"Oh, please, don't take this out on that beautiful little child you carry."

"I'm not going to. I'm just terrified that I'll have to deal with Justin for the rest of my life and my child will, too. If you found out about the pregnancy, he will. What kind of a life would it be for this baby to be afraid of his father? I'm pursuing adoption, for the baby's sake."

Dinky gasped. I squeezed her hand. We said nothing.

"My husband and I want to help in any way we can. Words can't tell you how sorry we both are." She wiped away the tears, smiled feebly, and turned to leave.

Buck had returned and was listening intently to Dr. Farris. "Unless God changes this young man, he won't change. I've been on that roller coaster with an addicted person, and it kills you little by little."

She responded, "You're right." Dr. Farris turned back around to hug Shelby. "I only wish I could do more. You're a brave young woman, whichever direction you choose for this unborn child. Thank you for not ending the baby's life. It is great pain that I consider the future without this grandchild." She turned to Buck, "I ask you to pray for my son. I know from the medical standpoint what you say is correct, but as a mother, I want wholeness for my tormented boy. If God could do that, well, I can't tell you how much that would mean to our family."

"There is always hope, I'll pray for Justin," Buck said.

She looked once again at Shelby. "If you decide to keep the baby, please consider including this set of grandparents. A child can never have too much love. I'm sorry I couldn't do more to secure your safety and peace of mind." She hesitated, and then started out the door. She summoned the attendant.

"Dr. Farris, wait. If you can get me into the jail to see Justin, I'd like to talk to him," Buck called after her.

She put her hand on the wall to steady herself. A brief smile formed on her lips. She pulled a business card from her pocket and asked for Buck's number.

"I'll get back with you as soon as possible. I'm not sure where he is, since he was injured and all. I'm not even sure he'll talk to me. Thank you so much. I'll call."

At home, Shelby rested. She divided her time between the couch and the bed.

"Mom, I can't believe how beautiful everything is. It feels welcoming, doesn't it?"

"I'm so glad you think so. When I think of the hard work and love that went into all the details, I see Buck, Kelly Jo, and Nathan everywhere. Dinky encouraged me all along the way. It's so good to have you here with me."

Buck kept her updated on Justin—with more charges accumulating, the authorities took him from the hospital to a jail cell. Justin had consented to see Buck. He told Shelby he was eager to talk to the boy.

I could tell that Buck was eager to make Shelby comfortable at home, too. He began calling the property Hollingsworth Estates. I guess that made him feel better as he continued spending his money on more gadgets to fortify the perimeter. We thought we'd enlisted—we were positive we were living in a fortress. I realized what I really knew all along. Once Buck got a focus, there was no turning back. His new passion was keeping "his girls" safe.

At one point in their conversation, I heard Shelby call Lexus, who quickly responded. She patted her head and rubbed her back. She held up the star that now hung from her collar. "The vet is right. She deserves a star. I think all I need is you and Lexus, Buck. You protected me."

"The Lord did it—He just allowed us to be involved," he shouted. She nodded and smiled.

During the next few days, we were seldom without company. Shelby was a knitting machine. She finished two scarves in short order. She showed Kelly Jo her lovely work. Kelly Jo reveled in the projects and asserted that Shelby needed more yarn. She picked out some from the new merchandise and sent it home with me.

Carter came for the weekend. He told Shelby about Alex and the pain the failed relationship caused him. Then he stated he should've been there for Shelby. He should've hunted the guy down and beaten him to a pulp before the scum had a chance to come after his sister.

"That's what Dad would've done," Carter stated.

"Oh, Carter, we can all look back and wish we reacted differently. I do," I said.

"Hey, big brother, when we were little and did something wrong, we knew we'd get into trouble. What did we do?"

"Don't tell Mom. Not even now." He laughed.

"What did you do?" I said.

"We'd meet in our secret hideout and agree on a tall tale," Carter said. "I think it was the way we wished things had been. We wanted to make you see things in a better light."

"Yeah, and you and Dad always saw through it. We never got by with anything. Other kids did, but not us. I know I have a lot of growing up to do. I'm not inventing any tall tales or blaming anyone else. My counselor works on that every session. I'm really working on making right choices."

"Wow, Shelby. When did you get to be older than me?" Carter asked.

Maturity had come with a price—a great price, indeed.

On Sunday, Shelby burst into the kitchen, dressed in good black slacks and a lime green sweater. I looked up from my bowl of Cheerios and asked, "Where are you going so early?"

"I thought Nathan's church started at 8:15. I'm ready. Why are you still in your robe?"

"It starts at 8:30. I was going to second service, but clean up my mess and eat something. I can get my act together rather quickly under pressure." I finished my comment as I raced out of the room.

I gripped Shelby's arm and guided her to the only vacant seats—up close. "I'm sorry we're late. We have to take our punishment," I whispered as we scooted into the front pew.

The praise band began playing, and we sang along. The service moved quickly to Nathan's sermon. He'd started a series on revival some time ago. This sermon centered on confession and cleansing. The message hit hard on healing your relationship with God through confession. He offered to pray for anyone who would join him at the altar. Shelby jumped to her feet and climbed over me, hurrying to the front. An older woman who often went forward followed. I rose to join Shelby but saw Nathan praying with her, so I slid into the aisle and went to the railing on the other side. I shut my eyes and began praying. I felt a bump on my arm, a nudge on my other side. I heard someone weep close by, a nervous groan from the other direction. When I glanced up, people surrounded me. Nathan crouched not far from me and prayed for a young man. Genuine worship erupted all around. Nathan ministered to those who lingered. I rose and crept back to my seat. Shelby remained on her knees. As others left the front, Nathan helped Shelby to her feet and cleared his throat.

"This is Shelby Hollingsworth. She has asked to speak."

"I've made a mess of my life. Really, I ran from God. Now I've confessed that to God, but I need to ask y'all to pray for me."

I streaked to Shelby's side and put my arm around her waist. Nathan stood on the other side.

"I desperately need God's guidance."

I'd been staring at the floor, but when I looked up, people were filing down the aisle and surrounding us. I saw tears all around.

Nathan prayed, "I thank You, Father, for the effective working of the body of Christ that we're witnessing. I ask You to continue this work now as we leave this place."

No one moved. He held his arms up and gave the benediction. A few people started back to their seats. Some in the pews moved toward the foyer. Finally, the band reassembled and began playing. Those in the front hugged and laughed. It was several minutes before the loving worshippers released my child.

Dinky cried when she heard what had happened. Buck put one large arm around Shelby and the other around me and squeezed. We sat in the crowded restaurant and beamed at each other. We consumed healthy doses of food and fellowship.

After the doctor gave Shelby permission to resume normal activity, she asked to see the apartment.

As she made her way into the apartment, she started laughing, "Oh, you have been busy, Mom. I thought you were up to something. You had that gleam in your eye."

"You started it when you suggested your bedroom furniture could stand a coat of paint. I needed to get rid of a lot of nervous energy. Your furniture happened to be the easiest thing to absorb my aggressions. I roped your brother into helping some. I knew you shouldn't be around fresh paint, so…what do you think?"

"I love it. It looks new and sleek painted black. Oh, Mama, the quilt." She rushed to the bed and hugged the quilt.

"It's a labor of love."

"Oh, look Aunt Claire, Aunt Betsy, Dinky. They all signed the blocks. I don't deserve this, Mama." She buried her face in the fabric. "So does this mean that you feel I'll be safe here?"

"Dinky and Buck gathered your things from their home so the place is ready. We'll talk about rules and come to an understanding. Right?"

"Got it. Never thought I'd say this, but rules are a good thing. I certainly learned that in the months I've been gone. Mom, it's been a long journey."

CHAPTER

33

Shelby and I scanned the bridal shop, hunting for the perfect gown at a good price. Shelby saw the dress on the markdown rack. We whipped it off the rack and raced to the fitting room.

"Mom, this is it. Not revealing but elegant. Look at the pearls all over the bodice. There's even a jacket. Here, try it on."

"I think it's meant for the mother of the bride, but it's perfect for my wedding dress. Did I see you carrying something else?"

"This evening dress costs less than a blouse at most stores. Try it on."

"It must be damaged. It's too cheap," I whispered. The sales clerk heard our conversation and showed us a slight pull in the skirt. I knew I could fix that.

Weeks ago, Nathan had asked me to go Da Vinci's restaurant. I'd planned to wear something old. Now, wearing my new black dress and waiting for my wonderful man to pick me up, I was ecstatic. I finished dressing before five. Nathan was coming at six. Shelby fussed over the necklace, the shoes, and my hair. The mist of hairspray was heavy as I peered into the full-length mirror in the bathroom. She worked with the wisps of hair, which were usually pulled away from my face, so that they fell softly on my skin. The gray streaks glistened. Shelby had applied eye makeup. I'd resisted her first attempts to glamorize me, but I gave in to the full treatment. Dinky had provided a black scarf with fringe to drape on my shoulders. She also insisted I wear her diamond earrings. I strutted back and forth, gaining confidence with the seldom-worn shoes. Shelby and Dinky sang "A pretty girl is like a melody," humming the rest as we giggled. At six on the dot, the doorbell rang. Shelby squealed as she opened the door. My handsome escort had arrived in a limousine. Nathan extended his arm to me, and we strolled to our coach. I sunk back in the lavish seat and squeezed Nathan's hand.

"What a glorious surprise. What's the occasion?"

"Da Vinci's, my dear. We have a reservation for two. A limousine is, of course, the only way to arrive."

I laughed nervously as we hugged. We drove through the streets of downtown Greenville admiring the glittering lights of the Christmas season. Last year at this time, the only cruising around town was in a frantic search to find Shelby. Her disappearance and Dinky's wedding had dominated every thought. This year, Nathan and I smiled dreamily as we exited the grand vehicle and advanced to the lovely hotel dining room, hand in hand. The maitre d' flipped my napkin and placed it on my lap, handing me the menu at the same time. He bowed and left the table after doing the same for Nathan. Nathan ordered for us. The service was superb. A waiter whisked the plates away as we finished each course. At the end of the scrumptious meal, Nathan nodded to the waiter. He brought a huge tray with a domed lid. As he lifted the lid, roses peeked out—too many to count. I'd lost track of Nathan while viewing the flowers. When I looked back, he was kneeling beside me. He reached across to the roses and picked up a ring in the center of the bouquet.

"Abby, I love you. Will you be my wife?"

"Oh, Nathan, yes." He placed the ring on my finger as a violinist came to the table and played. Everyone in the restaurant smiled and clapped as Nathan stood to his feet, pulling me to mine, and kissed me. The blush ran from my face to my toes.

"Are you ready for dessert?" Nathan said as the server placed a decadent dish before me. "I'll call the limo driver for our ride back to Traveler's Rest when we're are ready to go."

"I'll follow you anywhere, but let's not rush our chocolate."

I stopped by Buck and Dinky's the next day to tell them my Cinderella story. Dinky showed me a card Buck had received from Dr. Farris and her husband. She'd written a note, telling him how thankful she was for the change she'd seen in Justin since Buck began talking to him.

"That first trip was a little rocky," he told me. "When Justin recognized me as the shooter, I thought maybe that was the end of the visit. Instead, it piqued his curiosity. He couldn't understand why I'd waste my time with the guy who'd hurt his family. I told him I forgave him. That led to quite a discussion."

"How are things going now?" I asked.

"He vacillates between trying to pull my chain and really listening to what I have to say. He has a list of questions each time I see him. What excites me is he's doing the homework I give him. The chaplain even asked me to start a Bible study for more of the men. Apparently, the men have nothing to do while awaiting their trials, and the guards thought it might be good for them. Can you believe it?"

Ten days before Christmas, on an unseasonably warm afternoon, Kelly Jo hosted a gathering for the sisters at Polly's home. The precious sisters dressed to the hilt. Penny held court from her hospital bed. Several women from the neighborhood, the shop, and our church were there. The sisters graciously greeted Shelby, Dinky, and me. They escorted us into the formal dining room, where they had displayed pastries ever so tastefully. Kelly Jo beamed as she patrolled the table, making sure each serving plate was brimming with goodies.

"Pansy brought out her mother's Christmas recipes when we opened the café. Last month, she suggested we make some gift bags full of the family recipes. She wanted to thank everyone who has been so generous to them over the last several months," Kelly Jo said. "We've been baking for weeks. Patsy and Polly have been swamped at the café, so I've helped here. I had never made candy before. Abby, I've learned so much from these precious women."

"I take it you're doing more than just cooking. The house is sparkling. I hear nothing but praise for your work. In fact, Pansy says you are a member of the family."

"She has the cats at her house. Penny says she tumbled over the cat, and that is when her troubles began. Her doctor says she probably blacked out, causing the fall, but, either way, I was glad to see Miss Muffy find a new home. I'm not a cat person." Kelly Jo motioned for me to come closer. "Abby, guess what? In my quiet time this morning, I heard from God."

I was caught off-guard by Kelly Jo's comment, but her enthusiasm was catching. "What do you mean?" I said, almost in a whisper.

"I didn't hear His voice, but the thought didn't come from me, Abby. It was so neat," she said softly. "He reminded me how I got here—to Traveler's Rest, I mean."

"You told me your dad inherited the property your house is on, right?"

"Yeah, his grandfather left him twenty acres. We lived in the north Georgia mountains at the time. After the losers in my life, I moved back home to my dad's place. Well, Dad said he'd give my brother and I some of the land if we'd go with him. I didn't want to move, but the minute Dad said the name of the town, I changed my mind. You know, I was a traveler who could sure use some rest. Well, I hadn't thought of that for years, and then when I prayed this morning, it came to me. God meant for me to come here. Don't you see? Y'all showed me to rest in Him." She sighed and squeezed my hands.

"Oh, Kelly Jo," I cried. "I'm thankful you're my friend."

It took time to pry Shelby from the sisters. They were all thrilled with the thought of new life in our midst. They asked her favorite baby colors. I knew they would be planning a baby quilt soon. We spoke again to Penny as we headed for the door. The other sisters gathered to wish us a Merry Christmas. As we thanked them for the lovely afternoon, they each hugged us and gave us each a beautiful basket.

Dinky was the first to receive the generous gift. "Wait a minute, what's this?" she said. "We've already received your kind hospitality. Nothing more, please."

"We cannot thank you both enough for all you have done. Without you women, Nathan, and Kelly Jo, who knows where we would be?

We don't know how long we'll be able to stay in our own homes. We are thinking of downsizing and all of us living here in our parent's home—Polly's house, that is. You know, none of us has living children or husbands, so we are forced to make our own plans for the future. You have given us the luxury of making informed decisions without the pressure of time. We owe you so much. Thank you, from the bottom of our hearts," Patsy said.

I turned as we walked to the car to see the beaming faces of the sisters. Christmas cheer was all around us.

"Mama, I had the saddest conversation with Miss Polly," Shelby said, as we drove home. "She said she had to face the same decision as me when she was young. Everything was different then, and Miss Polly had no choice but to give up her child. Can you believe that her parents said the child's father wasn't acceptable because he was uneducated? They said he no promise of a successful future. Mama, her parents sent her to an unwed mother's home. They told everyone in the community that she was taking care of an ailing aunt in Virginia."

"That's what people did back then, Shelby." Dinky said.

"But, Dinky, she said she still sees her beautiful child as they took her from the room. She married somebody her parents approved of a year later, but never had other children. Oh, Mama, she carried the grief all those years. Her last comment was that nothing had taken away the pain, nothing."

I swallowed hard, but couldn't speak.

Dinky comforted Shelby. "Sweet child, the decision you make will have tremendous consequences for you and the baby. Just remember we love you and we are here for you."

As Shelby climbed the steps to her apartment, she said she wanted both of us to go with her to the next counseling session. I watched her walk away, and my heart ached for her. Would this child bless our family, or be a blessing to some young couple so desperately wanting to become parents? At future Christmas gatherings, would we look forward to toys under the tree and a child to watch in wonder, or would someone else have that pleasure? Would all holidays to come leave a deep longing for what might have been?

This was our third Christmas without Sterling. In some ways, it seemed forever since he'd been part of our lives. There'd always be a twinge somewhere deep inside when the holidays arrived. Sterling, who had been my entire life for so long, wouldn't be there to see how the kids were maturing. He'd not be there to be part of the laughter. He wouldn't be there to run to for comfort. And yet, there were sweet memories this year. They just mingled with the sadness, both magnified during the Christmas season. I relinquished the dreams of the past. Well, not altogether. They revisited me now and again, but I saw more than glimpses of joy in my world this Christmas.

I chuckled as I wrapped gifts with Shelby. She remarked how complicated our family tree was becoming. I agreed. Buck was my former mother-in-law's husband, but more like my dad. My real daddy was a new man—frail, but glowing from within. Nathan was my fiancé, but also Dinky's new stepson. My children's grandmother would soon be their step-grandmother as well. Go figure that one. Andrew would soon be my stepson and my children's stepbrother. Dinky and I had carried the Hollingsworth name for so long, and we would now both have Christopher as our last name. It would've been hard to comprehend had there not been so much laughter in it all.

My family was joining us for Christmas Day. For the first time, I looked forward to the event. Nathan and Dad exchanged emails on a regular basis. I didn't know exactly what they'd been saying, but my dad initiated phone calls to me often.

Our wedding was set for March, so there would be no rush. I could savor every moment. Carter came home two days before Christmas. He'd enjoyed living in Columbia since graduation, and he talked about the demands of the new job. I heard him tell Shelby he'd been on a couple of dates, but he wasn't interested in a relationship any time soon. Claire and Pete seemed genuinely thrilled for Nathan and me. Their children wouldn't be home for Christmas this year. Claire seemed to be handling the whole thing well. Kelly Jo and the sisters planned to come by on Christmas day so they could meet my family. Patsy and Polly had taken orders for holiday cakes and cookies. They couldn't keep up with the demand otherwise. We reminisced about the festivities of last Christmas as we looked through the wedding photo albums. We discussed the March wedding. Patsy wanted to make the wedding cake. She insisted her cake was the favorite at the shop.

We were exchanging gifts with Dinky and Buck at their home. It was our new tradition. This Christmas, I realized what an utter privilege life is. Yes, I had treasures in heaven waiting for me to join them. I was sure Nathan and Sterling would have been friends if they'd met on earth. Maybe they would be friends in heaven. All I knew was that what I was experiencing was heaven right here and now. In the glow of the candles and glimmer of the lights on the tree, Nathan sat, holding my hand as he talked to others, glancing in my direction. I squeezed his hand and felt warm as he kissed my cheek.

I relaxed in the glow of memories past and those in the making when Nathan leaned over and whispered, "You know, your dad isn't feeling all that well."

"He said something about some upcoming tests when I talked to him yesterday. He sounded as if there was surgery in the near future, maybe a long recuperation, too. Is that what you understood?" I whispered back.

"Yeah. It sounds lengthy at best. Your whole family is coming tomorrow for Christmas, right?"

"Right."

"What about having a wedding then?"

"Who's wedding?"

"Ours. We can guarantee everybody will be with us that way." Nathan chuckled as he looked into my eyes. "We already have the license, the rings, your dress, and the guests. All we need is the preacher and I know about 800 of them."

"One willing to preside at a wedding—at short notice—on Christmas day?"

"Give me a few minutes, and I'll see."

"You're kidding, right?"

"I'm dead serious. You could be Mrs. Nathan Christopher by tomorrow night. How does that sound?"

"Wonderful."

Shelby didn't miss a thing. She moved closer and craned her ear to hear more. As Nathan jumped up, moved through the gift boxes on the floor, and disappeared, she scooted into his abandoned chair. "What's going on, Mom?"

"What do you mean, Shelby?"

"Give it up, Mom. You can't stand my interrogation methods. Do you want to get Dinky into this?"

"Nathan and I are just making some plans for tomorrow. You know, Christmas and all."

"What about a wedding? I heard a wedding mentioned."

"Well, we are getting married, you know."

"Hey, everyone. Nathan and Mom are getting married tomorrow!"

With that, everyone attacked the situation like troops going to war. Nathan emerged from the entry hall in time to view the chaos. Gift-wrap was being snatched and placed in trash bags. Everyone was gathering their gifts and talking in high-pitched exuberance.

"What did I miss?" Nathan asked. "Is there a tornado on the way or something?"

"Shelby has great hearing, unfortunately." I chuckled. "Did you find a preacher?"

"First call. A friend of mine retired last June and lives in Spartanburg. He and his wife were going to be alone tomorrow, so they are looking forward to coming."

"So, you two are really serious about this surprise wedding, huh, son?" Buck bellowed.

"I am, if my bride is."

"Don't just stand there. It's early enough to call Kelly Jo. She can call the rest," I barked.

So, my three months of planning time narrowed considerably. Our Christmas meal would be the reception. I asked Nathan to call Daddy while I alerted Betsy. My kids and I scurried to my house to clean. Carter rummaged through my music collection for the songs used last year. Shelby searched through her clothes to see if she had anything that would stretch over her expanding tummy. Daddy didn't seem surprised when Nathan called him.

"Craziness like this doesn't run in my side of the family. That's for sure," he mumbled as he yelled to Katherine, "I'm definitely going to be at my daughter's wedding this time."

Wearing my creamy, long dress on Christmas morning, I peered into the mirror. If we had waited until March, I might've done more with my hair, and I might've had my nails polished professionally. Those things were unimportant. Betsy, Claire, and Shelby pulled me into a circle with Dinky, and we said a quick prayer. There was lots of giggling before we broke the huddle.

As the candles glistened and the music played, I walked into the hall. Tears streamed from my eyes as I took my daddy's arm and continued through the foyer.

As we reached the living room entrance, Daddy turned and whispered, "I love you, Abby."

I paused and hugged him. "I love you, Daddy."

He winked at me, and we continued into the living room. He stepped aside and stood by Katherine. I looked around the room before taking Nathan's arm. Shelby and Carter stood arm in arm, Shelby's other hand resting on the emerging belly, with Daddy and Katherine next to them. Andrew was next to Buck and Dinky. He smiled timidly. Kelly Jo and her daughters stood behind the wheelchair, with Penny safely in tow. Patsy, Polly, and Pansy sat on the couch, grinning ear to ear. L.J. stood close to Kelly Jo—interesting.... I guess she invited him, I didn't. My sister Eleanor and her husband sat prominently in the wing back chairs, flanked by their daughters. Betsy, Claire, and Pete smiled from their location near the preacher. Betsy's family stood behind Eleanor. For a moment, I thought I saw Sterling standing next to Pete, his face beaming, and his thumbs up. I turned and faced Nathan as we exchanged our vows.

ABOUT THE AUTHOR

Sue Carter Stout writes what she knows. A mother, grandmother, and former widow, she has faced many of the situations her characters do. Sue has a passion for teaching and speaking, and she is happily married to her husband of four years. *Traveler's Rest* is her first published novel.

LaVergne, TN USA
16 April 2010
179504LV00005B/10/P